BODYSNATCHER

The Untold Story of the Burke and Hare Murders

Carol Margaret Davison

**Ringwood Publishing
Glasgow**

First published in Great Britain in 2023

by

Ringwood Publishing
0/1 314 Meadowside Quay Walk,
Glasgow G11 6AY

www.ringwoodpublishing.com
e-mail mail@ringwoodpublishing.com

ISBN 978-1-901514-83-4

British Library Cataloguing-in Publication Data
A catalogue record for this book is available from the
British Library

Dedication

For Kestrel Zandra Davison,
my oxygen,
and the countless others
who have experienced
domestic and sexual violence

"Even Mrs. Radcliffe, with all her talent for imagining and depicting the horrible, has not been able to invent or pourtray scenes at all to be compared, in point of deep tragical interest, with the dreadful realities of the den in the West Port."

West Port Murders, published by Thomas Ireland Junior, Edinburgh, 1829

"This thing of darkness I
      Acknowledge mine."

William Shakespeare, *The Tempest*, Act 5 Scene 1, ll. 275-6

"Up the close and doun the stair,
  But and ben wi' Burke and Hare.
  Burke's the butcher, Hare's the thief,
  Knox, the boy that buys the beef."

Edinburgh skipping rhyme

The Scotsman, July 16, 1836

STRANGE DISCOVERY. About three weeks ago, while a number of boys were amusing themselves in searching for rabbit burrows in the north-east range of Arthur's Seat, they noticed, in a very rugged and secluded spot, a small opening in one of the rocks, the peculiar appearance of which attracted their attention. The mouth of this little cave was closed by three thin pieces of slatestone, rudely cut at the upper ends into a conical form, and so placed as to protect the interior from the effects of the weather. The boys, having removed these tiny slabs, discovered an aperture about twelve inches square, in which were lodged seventeen Lilliputian coffins, forming two tiers of eight each, and one on a third, just begun! Each of the coffins contained a miniature figure of the human form cut out in wood, the faces in particular being pretty well executed. They were dressed from head to foot in cotton clothes, and decently "laid out" with a mimic representation of all the funereal trappings which usually form the last habiliments of the dead. The coffins are about three or four inches in length, regularly shaped, and cut out from a single piece of wood, with the exception of the lids, which are nailed down with wire sprigs or common brass pins. The lid and sides of each are profusely studded with ornaments formed of small pieces of tin, and inserted in the wood with great care and regularity. Another remarkable circumstance is, that many years must have elapsed since the first interment took place in the mysterious sepulchre, and it is also evident that the depositions must have been made singly, and at considerable intervals — facts indicated by the rotten and decayed state of the first tier of coffins and their wooden mummies, the wrapping cloths being in some instances entirely mouldered away, while others show various degrees of decomposition and the coffin last placed, with its shrouded tenant, are as clean and fresh as if only a few days had elapsed since their entombment....

1.

Nelly

My Auntie Bridie used to say that life and death shouldn't run up alongside one another, but I've never known anything else. In my experience, opposites always attract and rub shoulders. Filth and beauty. Hatred and love. Darkness and light.

A true product of these experiences, I have played, for the most part, the role of death's midwife. It is, perhaps, a curious calling, but it is one I actively embraced for a time. With this pen, I hope to lay everything to rest. Once and for all. At least the facts of the case.

God only knows — and me with Him — that you can't exorcise the ghosts from yourself. There are memories we'd pay to be rid of, that we wish we could extract like abscessed, rotten teeth, memories that will haunt us to the grave. I have seen the monstrous machine called a pelican they use on such teeth. I have even been the victim of one. Sadly, no pelican exists for the spirit.

He — William Burke, my Billy — is my biggest bogey. Now he's everyone else's. The entire country trembles at his very name, especially the children, as well they should. They squeal and flee at the mention of him and the dreaded Dr. Knox, the dark phantasmal figure to whom they may be sold.

But Billy was *my* bogey first. *My* bogey, with the blackest soul this side of the Borders, as cold and as hard as anthracite. Colder. Harder.

That's not the way it was in the beginning. He

seemed the greatest godsend at the start. A miracle in the flesh. A loving, protective angel in man's clothing. I was overjoyed and overwhelmed. I didn't see him coming. Many who suffered fates worse than mine didn't either. I take some comfort from not being alone. Cold comfort.

The only way I can describe how it was *then* is that he was a conjurer. With just a few words and an intense look as if he could peer into the future — *our* future, he always insisted it was ours — he could fashion wondrous portraits of himself and me and who we might be together in that country before us in time, that country called the future. The best of all possible worlds. And nothing seemed impossible. He drew out of me the best I could be and I stood stupefied, mesmerised by his word-pictures as they assumed mystical flesh before my entranced eyes. Enthralled by the work of this word-wizard, I submitted wholly and completely, kneeling readily at his feet.

Charisma, someone I met once at the White Hart had called it. I never forgot that word. It sounded enticingly foreign as it rolled luxuriously off his tongue, just like the words used to roll off Billy's. In bygone days, sons would have been willingly uniformed and sacrificed, sent off to die for words such as he spoke, words that conjured up a better world, a more magical, enchanting world. A new world of freedom and possibility. One worth dying for. One worth killing for.

Ever engaged in crafting his own self-portrait, he was fond of saying that Scotland would never have signed on to the Union with men like him at the helm, nor would they have been at the throats of their exploited Irish brothers. Instead, we would have built our own new world together, here rather than abroad in all of those sunless, Godforsaken corners of the earth to which our life-long enemies had sent us to toil, fight, and die for a pittance, regularly left unmourned in mass unmarked graves. He knew this first-hand from the seven years he served as a batman in the Donegal Militia. (I can hear the echoes of his voice in mine here — his seductive Irish accent growing more pronounced as his lay sermon developed. He always said he missed his calling and many — myself among them — agreed.)

'Just look at what Scotland got without such men,' he would say, venomously, his urgent voice rising while his pointed finger gestured outside the pub to the noisy, dung-laden Cowgate beyond. 'Submission and sordid squalor.'

'Submission,' he would emphasise again, his animated face and arresting blue eyes searchingly crossing the pub and its lost souls in various stages of inebriation, standing or seated on low stools. They would come to rest, finally, on Fergie, the publican, who would nod in agreement with an exaggerated expression of sadness as he pulled the next pint.

'Who thought the Scots would become willing slaves to the English?' Billy would provocatively add, sourly shaking his head, his eyes lowered to the filthy earthen floor as if something lay buried beneath his feet.

'Willing slaves,' he would repeat again slowly, almost agonisingly, as if at a wake, emphasising the first word to bring his point home, his eyes slowly scanning the pub again, before he drained off his gill of whisky. At this, several pub-goers would swear aloud, then hiss or spit. Now it would take five thousand men like Billy — a man ever unwilling to submit — to turn things around.

In my experience, it had only taken one Billy to turn everything around. Within days of our meeting, my world had been turned irreversibly upside down, inside out. Meeting Billy skewed my whole world.

Everything grew richer, gained depth, became charged with a new energy. Monochrome became rainbow as I, once almost blinded by his hand, regained sight, pulled from out of my dead self, alive. At least, this is what it felt like in the beginning. Billy's visions seemed worth living — and dying — for. Then.

And, unknown to him, I have witnessed him murder and discovered numerous corpses. (There is much about which I have regretfully bitten my tongue and silenced my spirit. My pen, however, refuses to rest, a pen I learned to use just before meeting him those many years ago.)

I can now confess to having assisted with some murders, including and especially my own, although mine was long and painfully drawn out, something I failed to see at the time.

I should have said that at that harrowing twenty-four-hour trial to the wall of leering, hostile faces, especially those of the smug, judgmental women in freshly laundered dresses and immaculately polished boots. Boots I might have re-soled at one time or other had they had the courage to step out of their prim, sheltered houses in the New Town to enter my desperate, dilapidated neighbourhood. The same unsympathetic women who shocked me by applauding in the courthouse when the charges against me were found *not proven*. I now understand why. My release confirmed what they had come to hear: that no Scot — and, thankfully, no Scots-woman — had a hand in this nightmare. 'It was, as we thought,' they sighed with smug Presbyterian relief, 'those God-forsaken Irish.' I know those same women — and the whole of Scotland — have wondered about my role in these crimes. They couldn't care less about what happened to me. *Me. Helen McDougal. Nelly.*

Yes, I should have said, shamelessly, I have had a hand in killing myself … unwittingly. Doubtless, they would have laughed aloud, thinking me mad and ripe for the asylum.

If only someone had consigned me there years ago, I might have been better off. At least, I'd have been safer and she'd still be alive.

Instead, I feel like the living dead, my heart crushed, my life's essence drained.

Truth be told, I have been dead inside a long time. A fitting state for death's midwife, I suppose. A requirement for the job.

Perhaps through this account, I will regain some life and sanity, what little there is left of them.

Or perhaps this is the last of me spilling out onto this damp, crumpled page. That would just be my luck. With every inky last word, I am expiring, participating in my own undoing all over again.

***

Over the years, some have asked why I wanted *him*. Why, of all the men on offer, I chose *him*, a wild-eyed, flirtatious Irishman who ran hot and cold. What could a sandy-haired labourer in a shabby blue surtout coat and dilapidated shoes offer me who had once been called a braw, wild lass? I have always wondered why he chose me. Now, well after the fact, I have some answers.

And for those who didn't ask, I read these and other questions in their searching, penetrating eyes. Especially during that horrid, torturous trial.

The answer comes readily, is born of a basic human need.

I wanted someone to whisper with in the dark.

Only the women understand because only the women can understand. Only they who have known what it is like to be overlooked on the streets of this great, filthy, faceless town and treated worse than a dying dog, can understand the desire for such special notice and intense intimacy.

The strange thing is, it was Billy who first described me like that, and a sudden chill of excitement ran through me — then as now as I recall this — as if he'd pulled the words out of my head. As if he'd read my mind.

'You're the one,' he said. 'The special one I can whisper with in the dark.' He said those and a lot of other words the first time we lay together, all of them new to me, the person he claimed had inspired them. From the beginning, it was as if Billy was tutoring me in a new language or translating one that had never made much sense. After Rab's brutality and Ewan's rejection, Billy's was a foreign, enticing tongue.

He said each word deliciously slowly that first night, holding me firmly against him from behind, his breath warm, his deep voice resonating against the nape of my neck, stoking my desire to pull him closer.

You're the one I can whisper with in the dark.

Women melt over words like that, I can tell you, and I'm no exception. Coupled with tender embraces and irrepressible passion, we sign on for life.

As his hot wet mouth travelled along the back of my neck, his hands firmly clasping and unclasping my full breasts and swollen, eager nipples, his sex pressed against me through our clothes. I remember melting into him, wet with expectation, my legs trembling as the layers of clothes hurriedly came away, his hands madly swimming over and under my skirt and petticoat as we fell into each other.

For years, we shared much of the same passion, until those few last when, with his wasting illness, he became but a husk of a man, the old Billy left behind like cast-off clothes, a person no longer recognisable, at least not to me.

But, then again, I am barely recognisable now, even

to myself.

I have whispered throughout this entire ordeal, even in Billy's absence. And I'll whisper until I'm dead and buried to that once-upon-a-time tender-but-passionate Billy of those early delicious days who could utterly undo me, even — perhaps especially — after our mad and frequent fights.

He undid me alright. (And what, exactly, I still wonder, did he do with her?)

After all that has happened, I have whispered to God, pleading for answers, a shred of something to hold onto.

But it would seem no one is listening.

The story of my life.

2.

Billy

When you asked for a confession, Mr. M—, I couldn't help but repress a smile, finding the idea absurd and amusing. A *requested* confession? A *remunerated* confession? Rather it should be granted willingly by a remorseful, agitated sinner unsure of their standing with God, one perched, trembling, on the precipice of the next world. No?

I have given much thought to it — the next world, that is — and being confirmed in my righteousness for enacting God's will on earth and assured of my reward to witness His eternal glories, I hardly qualify.

Did you not think I might confess voluntarily and free of charge? Where could I, imprisoned now in this rank, dark condemned cell in Calton Hill Jail awaiting public execution, possibly spend the money?

Well, you had me figured out on one count, at least — I don't do anything free of charge.

Whether this is a confession, a vindication, an indictment, a sublime ruse, or otherwise, I leave it to your dedicated readers at the *Edinburgh Evening Courant* to decide. Some of them might get the point. I do intend to make at least one. My first confession from a fortnight ago on the third of January made to the three serious gentlemen — the Sheriff, the Procurator-Fiscal, and the Priest — was of an entirely different nature as it was required by law.

'Stick to the facts,' they tersely advised me while adjusting themselves upright in their high-backed chairs opposite, their well-manicured hands calmly at rest, unlike mine, in their laps. And so, I did, thinking the whole time that the facts never really do add up to much. They aren't the most important thing, offering but a mere outline of a person's history, a measly skeleton with no meat on the bone. In stark contrast, what people think happened, the fictions they live by, the stories they tell themselves before and after they act, that's where the meat lies, the heart of the matter. You never get to the heart of a man by asking him what he does for a living. He's likely just to spit in your face or turn his back. Ask, instead, what he dreamt about when he was a wee laddie. But, then again, as I have found out the hard way many a time, the likes of you simply don't care to know the likes of us. We are invisible despite our multitudes — troublesome ghosts, even while standing directly in front of you in the flesh serving your insatiable needs.

And what needs, I have wondered, might this story serve?

At least your expressed interest seemed to lie in another direction. Your directives that I *go beyond the facts* struck me as a novel and challenging idea, one entirely in the line with my way of thinking.

I repeat now what I said then:

All I ask is that my Nelly gets the agreed-upon ten pounds. That's the least I can do for the only person who ever stood by me despite never fully understanding me — and that for ten years now. She's a good girl. A little rough around the edges sometimes and a wee bit willful and jealous, but obedient when it matters most and all is said and done. There are some who should be in here with me, but Nelly isn't one of them. Trying her for these crimes and placing her in the Edinburgh Tolbooth for two days took its toll. You wouldn't know it, but she's been to hell and back and isn't strong for that sort of thing, especially since the baby died. I've sent her, as advised, my few things of

11

value. She won't get much for hawking my old watch unless she tells the buyer who once owned it. But then there's sure to be questions about how she secured it, placing her in some danger, something I've tried to spare her throughout.

As I said when we first struck our bargain, Mr. M—, *I trust you'll get the money to her somehow.* Dr. Knox still owes us five pounds having only paid us half for the last body, but I fear Nelly will never see my share.

Ten pounds. Funny figure that. The going rate for a shot during the winter months. Only seven or eight pounds during the summer (with that harridan Margaret always taking her one-pound *rental rate* off the top). The resurrectionists have a tougher time of it with the ground frozen and the incredible amount of physical labour, so they are compensated accordingly. Fortunately, I've never had to stoop to such desperate, foul, labour-intensive measures, although such rank work does pay off in the end, I can assure you, making as much as three years' worth of pay for most folk. Still, I feel sorry for the poor, suffering wretches who are driven to it.

So here I am voluntarily putting myself on a different slab for the same amount, plus my daily bottle of laudanum, my last, most loyal love. 'My amber darling', as I like to call her, smuggled in by the enterprising sentry who turns a blind eye to my scribbling while the Bible lays open before me. I have heard tell that Dr. Knox has a Bible at his bedside but I, for one, doubt that it's ever been opened or read, a rich irony for one who claims descent from the fanatical John.

Trust me, Mr. M—, I am deeply grateful for this provision, as you will be for this illicit manuscript. Without the drop, I am regularly sleepless until the wee hours in this bone-chilling, stinking damp without a fire, while subjected to the prisoner's coarse bread and water fare. Especially under these atrocious conditions, with my guts wracked and ankles shackled to the gad running horizontally across my cell about half a foot above the floor, this tale needs some lubrication. Most things do in my experience of them, as life, for the vast majority of us, is truly a bitter mistress. Judging by your face and shoes, you've never been acquainted with her, and have simply chosen, whenever necessary, to turn a blind eye, like thousands of your well-heeled brethren. Unless, of course, staring her in the face might catch a headline. How I have laughed aloud over some of your recent papers thinking, wryly, that what's news to you is commonplace to us, we whose children die gruesome, torturous deaths by the day. It takes a lot to shock us, our lives being an exercise in desensitisation from the cradle to the grave, our senses being, slowly and painfully, crushed out of us. What, after all, are feelings but a liability in the mad scramble to survive? And so, we are divested of our God-given senses over time — by God's creatures no less, those set above us to care for and protect us, our examples to follow. Some examples.

Take me, for instance — a typical product of this environment. I feel, at this stage, utterly senseless, my heart but a phantom. I have vague recollections of sensation … on my bad days.

I am led again to wonder, as I did in your presence, aloud, when you made the request that I unburden myself of the full and true story: what lesson will my story serve?

The very same creatures who devour this confession or consign it to the rubbish heap are sure to smugly condemn me, expressing astonishment that such as me exists. 'Look around you,' I would tell them if presented the opportunity. 'Take a minute from your bed-warming pans and well-stocked and ordered pantries and libraries and really look.'

What a lesson indeed!

First, I will subject myself to mental dissection in this battered red notebook you've provided, then to a public, spectacular, and medical dissection for Edinburgh's eager viewing pleasure. No doubt, Edinburgh's fashionable will be granted the best seats in the house. Justice must, of course, be served — or, at least, be seen to be served while rich people line their pockets. Appearances must be retained. Appearances are everything after all. If nothing else, God has an impeccable sense of humour. It would seem he shares that with our justice system as I have learned that my dead body is to be dissected — anatomised, as the good doctor calls it — in the very same manner as those of my victims. By that butcher, Dr. Monro, no less. Could anyone write a more fitting conclusion? I think not.

And this case is riddled with a raft of bloody ironies. That Hare, having turned "King's Evidence," which granted him immunity from prosecution, gets off Scot-free is a consummate, bloody irony. If I harboured any doubts that the penal system was broken, I would be convinced of it now. That that empty-headed wastrel who can't write a word and has never strung more than three sentences together at a stretch, at least not in my hearing, could relate the narrative of our business enterprise, is astonishing to say the least. Unthinkable in fact. Nelly and I nicknamed him the Mute for a reason. 'My fine Irish brother', as I so often referred to him, my tongue firmly planted in my cheek, is nothing if not a man of few words. His wordlessness goes hand in hand with his mindlessness. While I was the brains behind the operation, his brute strength was vital. And now he walks? He must be fair chuffed thinking he's outsmarted me. Well, the Scottish people might be led to believe, following the opinion of the legal folk, that

14

a man of twenty-one must have been apprenticed to a thirty-six-year-old madman, but they would do well to rethink that theory, lock their doors, and tremble with fear because, upon his release, I can assure you, my man Hare will get up to no good. And by *no good* I mean one thing and one thing only — violent crime. He has cultivated an appetite for it. *It is his dram.*

And what, you're probably wondering, besides whisky and women, is mine? I do intend to elaborate, so please bear with me, but the short answer is character — the mining of character. While the good doctor has fixed his lens on the body with all of its physical properties and appetites, I have turned my attention to the greatest mystery of all — the mind, the personality, the spirit that animates our fleshly bodies, as my former minister friend, the Reverend Dr. Dixon, described it. We each carry a world within us, a rich and fascinating world impenetrable to science and its army of sharp, meddling instruments.

My engagement in this body business has taught me one thing for certain: the heart of the matter does not lie at the heart of the creature. The physical frame is mere window dressing, a costume that clothes the character, without which we are but shots really — or *cadavers,* to use the good doctor's word.

The uniqueness of character has long fascinated me, especially in this foul drain of a city where we are regularly reduced to disposable, replaceable, working brutes. What, I continue to wonder, makes a person tick, especially while we inhabit the flesh in such an unholy sewer? What undoes us on life's agonising treadmill? What sets our hearts racing, making us wish we had another twenty years to live or, to take another tack, that we had never been born?

The good doctor and I have our mutual fascinations but we do not share a way of seeing. My experiments, undertaken by one on the brink of death by disease, had different results, yielded other conclusions, because I believe I have asked the right questions. I can assure you my answers have come at a great cost. All I ask is that before you judge me, you consider what it must be like — *really like* — to walk, even just for a day, in my shoes.

***

My motto has long been 'Show me the shoes and I'll show you the man'.

A philosopher by inclination and a cobbler by trade, I have spent a lifetime studying men and their shoes, especially here in this realm of squalor known as Little Ireland in the West Port, and I can tell you one thing for certain — like so much else in this life, it all comes down to the pocketbook. We, desperate drudges, must leave nothing to waste, especially if we want drink and tobacco. Were you aware, Mr. M—, that, with the assistance of a skilful, inventive cobbler, a single pair of shoes can actually last a man a lifetime? Not so with a bottle of whisky.

We poor scavenging Irish might be said to shuffle the brogue in a different sense for a lifetime, and a lifetime might be revealed in a shoe. With their various styles of stitching, different qualities of leather and sole, shoes reveal much more than a person's size and gait. Character emerges in a man's shoes, is written in them, ground in over time. Does this one walk upright and with purpose? When life requires it of him, can he go the distance, or does he move reluctantly along, his shoes dragging beneath his feet? Shoes tell a story all their own and, as only a hawking cobbler knows in this damnable rookery, the vast majority of us are walking in dead men's shoes. Given the great number of poor who waste away in this God-forsaken, cobble-stoned hellhole, there are more than enough dead men's shoes to go around.

Over the course of many months, I painstakingly perfected my death method like the good doctor has his surgical techniques, ever careful not to falter in the face of my dreadful business. Having learned during our first sale that a shot must be delivered naked or we risked arrest for theft, from the first murder to the last, I have scrupulously prepared the bodies. But it occurs without fail. During a routine moment of my operation, not the one you might expect, I regularly falter — when I must remove the victim's shoes.

It is only a few days afterwards, always days of mental fog and crippling physical fatigue, having swallowed many a gill of whisky and countless doses of laudanum, that I can bring myself to re-sole them.

3.

Nelly

I have heard tell of people who can remember being born, who recollect striving upwards towards a lustrous light, emerging through murky, blinding fog into being, but I'm not one of them.

Tales of welcoming, cradling arms, swatches of sky. Your regular pub tales.

When I was in my cups, I could hardly remember the day before yesterday — or even yesterday.

I have sworn off that now given all that's happened. The drink was long a part of my problem. Perhaps all of my problems. I have to blame something. That's what he did. He always blamed me. For everything.

I didn't see that coming in the beginning. How could I?

Now, without the drink, all of the memories — of Billy, my mother, my childhood, Rab — flood back and consume me. Claustrophobic and toxic, they persecute me at night in my box bed (like the one where *she* died), sitting atop my chest like a riotous night hag stifling my very breath. More often than I care to think, I have lain awake sweating, choking and gasping for air, praying for release from their suffocating embrace.

The time has come to sort them out in a bid to make some final sense. Of them. Of my life. Of everything.

I'll settle for anything. Always would. I can see that now.

I remember no bright, dancing, beckoning lights or swatches of indigo sky. And cradling arms would be a dream, not a memory. The strongest impression is of an odour, a foul incongruent odour of human and animal waste, dank earthen hovels, burning peat, and lavender water — the last, pungent and piercing, trying to mask the rest. A strange mix. The essence of Scotland in a sense. The essence of Scotland in a scent. One that I recall with pleasure, a type of childhood joy. Even now, a smile emerges at the thought of it. Although it beggars belief and was certainly short-lived, there was a time when I felt happy to be alive, a carefree time when I ran endlessly up and down the slag heap behind my grandfather's cottage in Redding amidst the bracken, heather, and wildflowers. I remember being in awe at what could grow out of coal slag. Once, I spied a cream-coloured orchid veined in light pink that resembled a butterfly. It took my breath away sitting there on its own. I studied it for what seemed like hours, revisiting it for days afterwards, until it withered and died.

Sounds also abound in these early memories, my Auntie Bridie's singing (the only nice thing about her) rising above the rest. Memories of her haunting sombre lullabies exquisitely cut my soul in half, granting me a strange, sad ecstasy. Capturing as they do the essence of my childhood and my relationship with Billy, they serve as the chorus of my life.

***

From what I can tell, God has ignored me my entire life.

Pray as I would, bargain as I might, no God has ever answered my prayers. Perhaps he is deaf. Or careless. While wee Morag Newell's daily Hail Marys were rewarded with slow, passionate kisses delivered by Tam McLean privately in the laneway behind her Auntie May's cottage, followed by a sudden marriage and two wee weans, I was left empty-handed and alone. But perhaps my demand for protection was too great. Perhaps there are, as I have long suspected, serious limits on what God can do in this world, especially for women.

Thinking things would change if I turned Catholic, I asked Morag to loan me a rosary and teach me the Hail Mary. I created a hairshirt out of horse's hair, a rusty needle and thread, and one of my grandfather's cast-off shirts. It didn't look like much to the uninitiated, the inattentive, but I knew God would recognise my intention.

I also knew that my Auntie Bridie who, despite her name, despised Catholics with a hellish venom that defied description, wouldn't, so my time of worship had to be chosen wisely.

When she went potato picking or out to the market and I knew the house would be empty and quiet for a while, I would kneel in that hairshirt in front of my makeshift altar in the hearth, and recite in a low but feverishly dedicated whisper:

Hail Mary, full of grace, the Lord is with thee;
blessed art thou amongst women, and blessed is the
fruit of thy womb, Jesus.
Holy Mary, Mother of God, pray for us sinners,
now and at the hour of our death. Amen.

Try as I might, I could never actually imagine Mary. She seemed so far removed from the reality of my life. I would picture her hovering with a halo in a haze of blue smoky light, her eyes strangely transfixed on the unseen heavens above. I didn't even know a Mary, had never even met one. The person I would imagine was my long-lost mother, of whom I had no visual memory, whom I didn't then know was actually still alive, my grandfather having fatally announced, with a sombre shake of his bowed head on several occasions, 'She's dead to us'.

Unlike Isobel White who saw the Virgin all aglow at the foot of her bed one Sunday night, a cream chiffon gown with pale blue overcoat and veil framing and floating around her, her sorrowful eyes and arms raised imploringly to the opening, beckoning, heavens above, my Hail Marys did not result in a mother's warm enveloping embrace. This yawning black hole in my life left by her absence remained open before me like a gaping grave. But I stood firm, as is my way, praying fervently that she would magically reveal herself to me one day.

I look back painfully at those desperate acts of entreaty with a certain realisation: there are some things for which prayers cannot be fashioned. There are some things that render us mute.

***

And then, when I least expected it, my prayers were answered.

My Auntie Bridie had raised me and by raise I mean she had put food on the table (we never went without), taught me basic cooking and cleaning, and skelped me hard and regularly to teach me right from wrong.

Given her strict regime, Bridie's loveless house resembled a soldier's barracks or, as I have thought many times, smiling at the irony, a nunnery, at least, as I conceived a nunnery to be. I never once thought of Bridie as family. She gave me ample reason not to. We were strangers — in spirit, especially — brought together by need.

The one thing I know for sure after years of living with her: there is no place colder or more hostile than a house barren of love, and Bridie's barrenness filled her house to icy suffocation. Hell seemed joyful by comparison.

Despite my efforts at that time, I couldn't figure out the source of her coldness.

From a young age, I sensed she resented, perhaps even hated, me. There was venom in the manner with which she told me, at the height of her many rages while she thrashed away at me, sometimes armed, sometimes unarmed, that *she* was not my mother. She would hurl this information at me, zealously repeating the words as if I were defiantly resisting belief. Through her narrow eyes and flying spit, she seemed to be thinking back through some old memory, a memory that had her firmly by the throat, refusing to let her alone.

My grandfather told me when I was five that my mother was Bridie's sister Maeve, his other daughter, who had hurt Bridie in some horrible, unforgivable way. The offence was so grievous, he said, that it could not now — or ever — be set to rights, do what he could. He never mentioned the unpardonable crime to her and only later revealed it to me. Despite this offence, Bridie stepped in to take care of me at a time when Maeve was not able, showing what seemed to be some mercy. He doubted whether Maeve, whom he secretly told me was his favourite daughter, his younger girl, the one who looked more like her Irish, Roman Catholic mother, would have done the same had their circumstances been reversed.

I wondered often about this offence, but not then knowing the horrible havoc men can wreak in women's lives, never considered another's involvement. Try as I might to get my grandfather to talk about Maeve, he refused, saying simply that she was his dark-eyed, braw lass who had gone down the wrong road, a road from which she could never return, a road he prayed to God would never be mine.

It wasn't long after that Bridie pointed out a woman to me on the main road and declared, 'There she is.' I knew immediately whom she meant.

The young woman was seated outside the local gin shop, her long navy skirts ragged and muddied, her eyes downcast, her dark hair dirty, stringy, and unkempt. A quick glance at us revealed an intense set of black eyes that looked strikingly like my own. While I stared right back at her, eyes unwavering, she looked straight past me as if I wasn't even there, as if I didn't exist.

I saw her several times on the main road after that and stopped to stare at her each time, even pulling away from Bridie once in an attempt to get some reaction from her, some sort of recognition. I remember smiling at her while standing only feet away and holding out my hand, red raw from dishwashing, but she just turned away, ignoring the gesture, refusing the contact. Whether her reaction was born of shame or embarrassment I can only guess. Her eyes seemed queer, unable to focus, capable only of looking through me. I have seen countless empty eyes like that since, some belonging to the smallest of children. Life experience has a way of gathering up around the eyes: some may be windows, most are doors.

If ever a person was an impenetrable fortress, that person was my mother.

And one thing was clear: I was no one to her.

Every time afterwards she seemed a different woman, one who grew paler, thinner, and more haggard, her clothes increasingly faded and shabby, her gait slowing. She looked ill and dejected which, in combination with the drinking, destroyed her looks and health. And she was drunk every time that I remember, stumbling about the roadway, her arms outstretched like a blind, disoriented woman afraid of falling down. *She is a walking ruin*, I thought to myself, the hot tears running down my cheeks as I recalled her face later in private.

Careless is the word that now comes to mind. *Careless* — about herself, the world, everything. She was certainly careless when it came to me.

I now know the state she was in. Indeed, over years I have come to know it as intimately as a bedfellow. It's the one where you give up on everything because it gave up on you. You yearn for obliteration, believing you'd be better off dead and, for all intents and purposes, you already are.

***

My mother died on what seemed a day for dying, one oppressively dark and rainy with bone-chilling damp.

The hard, urgent raps at my grandfather's cottage door came in the forenoon. When he answered, a dark, rain-soaked man hurriedly carried my mother, unconscious, her skirts slick and dripping, into the back room, the location of my grandfather's bed. He and the man he called Rab exchanged a few words in hushed, urgent whispers, punctuated by worried glances at me, after which Rab left suddenly. I overheard one word in the frenzy of their discussion — Maeve.

I hesitated to enter the room and look more closely at her. Sensing the gravity of the situation, I tiptoed in after a few minutes and sat down at the foot of the bed. Her laboured breathing, fevered mutterings, and sickly pallor told me everything. My grandfather uttered the words, 'She'll no be long for this world.' At one point, she sat straight up, gesturing at something in front of her, some*one* I thought. I remained silent as death approached, watching nervously for the ghosts I'd heard so much about as my grandfather persuaded her to lie down again and calm herself, then sat down beside her, stroking her forehead and tangled, thick mass of snaky, wet hair. I had never seen him cry as he was doing now, his tears falling steadily as he repeated the words, 'wee lassie, wee lassie, what have you done?'

My mother lay still, her laboured breathing subsiding as she stared up at him, her eyes bloodshot and sad.

'You've been more sinned against than sinning, wee lassie, I've always suspected,' my grandfather said. 'You never told me the whole story. What was done.'

After a time, my mother's eyes fell shut. She didn't seem to be breathing at all. It was then that I did what came naturally: I crawled up onto the bed beside her and cuddled into her breasts and belly, my free arm clutched around her waist, my face pressing into her neck. My grandfather said nary a word. Despite the strong scent of urine, alcohol, and sour sweat that accosted me, I just lay there, leaning in as close to her as I could. She whimpered a bit over the course of the next hour while holding my grandfather's hand, muttering a few words at intervals. The only ones I could make out were *sorry, so sorry*. As she uttered each word, my grandfather tried to calm her, stroking her forehead the way he did to me when I was sick, telling her she had nothing to be sorry about. He was the one who was sorry, he said, his face awash in tears. I watched in pain as he leaned in close to her, wracked with sorrow, weeping as he kissed her repeatedly on the forehead and asking her forgiveness. With the little energy she had left, I felt her repeatedly squeeze his hand, a signal of her acceptance of his penitent words.

A few long minutes later, just as I allowed myself to cry, my mother lay calm and motionless.

After fixing her dishevelled hair and kissing her a final time on the forehead, my grandfather stood up and said, 'it's all done now.' Then he left the room. He returned some minutes later with a damp cloth, a knife, and a wooden, oblong box I'd never seen before. I watched intently as he leaned down, gently wiped my mother's face, touched his lips to her cheek, and clipped several thick locks from her mass of dark, matted hair. Then, moving to the bottom of the bed, he cut a big swatch of cloth from her long, ragged skirt. After laying this piece of cloth flat on the bed, he removed a small wooden soldier from the wondrous box containing many others, then carefully wrapped the cloth around the doll. After cinching it in at the waist and securing it with some sort of glue, he did his best with his cobbling tools to etch in a face. Lastly, he glued some of my mother's hair on its head, pressing it on firmly. Then, looking at me tenderly with care and deep sadness, he told me the doll was mine.

'It's a keepsake of sorts, hen, although not much of one. You'll have to wait a while till it's ready and the glue dry. You stay with her now and say your good-byes while I find something to put this wee one in.'

A while later, as I lay beside my dead mother awaiting the arrival of my Auntie Bridie to help wash and wrap the body and lay her out, my grandfather handed me a small wooden coffin with a lid lightly nailed down with brass pins. Inside was the delicate wee doll, snug and secure. I liked the way it cradled comfortably, box and all, in my hand.

While someone else might have built a bed or a house for a doll or a small chair, my grandfather had built a miniature coffin. It didn't strike me as unusual at the time. Even now it seems the only safe place.

I put it away knowing it wasn't for the eyes of Bridie who arrived home a short time later. Having exchanged a few whispered words with my grandfather at the bedroom door, she entered menacingly, scowling at my dead mother on the bed. Approaching her with a look of anger, her eyes flashing and throat constricted, Bridie stared down at my mother's pallid, waxy face as if she still had the power of sight and could recognise her.

'Serves you right, you damned whore,' she whispered angrily through clenched teeth and choking, uncontrollable sobs as if my mother were alive and capable of hearing.

'Show some respect for your sister, lassie, and for her daughter who's lying right there taking all this in,' my grandfather said, raising his voice, which was not his way.

'She's beyond this world now,' he said more quietly, glancing over at me. 'And it won't be long until it's our turn.'

But Bridie paid no heed. Turning again towards the body on the bed, she angrily spat out her next words — 'Serves you full right, Maeve. You always thought you were better than me. Well, look at you now.'

As Bridie's words hailed down around me, I mouthed the Hail Mary and later, after Bridie left to make supper before preparing the body and arranging for a sin-eater, I caressed my mother's soft eyelids with my fingertips, stroked her forehead, and lovingly kissed each cheek, the way I always prayed she would do to me. I did this a few times until, overcome with grief, I pressed my face into hers, my sobs uncontrollable.

After some minutes, I pulled back to consider her face up close, the face I had longed for, the gaze I had desired. While I received no such look now, a tremendous feeling of peace washed over me as I lightly stroked her face and eyelids. Despite their rubbery feeling and the moment seeming unreal, a feeling of warm comfort flushed through me from head to foot. It was as if I were looking at my own face. There was no doubting our relationship now that she was up close. She was *my* mother. I could see that I was *her spitting image* as my grandfather had told me so often.

Basking in the intimacy and calmness of the moment, I kissed her softly and lovingly on the lips, cheeks, and forehead. But my peace fast turned to fright when, as I pulled back to look at her, I beheld tears streaming down her cheeks. For one brief moment, I thought I was witnessing a miracle, that by some incredible magic she had returned to life. Disbelief and joy overwhelmed me as I frantically touched her face with my fingertips, whispering 'Mama' in horrified amazement.

But my mother just lay there, motionless.

It was then I realised that the tears were my own.

Hours later, in the eerie silent darkness of Bridie's freezing, heartless house, I faced the finality and reality of my mother's death, feeling myself more deeply alone than ever. Try as I might, pray as I might, Maeve, my mother, ever absent and distant, could never be brought back to life and returned to me. Along with her death went my childhood hopes to experience a mother's care and love. I fought back the waves of sobs as I swallowed that acrid, bitter truth.

Hours later, as the sun rose, I fell asleep to my internal recitation — *Pray for us sinners, now and at the hour of our death. Amen.*

From where I sit now, having finally found my own words, the process of a lifetime, I pray she rests quietly in a safe and peaceful place, she who, like me, had suffered the loss of all things.

'Please God,' I would entreat Him, 'cradle her safely in your arms. Rock her gently. Hold her close.'

4.

Billy

There are some people that should never be born. Waste of space on this earth. Waste of breath, really. Better off dead than alive. Certainly, worth more that way — at least to me and the likes of me.

And I have heard the good doctor say they are *worth more to science*. I bit my tongue when he said that the first time, that man who fancies himself a martyr to science. I bit it so hard I had to dip it in whisky for nearly an hour after we'd sorted out the payment and left. It ached and stung for days, being extremely tender to the touch. What a godforsaken sham, a lie if ever one was told. Science couldn't care less about curing the bodies of us poor sick souls — those who remain alive to scrounge every day like mongrels in this vast cesspool of a city and who, like me, have experienced insufferable pain from brutalising labour and the diseases that overtake our battered bodies.

Say worth more to the rich, good doctor, and you'd be getting closer to the truth, I thought silently to myself. It's like everything else as I've found it to be — a right, bloody poor exchange, one where down-and-out drudges like me are sacrificed to the interests and habits of rich, greedy, privileged folk like you. Nothing new there.

'It's the same sack of potatoes,' as my mammy used to say, 'and chances are there's a hole at the bottom of it.' Such was the optimism of folk from County Tyrone.

Science couldn't care less, nor could our earthly

masters who need poor, desperate drudges like us to get everything done. We are key to the operation so must be treated like idiotic cripples, incapable without a master. We do the dirty work better — and cheaper — when we believe we're mindless and desperate, when we're kept mindless and desperate. And God knows there's a lot of dirty work to go around in this sun-forsaken shitehole. 'Clean' and 'work' never did go together in my experience of them. I've never had a sense of clean but for that one time when we went to see Doctor Knox at his home in Newington and the housemaid — all prim and proper in her bright white apron and crisply ironed uniform — shot me an alarmed look like my very gaze scattered filth about the place. And you would have thought it was *her* place, she seemed so proud and protective of it. I imagined her as a shot then I can tell you, that self-righteous look etched on that slag's ugly, judgmental face for all eternity. In my business, timing is everything and you can be in the wrong place at the wrong time. *Remember that, priggish Sadie. See, I remember your name, because your mistress had addressed you as I stood at the door. And, trust me, I could pick you out of a crowd. Count yourself lucky that you didn't spend your free time in my neighbourhood, or you might have ended up in Surgeon's Square in another capacity.*

I think Sadie would find, if she took the time to study us both, that the good doctor and I actually have a fair deal in common. You could call us brothers of a sort. At the tavern with the Mute after a rough day's work in the body business I would have called us *blood brothers* and heard a vicious laugh in response, one informed by our shared dark secret. Even the Mute, like your dedicated *Courant* readers, knew that the educated Robert Knox, being a doctor after all, the most famous anatomist in Edinburgh, must have noticed the particular freshness of the dead subjects

30

being delivered to him, fresh subjects with no signs of disease or wasting illness. Indeed, this was one of the requirements for the sale. I heard him comment about that on both occasions where I watched him painstakingly inspect the bodies, top to bottom, front and back. And yet, certain questions were never asked. Not once. Funny thing, that.

Did the cat get your tongue, good doctor — you, who, it is said, eloquently mesmerise your student audiences?

If the plain truth were told — and I do like to tell it, especially with a full jar in hand before a rapt, drink-charged audience well into the wee hours — Edinburgh is, itself, a type of death manufactory given the dozens whose lives are destroyed here by the day. Take the horrifying case of the climbing-boy James Thompson, trapped in a chimney in Albany Street and then slowly and excruciatingly killed, pulled to pieces with a rope by a vicious master-sweep trying to extract the wee boy's body from the black, soot-lathered hole of the chimney. Or the countless children on whom parents take out insurance before dispatching them by the quickest means possible. And I know that my mammy would have a right, good belly laugh knowing that so many dedicated hard-working folk are putting themselves into an early grave trying to make their burial society payments.

I can hear her now, as I imagine describing the madness pervading Edinburgh.

'Have you ever heard the like of it?' she would chortle uncontrollably, the tears streaming from her eyes as her hands busily peeled potatoes into her apron.

'Such is the fate of the great unwashed,' I would remind her, the wry, critical smirk coming over my face.

'And here in Edinburgh, as in the rest of this misguided country,' I would state with emphasis, on the brink of launching into one of my layman's sermons, 'the great unwashed are the great uneducated.'

This would have met with pained laughter as we shook our heads pathetically.

But sitting here now, on this side of prison bars, my laughter has ceased.

Like those who, armed with pikes, muskets, and pistols, stood up for liberty nearly a decade ago at the Battle of Bonnymuir up the road in Falkirk near Nelly's people, I have spent these last many years trying to think for myself.

You can see where that has brought me.

Some of those *traitors,* as they were branded at Falkirk, had fought at one time, as did my brother Connie and I, on behalf of this misguided country. For their valiant efforts, Andrew Hardie and his associates were either summarily executed, like their good covenanting brothers before them, or transported for levying war. May they all rest together now in heavenly peace.

Once said faithfully, but now only in hope and out of habit, I repeat:

One day, we shall be reunited, my brothers, in a far, far better place.

***

Edinburgh. Auld Reekie. Athens of the North. A two-faced harridan of a city, if ever there was one, with its Old and New Towns. It shouldn't surprise you to know, Mr. M—, that I have rarely visited the New Town, and then only briefly and under the cover of darkness. Its precise streets and immaculately arranged and cultivated gardens serve as a stark contrast to my regular haunts in Edinburgh's decrepit dark underbelly. Crossing one of the bridges connecting the two Towns is like traversing two worlds, two different historic eras. It is like moving from heaven to hell. The contrast is horrifying, the idea that such a chasm can be bridged, stupefying. One would sooner believe in God.

I well remember, going on six years now, after work on that bloody Union Canal was complete, my introduction to this maze-like city of confusion with its rat-infested closes and wynds. I recall wandering aimlessly during those early weeks after coming in from the Haymarket, sometimes at night, sometimes during the day, always alone. I felt embraced at first, my curiosity seduced, each road, like a distinctive lady of the night, beckoning me on, enticingly. But, as everyone knows who has walked them, Edinburgh's maze-like closes have a curious way of closing in on you, of swallowing you up whole, a fitting gesture in this sprawling, hostile monster of a city shadowed by a gloomy fortress. I have met many — children especially — who are unaware that anything exists beyond Edinburgh's walls or that they can actually leave. Especially here in this West Port, they think the Flodden Wall impassable.

What was built as a fortress city, remains, for many vulnerable and downtrodden folk, a fortress city.

In its excess of precipice-style streets and precariously structured timber-fronted tenements, just when you thought you'd reached the lowest hovel on the lowest close, you find you can descend even further. Follow me along the Cowgate to the South Bridge vaults, where taverns and other shopfronts, one of them a cobbler's, are carved deep into the recessed arches of the bridge, the putrid air from the middens inside enough to catch hold of your throat, stifling you. Accompany me to my neighbourhood of Little Ireland, which encompasses the Grassmarket, the Cowgate, King's Stables Road, and the gorge known as the West Port over which the castle towers like a menacing overseer. Despite recent so-called *improvements* to this crush of habitations, this chaotic marketplace of tanners, corn merchants, tobacconists, candlemakers, and hawkers of all things imaginable — old clothes, human hair, skins of every variety — it remains a domain of outcasts, unwanted, dispossessed — some have called us *hangers on*. I could never figure out what we, who have nothing to show for ourselves save for a few clothes and a pot to boil potatoes in, were hanging on to. There are such cellars of misery here that your good *Courant* readers would shudder to think about, let alone enter.

It seems only fitting that, in this sublime, decaying city where the rich dead own more land than the living poor, one should stumble into a cemetery at every turn. Here we struggle, we who exist like ghosts perched on the precipice of picturesque graveyards in which our bodies may never be interred, our lives never commemorated, Edinburgh tightening up like a noose around our collective throats. A drunken man could be forgiven for thinking he'd died and entered hell itself if he woke up after a night of excess in this West Port, the old gallows seated at its eastern extremity, the overwhelming stench of animal putrefaction from Tanner's Lane inescapable, retch-inducing.

I see them up close every day, these poor, dying folk of Edinburgh, desperately trying to avoid the charity workhouse on Bristo Street. They are but wraiths, hypnotised by famine, disease, and brutality, the bottle and the drop being daily, necessary crutches providing them the fastest way out of Edinburgh. And they'll do anything to get them, says yours truly, an ever-desperate brother now riddled with the cancer who'd do what was necessary for his *wee drap of medicine*.

Edinburgh has now seen, since our arrest and trial, what desperation can do.

Serving as my own counsel, I should have said in my defence, 'Edinburgh drives most people to drink, but it drives some people to murder.'

But they directed my responses then, as they did everything else in my life up until that point, so I'm saying it now.

It feels right that it finally be committed to paper.

5.

Nelly

My mother was buried on the parish in an unmarked grave two days after she died and, within the month, in the same damp, dilapidated church, more than a decade after she'd planned it, Bridie married Rab.

Apart from the scrawny, lisping preacher in his worn, creased breeches who performed the ceremony, I was the only one in attendance. Make no mistake, I was there out of duty, at my grandfather's request.

Their courtship had begun the day of my mother's interment when Rab, instead of placing the flowers he'd brought on my mother's grave, gave them to Bridie. My grandfather, who witnessed the act, not wanting to disrupt the solemnity of the funeral, said, in a low serious voice, unmistakable in its outrage, 'This is no the time to woo, but you were never one for respect, were you, laddie? She's no even been buried yet.'

To these statements, Rab paid no heed. After the funeral, he came around every evening with small gifts and food offerings to take Bridie out for walks. If the cold-hearted Bridie can ever be said to have looked happy, it was then, during that short period of courtship. While she was still miserable around me, it seemed a subdued misery.

While I didn't understand the change that I saw in Bridie then, I understand it now. Men can make a hell of a woman's life, or a heaven. With one dramatic, unannounced entrance or exit, they can change its entire course.

Ever patient in the face of my grandfather's stubbornness, I managed, over those few short weeks, to uncover details about my mother's life. My grandfather swore me to secrecy as he told me that Rab had been engaged to Bridie, but then took up with my mother who soon became pregnant. My mother began to stay out into the wee hours and drink, which was not her way, but after my grandfather intervened, she agreed to stay off the gin until the baby arrived and give me over to Bridie. Some days were bitter battles, he told me, as he had to lock my mother in his cottage to keep her from leaving the town as she, on many occasions, threatened. Several times, he said, he feared she might do harm to herself, or to me, while trying to escape. Rab only came to see her once, having been barred after a violent argument when my grandfather told him he never wanted to see his lying, cheating face again. Much to his amazement, Rab complied — until the day of my mother's death.

I wasn't certain of my fate once Bridie married. I suspected my grandfather would take me to live with him up the lane so that I wouldn't be underfoot, but Bridie surprised me one morning when she said that Rab wanted me to stay there, with them. From the look on Bridie's face, that idea also came as a surprise to her. I sensed they'd fought over it, which gave me even more reason to resist the invitation. I wanted to stay with my grandfather and help him out as best I could, but when I raised the matter, he put me off saying he was worried about his health and now was as good a time as any for me to have the family I'd always wanted.

'You need someone long-term to take care of you, lassie. I'll no be around forever.'

A couple of years earlier, my grandfather had been badly injured in the coalmine where he had worked for over thirty years. The person in charge of the windlass that lowered the baskets into the pit had lost his balance one morning, rumoured to still be drunk from the night before. This brief loss of control left my grandfather and his friend Jamie Baird scrambling to grab hold of the wall to right themselves. My grandfather counted himself lucky. While Jamie had fallen to a horrible death, dozens of feet below, his body mangled, his face smashed almost beyond recognition, my grandfather had only been maimed on his left side. While that arm never lifted another pint and he walked with a limp, he was thankful to be alive.

'How could I possibly, being a useless cripple, look after a young lassie?' My grandfather's words, part apology, part justification, ring in my head to this day. Little did he know what he left me to.

I wanted to say, 'How is it you can still work?' but I thought better of it and bit my tongue. He was my cherished grandfather and the only love I'd ever known.

I pleaded nonetheless, saying that I could help him. But he was a ferociously independent and stubborn old man who, especially since the death of my grandmother ten years earlier, had convinced himself that he didn't need anyone.

'No one,' he would say every time her name was mentioned, 'no one could replace her. She was my forever lassie.'

He didn't mention my grandmother that day, but I could see that he had made up his mind.

So it was that I went to stay with Rab and Bridie.

I worried about Rab whose relationship to me remained unclear and around whom I felt instinctively uncomfortable. How was I to address him? Although he had never said so, he was my father by blood, but in terms of affection and duty, no father to me. Over the course of my life, I have received more affection from strangers and, as my grandfather had told me, Rab had never paid a single shilling towards my keep.

'Lassie, he's a man forever in and out of work — more out than in — and long wedded to the bottle. He can hardly keep himself.'

As was my way, I decided to let the matter sort itself. Having been ignored by Bridie, in whose house I had learned to live like a ghost, I kept well out of the way and quietly went about my business.

For a time, that strategy worked but, true to the story of my life, all comfortable arrangements soon came to an end.

***

It was just a few months after Rab had moved in and gotten to know the rhythms of the household. I returned home late in the afternoon after cleaning my grandfather's house and running a few errands. Rab usually wasn't back until after sundown when Bridie had returned from Mrs. Hamilton's where she worked as a housemaid. Sometimes he didn't return at all but when he did, he was drunk.

Bridie and Rab were already having rows and Bridie liked nothing better than to blame them on me. I loved nothing better than when the cottage was empty. I took full advantage at those rare times to read some pages in the tattered copy of *The Pilgrim's Progress* given to me by my grandfather who had been teaching me to read. Whenever the opportunity presented itself, I escaped into the pages of that other world, imagining myself in the body of another person, especially one having fantastical adventures. I was a slow reader and sometimes had to ask my grandfather to help me figure out some words when I went to visit him. I felt myself on the pilgrimage with Christian in this dream-tale and had rushed home to pick up where I'd left off — where Christian first encounters Apollyon.

But this day, something was wrong, different. I felt it from the moment I entered. There was another presence in the room. I saw nothing initially but, glancing around, I caught sight of Rab as I closed the door behind me. He stood at the hearth where the fire had been started and stoked hours before it should have been.

When I thought about it later, I realised he was on the look-out for me, waiting.

'Hello,' I whispered, startled and barely audible, before trying to move away.

But he, amused by my awkwardness, would have none of it. In a voice that was uncharacteristically calm and kind, he said, 'Come to the hearth wee hen and get warm. It's cold outside.'

It was the term of endearment, hollow and foreboding, that sent shivers through me. Something lay behind it. He had never addressed me in a kind manner. Never before had he even noticed me. Most worrying, never before had we been alone together, for which I was thankful. My mind ran in several directions at once. I knew Bridie would have my head for kindling the fire so early. She was a witch for such details as the careful meting out of our little coal allotment, and I was the one entrusted with this important job. Now, Rab had upset the usual arrangements and I would be the one to pay for it with a sound thrashing. I dreaded the thought: unthinking and usually with painful consequences, Bridie used whatever came to hand to beat me — a metal brush, a hard, dirty shoe, her red, rough hands. As much as I feared her punishments, I was more afraid of what lay before me. Something didn't feel right.

'I'm not feeling well, and I need to lie down in my room,' I insisted, trying to move away again. But Rab sensed a lie and was persistent.

His next words, uttered as he sat down on the stool in front of the fire and as if he hadn't heard me, sounded more like a command.

'Come here.'

His words were like blows, so I did what I was told. Rab, impatient, rose and pulled me into the front room where he once again sat down on the low stool. Still standing, I tried to free my hands from his crushing grip. As he looked into my face, the putrid odour of alcohol on his breath hit me hard, turning my stomach. I thought of my mother and the stinking, noisy pubs I passed the few times I saw her. In an instant, instinct kicked in. Fearful and sensing that Rab was about to get angry, I reminded him that Bridie would soon be home and expecting dinner on the table. His response was immediate and detailed, betraying how carefully he'd planned things out.

'Not tonight, she's not. She's helping Mrs. Hamilton until late, remember?'

He said the words calmly, followed by an amused laugh.

Feeling trapped and desperate to get away, I told him my grandfather was expecting me to go to his house soon to drop off a few things.

'You know him,' I said, issuing a warning, 'He'll be worried if I don't show up on time. He'll come looking for me. He'll come here.'

But Rab just laughed again, squeezing my hands even harder.

'Fridays are always your grandpa's pub night, lassie, you know that. So, let's get comfortable. C'mere,' he said, pulling me roughly onto his lap before the fire, my back against his chest.

I had no choice but to submit or risk my arm being broken, so I sat frozen, my body tensing up and my gut tightening as Rab began to stroke my hair with his filthy, calloused hands. My stomach turned as he pressed his slimy, stinking lips against the side of my face and up against my mouth.

I tried to scream as he groped me, one hand clasping my waist while the other struggled to remove my short-gown and muslin dress.

While I usually hoped Bridie would stay away from the house, this time I prayed for her to come home.

As I pulled my head away from his stinking mouth, Rab started pulling at my clothes, careless of damage. My shift was badly torn as it caught my knee. I crossed my arms in defence, trying to cover up my breasts. It was then, never having been exposed to the eyes of anyone since my body started changing, especially a man, that I began to cry, pleading with him to stop. But Rab was deaf to everything, and I saw he had somehow pulled down his trousers. Only my drawers remained on when he wrenched me back onto his lap. I grew tenser as his strokes grew more intense, squirming and trying to pull away as I felt something unfamiliar pressing up beneath me. Rab's arms held me so tight I thought my ribs would break. I could already feel the bruising from his fingers and wondered, my mind racing, how I was going to explain them and my damaged shift to Bridie.

I struggled to breathe as he roughly turned me to face him and stuck his thick, foul-tasting tongue into my mouth, gagging me. As he fought to pull my drawers off, I fought back. Pain shot up my body as I twisted my left leg trying to stop him. When he clasped his hand over my mouth to silence me, he stopped me from breathing. Just as I feared he might suffocate me, something hard pushed up against me. It seemed to tear open my insides. As I bit Rab's hand in order to draw breath and reached down to push the unknown thing away, my hand emerged, slimy and blood-streaked. I gasped when I saw it, inhaling deeply. I was a limp doll in Rab's straitjacketing arms. To the sound of his rhythmic grunting, and with pain surging through me, I fainted.

When I came to, I was laying on the floor, shivering uncontrollably, my clothes strewn about me. I looked up to see an angry Rab standing over my naked body. I tried curling up to cover and protect myself, but he wrenched me onto my knees, and holding his face close to mine, he spoke, menacingly, 'This was your fault, you hateful wee whore. You've got your bloody mother's eyes. She thought she could refuse me too. She kept reminding me of my promise to that dour drudge of a sister of hers. But I showed Maeve, he said, grimacing. Even when she said no — because she did say no, she would say no, she always said no — I showed her. Just like I'm showing you.'

With this, he laughed and spat at me as I, still shaking, sought to cover myself.

Throwing some clothes at me, he said, 'Make yourself decent and get dressed. You wouldn't want Bridie to see you like that, would you?'

Later, after Bridie returned and went into the kitchen to put away some shopping, Rab turned to me with a snide smile on his hateful face. When he knew he'd caught my eye, he lifted his index finger, placing it firmly against his lips.

I felt sick as I looked away, knowing that, like my mother before me, I would be forced to keep his dirty secrets.

***

The weeks that followed remain a sleepless haze. The first few days were the hardest as I tried to conceal my bruises and injuries from Bridie and my grandfather. My drawers were streaked with blood for several days. A severe burning and stinging plagued me, especially when I peed. My left leg ached constantly and my ankle was sprained, making any movement difficult, but I did my best to try to walk normally. I was terrified that Bridie would find out and that the horrible events would be blamed on me.

'Just like her wanton, whorish mother,' I could hear Bridie tell my grandfather, revelling in her nasty, judgmental words.

Night after night, sleepless and weeping and biting my pillow pretending it was Rab's throat, I struggled to process what he had done and said to me. I now understood my mother's actions over the years, her life turned into a living hell, tormented and violated as she was by this brutish monster of a man. I ached to tell my grandfather the truth about my mother whom he had rightly surmised was more sinned against than sinning. But this would mean telling him what had happened to me, so I thought better of it and bit my tongue. I knew if my grandfather found out the truth he would find some way to kill Rab, damning his own life in the process. I couldn't run the risk of sharing Rab's dirty secret.

Besides — and I can admit this now — I was convinced it was my dirty secret too. Perhaps I was just like my mother in some bad, horrible way that I had yet to fully understand. Perhaps I had some hidden way of attracting bad men?

Over the following weeks and months, I wrestled with my demons over my role in it all. Why, I wondered, had God brought me to that house? Was there something wrong with me? Something perhaps even evil about me? 'Like attracts like,' my grandfather was fond of saying. I turned those words over in my head many a time, struggling to understand their meaning.

At other times, I was consumed by violent thoughts of revenge. I prayed fervently for Rab to lose his safety-lamp or be trapped in the pit where he was working. I prayed feverishly to Mary, my body rubbed raw with my hairshirt, to let him drink himself to death in the pub or find himself on the wrong end of a fight, the very bloody, brutal end. I begged God to let him die by alcohol poisoning the way that Ida Newell's husband had just a few months earlier. But my prayers were futile and fruitless. In desperation, despite knowing self-murder was a sin, I offered my own life as a sacrifice. What did I have to live for?

I was fervent like Christian. I had Faithful by my side. Apart from reading *The Pilgrim's Progress*, I prayed relentlessly every single day. My life collapsed into a desperate cycle of working, reading, and praying. I was sick and terrified every single minute, preparing myself for Rab's next attack.

Despite my fervent prayers, he remained alive and uninjured.

***

In the months that followed, the horrors continued. Rab's assaults increased in force and frequency along with the threats to tell Bridie, if I failed to arrive at the house when directed, that *I'd been seducing him, showing myself to him naked and inviting him to lay with me.* The worst thing was I knew Bridie would believe him. Terrified by this prospect and sick with despair, I stopped eating and bathing, all of which called Bridie's ire down upon my head.

'They'll be saying I can't look after weans, and that it's a good thing I never had any, if you run about with such dirty clothes and matted hair. You look more and more like a dog by the day.'

And then she added, in her gleefully menacing way, 'More like your mother.'

Rising to the height of her tirade as she slapped

45

frantically at my legs with her heavy leather shoe, she added, 'I might've known you'd turn out like your mother.'

It was about that time that I gave up on God and Mary and turned, instead, to a different power. Telling my grandfather I had a friend in the village who had died and I needed something to remember him, I asked him to fashion another toy soldier as a companion to my mother's doll. I asked him to colour its hair short and black and make a coffin for it. I'd already made its clothes from one of Rab's old shirts.

Over the months and years that followed, I inflicted countless abuses on that doll. I started with a naming ceremony followed by a baptism by fire, speaking Rab's name aloud and wishing his soul into eternal hellfire as I rapidly circled him over and into the flames with Bridie's cast-iron tongs. I then dunked the doll into a pail of dirty dishwater to put out the flames. Nightly, I took special pleasure securing that doll, slightly charred, into his coffin bed, stuffing in, for good measure, several stifling, dirty rags I'd used at my chamber pot. Then, I'd bury him deep in the fireplace ashes and soot, only to recover him the next morning to conduct further fantastic abuses upon him. There wasn't a wall in the house he hadn't been slammed up against or a table from which he hadn't been violently thrown. I'd even taken long sewing pins from Bridie's basket and, with the aid of my grandfather's mallet, pierced him through the head in various directions. I laughed aloud one afternoon as a section of his head flew off.

But the weeks passed, fast becoming months, and Rab continued healthy.

Finally, with a courage that came with age, I determined to take matters into my own hands. It was clear no one was coming to save me. Then as now, I was on my own as I faced the City of Destruction. I was left to save myself.

One day, when my friend Colleen sent me to buy strychnine at the chemist's for a rat problem, I thought about poisoning Rab. I remember weighing out the options, considering whether to use the strychnine on him or myself. I finally rejected both options worrying that if I killed him, I would be discovered and hanged. As I imagined the verdict being read and the noose readied, I also realised I couldn't bear to see my grandfather suffer.

I have learned that there are ways to defy the devil when you can't defeat him. I have had a lot of practise. When Rab violated me, I learned to look straight past him and play dead, the way my drunken, self-medicating mother must have done over those many, unbearable years. *Channelling* is my word for it. It involved concentrating my whole being behind my eyes and thinking myself out of my body. The minute Rab's hands touched me, I could withdraw from my own flesh, rising above the scenes of his painful and humiliating crimes. Without moving my lips or opening my mouth, I would curse this repulsive man at a safe remove, wishing him dead and buried in the deepest, blackest grave, one that would swallow him whole, strangling him breathless, stifling his voice as he had so repeatedly stifled mine. Stifling *his* ability to say no.

I cursed him countless times under my breath as his breathing grew loud and uncontrollable, and I imagined tearing open his throat with my teeth. I delighted in the idea of his perishing from blood loss, slowly and painfully, before my entranced, delighted eyes. I remember looking directly at and through him, taking pleasure in the thought that, unknown to him, I had killed him in exacting and excruciating ways, countless times.

I learned to revel in the knowledge that Rab could

47

not know and control everything. My mind and imagination remained my refuge.

The devil is a brutal taskmaster who teaches hard lessons, like the fact that the most precious things do not lie in the flesh. We are deceived in such notions. Wounds heal and the body recovers, but the spirit is another thing entirely. You would give every guinea you had to protect it, if you had the guineas, and if you were given the magic and the chance.

Sadly, as in my case, you never are.

My nightmare with Rab caused the very air around me to change. In place of the lightness I once felt, Rab constricted me, making it difficult to breathe. He left me pregnant with fear and rage. What I remember the most is how he made me hate my own body. Try as I might, I could never wash his filth away.

Looking back across the years, I can say that my body has recovered from Rab — from Rab and Billy, and their ilk — but my spirit never will. If ever a spirit was shrouded and scarred, it is mine. It has been my horrible fate to become versed in the twisted and tormented ways of bad men, tutored in their sickness, and tortured to stay silent. I lay smothered beneath their dirty, guilty secrets, secrets I now know were theirs and not mine.

For a time, my voice went unheard, but I am finding a new one here in this journal, a sombre and sober one, as I try to make sense of the senseless, the goal of all writing.

***

'C'mere.'

His calm tone suggests an intimacy between us, a grown adult and a young girl, once twelve, now fourteen. It suggests that I am acting freely, and that he is doing nothing wrong.

But I know better, having tried each time to resist and reclaim my own body. Once, my channelling failed and I wildly bit him on the arm, hard and deep, drawing blood and leaving fleshy, ragged marks where my teeth had managed to cut through. He was as shocked as I was at that moment. I recall his rage as he wrenched me up onto my feet so brutally, pulling out some of my hair. I managed not to cry despite the sharp pain shooting up my back. Never once did I let him see me cry but, privately, I wept for days afterwards, my head being horribly tender to the touch.

A lack of power can be felt in the body, in the gut. It even reaches deep into the spirit. To enter Bridie's cottage was to be at the mercy of a merciless man, to be suffocated in the sunless, dank coal-pit of his sick and miserable life. Until Billy, Rab was the darkest soul I'd ever had the misfortune to meet. Given his lack of control, I feared for my life every time he touched me — and for my grandfather's, whom he had threatened to hurt if ever I spoke about what was being done to me.

This time, as he forces some whisky down my throat, a drink for which I have developed a taste, I vow that this will be the last time, that I will flee somewhere, anywhere, come what may, to save myself. But the next words out of his stinking, vile mouth, stated in such a matter-of-fact tone, stun and silence me, throwing my thoughts into confusion.

'You've got a baby in your belly, you wee whore.'

My gasp is so audible it startles me, sounding as if it came from someone else. I choke, finding myself unable to breathe, the air sucked out of the room. As I process Rab's statement, I am glad for the drink and the calm warmth it provides despite the shock of his words. I crave more.

His next words make my heart pound hard in my

chest.

'Can you just imagine what Bridie will do when she finds out?'

I am only fourteen and naïve, still ignorant about the possibility of babies. I feel sick as I try to understand his words.

Perhaps there is some truth to them. Perhaps, and this idea sickens me the most, Rab, who has forced *my* body to do *his* will, knows more about my body than I do. My belly has been swollen in recent weeks, a change I don't understand. I am relieved that this change has not yet been noticeable thanks to my loose shift.

I realise that the cramping, thick, messy bleeding that started late last summer has stopped for some months. This must be a sign, but I wouldn't know as there is no one to speak to. Where I gave thanks that the blood stopped as I feared I was dying, I am now terrified. To the endless list of reasons I hate Bridie, I add the fact that she never taught me anything about the workings, the cycles, of my own body. I vow to learn more and help myself.

Half an hour later, after Rab is done with me, he slaps me hard on the belly before leaving and says, emotionless as usual, 'You'd better see to yourself. You don't want a brat at fourteen and you'll have a lot of explaining to do.'

***

The next day I undertake the necessary, final ritual of burning Rab's doll to cinders in the fireplace. I gather my few clothes from Bridie's house, along with my mother's coffined doll and tattered copy of *The Pilgrim's Progress*, and make my way up the lane to my grandfather's cottage. It is very early morning and I know he has already left for the pit. I can't bear to see him but have planned to tell him I love him and not to worry. As the magic of writing is a skill I don't yet possess, never having stepped foot in a schoolroom except once to clean it, I leave my message by way of a small arrangement of wildflowers on his pillow, one of my childhood rituals of which he was fond.

I have also come with another purpose in mind — to retrieve the box of toy soldiers that he has promised me upon his death. I discover them on the bottom shelf in his kitchen wall-press, the wood cover securely fastened, alongside his few cobbling tools. Before I secure them away in my sack, I count the number of remaining dolls to make sure none have been removed. I realise I think of them as a family, connected to my family. They are my only inheritance.

With my few things packed, I lie in my grandfather's box bed for some minutes for what I know will be the last time. I bite my lower lip to keep myself from crying but the tears come regardless. I recall him reading to me here, covering me up and comforting me when I was sick. As I remember his caring last words to my dying mother in this bed, I become racked by sobs. Of everyone I have ever known, I hold no one closer to my heart than this strong but humble, fiercely caring man. I would sooner die than hurt or disappoint him. I briefly compare him to Rab, wondering how God could have fashioned both of them.

God continues to confound me.

But now is no time for thinking. I kiss the pillow gently three times as I have done countless times before, place the wildflower arrangement lovingly on top, and make my way, one last time, through his cottage door.

This goodbye is keen and bittersweet and overwhelming as I leave the ghost of the girl that was me behind.

The minute the word *baby* was mentioned, I knew where I was headed. It was the only place I could go, the only other place I'd ever been — several miles down the old Redding Road to Maddiston, the marital home of my cousin Ann, daughter of my uncle Derek, my grandfather's only son who left home, never to look back, when he was only fourteen. I remember thinking, as I tramped along the road, that I was following in his footsteps. This family had its patterns.

My feelings were mixed as I walked, blind to the beautiful natural world surrounding me that was in the full throes of spring. As happy as I was to remove myself from Rab's brutalising hands, I was heartbroken about never seeing my grandfather again. He had been my rock, my guiding light. I could never bring myself to tell him of Rab's abuses. I knew he would kill him and end up in jail. My leaving, I told myself, protected us both.

Bridie had only taken me to Maddiston twice, the last time five years earlier. Both trips were cherished memories as I spent my time playing in the fields and talking with Ann, then sixteen, whose knowledge about the world seemed boundless. She answered all of my questions and even knew some family secrets about which others never spoke. She told me how my grandmother, around whom there was a veil of silence, was a Catholic who had died, it was whispered, by her own hand after her fourth child died in infancy. Some said she was simple-minded and the baby had nothing to do with it. Ann and I discussed that possibility and decided we knew better.

Never before had I met such a storyteller. Ann's imaginary tales enchanted me, a child ignorant of goblins, witches, fairies, and dragons. Was it any wonder that, when the time came to leave, I refused to hug her good-bye, and cried my eyes out as Bridie and I made our way back home? I sobbed for days afterwards. In saying good-bye to Ann, I left behind a newly discovered world of magic and fantasy, one it pained me to lose. Life wasn't fair. I resisted and resented being pulled away from this longed-for older sister. But Ann remained caring and charming to the end, secretly handing me a small, polished purple stone as I went out the door. When I carelessly lost it some weeks later, I was inconsolable. It was as if I'd lost a family member and had gone into mourning. I vowed never to tell her of my crime of losing that special stone, fearing she would forsake me for my carelessness, and read that loss as my betrayal of her.

I remember praying, as I approached her door, that she wouldn't ask about it.

As I watched a wee bonneted child and her mother disappear down a nearby laneway before I reached Ann's house, I was reminded why I had come. Babies. Ann was the only person I'd ever talked to about babies and now she had two of her own. Unlike when I was younger, the very word now terrified me, and I hoped that Ann would know what to do. While her man had agreed to marry her once her first pregnancy came to light, I had to conceal the shameful story behind my situation.

But my reception was not what I'd hoped. Ann was greatly changed. Within an hour of my arrival, after disclosing my circumstances over tea, a clearly agitated Ann, who couldn't stop fidgeting, let me know that I couldn't stay. It was impossible, she said. I thought I heard her voice break up as she said it. As she scolded her boisterous wee boy who was noisily scampering about the cottage, she rocked her crying baby and told me that her husband, who was then away at work in the fields, hated her family and kept her from them, even though they lived nearby. He would be angry if he learned she'd been talking with me, *a cousin on the cusp of disgrace.* I winced, visibly, at this description from a woman who, just a handful of years earlier, was in my shoes. When she promised not to tell my grandfather what state I was in if he came looking for me, I winced again.

Stung by her words, I barely heard her as she told me the name and address of a woman a mile out who might help with *my predicament.* I didn't know what sort of woman this could be who might help a poor young stranger expecting a child, but I was thankful she existed. A painful sense of being utterly alone came over me as I embraced Ann and wished her goodbye before turning to the door. A profound sadness overtook me as she pulled back, this girl I once loved like a sister, now an unsympathetic, judgmental woman.

After tucking away the packet of buttered bread and cheese she gave me for the road, I began my walk toward Muiravonside Wood where I had been directed. For a few short moments, I considered turning around and heading back to Redding but the horrible image of a naked Rab and Bridie's hostile face accosted my imagination. That's when I heard the voice. There was no doubt it was a woman's. Distinctly and forcefully, it said, 'No'. Startled, I looked around, thinking it came from someone nearby. But there I stood, all alone on the road.

I had heard tell of people to whom God had chosen to speak, but I knew this was not Him. Besides, I didn't think then that I was someone to whom He would speak.

Although I had only heard my mother's voice briefly as she lay dying, I knew instinctively it was her. Her next words were unmistakable and unwavering: 'There is no going back'.

Exhausted and desperate, my fond memories of

Ann shattered, I heeded my mother's words. Despite my fear of the unknown and my aching feet, I kept walking.

6.

Billy

Some ideas reveal themselves as if they were part of God's great plan, inspired from above. Such was the way with the idea to sell the bodies to the anatomists at Surgeons' Square. It was a cheat really. Landed in our laps. Basic arithmetic: Old Donald succumbed to dropsy in the Hares' tramp house when he owed them four pounds from his army pension, and his corpse was sold to clear the debt. In the face of a problem, we found a solution. Or it might be truer to say I found a solution although I relayed it to the Mute in such a fashion that he thought, by the next morning, in the haze of his hangover fog as he presented it to that cunt Margaret, that the idea was actually his. So it always went with the Mute.

'The militia sold some of its dead to the surgeons,' I had told him. 'That's how we got rations some days.' Had Hare actually listened to me at the pub, he would have known this months earlier, but something gave me cause every day to wonder at the Mute's intelligence.

'And I have heard tell of many an Irish wake where the corpse was spirited away before the burial could actually take place. Seems the family was too drunk to notice … or simply too desperate for more drink. The dead were made to pay for their own send-off.'

As Hare's unsettling smile spread across his ghastly, scarred face, I knew the deal had been sealed.

'Desperate times call for desperate measures,' I pronounced, to which the Mute responded menacingly, his smile growing wider in his big, heavy head, 'And a debt's a debt.'

Although Margaret had offered Nelly and me free lodging until we *found our feet in Edinburgh*, the Mute's words also seemed directed at me. It was time for Nelly and I to earn our keep. I would agree to that as long as Nelly would be kept in the dark. I well knew that would be an amazing feat for these two tongue-waggers.

'A deal's a deal,' I agreed, and thought to myself, 'including those, like this one, made with the devil.'

***

Around daybreak the next day, the Mute and I made our way through the Grassmarket, up the Cowgate to the South Bridge towards Surgeon's Square. It was a frigid December morning with a light snow and I remember wishing for some thick moleskin trousers and a new woollen bonnet as my eyelashes started freezing together as we battled the bitter wind up the Cowgate. Even the stench of manure and human waste seemed blunted by the cold air. As agreed in advance, I did all of the talking, approaching a trio of young people, obviously students as they were dressed in frock coats, to inquire as to where we might find the Professor of Anatomy.

'That would be Dr. Monro,' one answered readily, eyeing us curiously in our shabby labourers' clothes, wondering, I could tell, as to our presence on University grounds. After telling him our business, he added, 'But you'll get more money from Dr. Knox.'

These words caught our attention. Hare turned and looked at me, winking discretely, his hideous smile fast forming. I asked where we might find this Dr. Knox, to which the young Paterson, as he introduced himself, replied, 'Surgeon's Square. Ten Surgeon's

Square.' He pointed to a clean white building opposite with what appeared to be a small belfry on top. A winding garden walkway led up to the gate.

'That is Knox's Anatomy School. I am the good doctor's assistant. But you must return after dark and knock discretely.'

We told him that we — John and William, as we called ourselves — would be back early that evening and that he should expect us.

By the time we returned to Hare's flophouse at Tanner's Lane, the carpenter had already delivered the coffin, deposited Donald inside, and nailed down the lid. Not wanting to appear too conspicuous, Margaret had hired three saulies to mourn the old soldier, and when they retired next door for a few drams, Hare hastily pried open the coffin lid with a chisel borrowed from a neighbouring tanner and helped me move Donald's body to my bedroom in a sack. Margaret decided that mine was the safest room for his storage as it was an inner apartment on the main floor that looked out onto a pigsty and a wall. It certainly seemed the best choice as I had lived there for some months and had never seen anyone outside the window. Still, an inner voice cautioned, anything could happen. We had to be careful.

I was less concerned about strangers discovering our plan than I was about Nelly. She would be shocked by my actions, sickened in fact. A lack of respect for the dead went against everything I had ever professed to believe. Hadn't I condemned the sale of soldiers' corpses during the war? Hadn't I called the people who had sold them criminals? Wasn't Nelly shocked that we had gained rations from their sale?

Nelly had also befriended Donald the very day we'd moved in, going out on a whisky run for him almost immediately and then sitting up in his room to talk, which was something unusual for her as she was generally withdrawn, except when she was drinking. She returned over an hour later, tearful, saying he reminded her of her beloved grandfather.

Given a bad row we'd had one night, I also knew how Nelly felt about dissection or, as she referred to it, *the public and shameful cutting up*. She was also concerned about *the ultimate violation,* as she called it — the utter disregard for spiritual resurrection, the life to come. The body must be kept inviolate, she told me, as if I wasn't well-versed in God's word. 'There can be no dissection,' she said, as if schooling me, 'or there can be no resurrection.' Despite all of her wrestling matches with God, as she liked to call them, she remained a believer. But I suspect it was the disrespect shown to the body in this life, on this side of the grave, that upset her the most.

Perhaps I was just nervous but, as I waited for nightfall, I sensed that Nelly suspected something. To keep her out of the way, I rose early and sent her up Bell's Wynd, further away than usual, to hawk shoes for the day.

Thankfully, all was going as planned with Donald, although my heart was racing like a whippet's as the Mute and I scrambled to fill the coffin with tanner's bark stolen from the adjacent laneway, before re-securing the lid. I scrutinised the saulies closely upon their return to ensure they didn't suspect anything. They seemed fairly sauced and jovial, noticing nothing. One raised his cap and declared Donald *a poor old soul gone too soon* before he scrambled back into the cart with the coffin and headed up the Grassmarket towards the burial ground.

Doing as Margaret told her after she returned home, the unsuspecting Nelly cleaned out Donald's old room. When she came down later, she told me the place *stank to high hell* and desperately needed airing. She had salvaged a couple of shirts for me that, with a bit of sewing, would do the trick. While I didn't relish the thought of wearing Donald's old clothes, I couldn't let on for fear that Nelly would sense something was wrong.

After Margaret picked up some tobacco, the four of us made our way over to the White Hart. The Mute and I threw back a few gills of whisky before hitching his old mare to the cart where Donald lay buried beneath layers of sacking. We stopped briefly at Bristo Port to compose ourselves with a brief smoke. For the rest of the journey, my mind raced from one potential obstacle to another, the terror of being found with a dead body in the cart, plaguing me.

As we approached Knox's school, I resolved to consider all of my answers carefully should we be asked any questions. Stopping the cart in a shadowy enclosure by the door, I looked warily around for passers-by. Apart from a few students heading towards the Cowgate, no one was around. I worried that Paterson may have forgotten our arrangement and we'd have to return to the West Port with the dead body, which would soon begin to rot, in tow. Thankfully, Paterson answered the door almost immediately after we knocked. Hare and I hastily removed the body from the cart as Paterson ushered us in. We negotiated the awkward, heavy sack between us down a long, narrow hallway into what Paterson called the anatomy theatre.

As we entered, our footsteps echoed loudly up and down the cavernous, candlelit room. A solid oak table, the room's focal point, stood before us, and we placed the sack down lengthwise upon it as Paterson directed. In the dim light, I discerned a gallery of seats rising up around us. For a few moments, I considered the prospect of sitting in one of those privileged seats. I imagined pursuing an entirely different path had fortune smiled upon me. But an inner voice reminded me that my calling was to the Church rather than to medicine. I remembered from terrifying childhood sermons how science could lead down the devil's highway. These reflections were interrupted by Paterson who asked us to remove the body from the sack and lay it out on the table. Although he spoke in a normal tone of voice, it echoed eerily throughout the room. Doing as directed, we pulled Donald, clad only in a tattered shirt and long underwear, free of the burlap sack, placing him face upright on the wide, solid table before us.

Paterson gasped when he saw him, startling me something fierce as I feared he suspected foul play. With an urgency in his voice, he told us to remove Donald's shirt and underwear. He expected the doctor any minute, he said, agitated. We reacted immediately, doing as we were told while he explained that under Scottish law, possession of a corpse is not a crime, but possession of their property is. 'From now on,' he said, looking directly at me, I noticed, rather than the Mute, 'the bodies must be delivered entirely unclothed.'

'Remember that,' he repeated. 'Naked, or not at all.'

I tried to process all three suggestions together — that transporting a dead body through the streets of Edinburgh was not a crime, that being in possession of a dead man's clothes was considered theft, and that we would, in future, be delivering more bodies. I didn't know which idea was more surprising, and I ran through them in my head as I stared towards the edge of the dark, scarred table in front of me, nervously gnawing at my lower lip, glancing up from time to time.

Within minutes, I heard footsteps and a balding, monocled, man, whom I knew must be Dr. Knox, emerged from out of the inky hallway and walked over to the table. His severely pockmarked skin became more apparent as he approached. What little remained of his scraggly hair was curled and hanging untidily about his neck and shoulders. His clothes and demeanour struck me as oddly out of place. Standing there in his black frock coat and bright burgundy waistcoat, he seemed dressed for an evening's entertainment in a very different kind of theatre.

My wandering thoughts ran to another extreme. Even though he didn't look at us directly, and I felt uncomfortable being on the side of his monocled eye, I felt anxious in his presence, my fears growing by the minute that he might alert the baillie about our possession of a dead body. Even paupers could be buried on the parish. Why hadn't this one? This was the type of obvious question I knew I would be asking or, at the very least, thinking, if I were standing there in his shoes. My mind would run even wilder, I thought, if the scarred and demented-looking Hare were standing in front of me, the body of a recently deceased man stretched out before him.

My palms were growing sweatier by the minute, my throat more parched. I craved a dram. Or three.

Dr. Knox seemed to have swallowed a few drams himself recently, I thought. He appeared slightly intoxicated standing beside us, muttering to himself. He proceeded to move around the table, pressing and prodding the body lightly with his fingers, occasionally lifting and closely scrutinising a limb. I watched in wonder as he picked up a candle and carefully manoeuvred it above and around Donald's body as if conducting some strange religious ritual rather than a medical inspection.

I studied the good doctor closely as he stood before me, this curiosity of a man who, with a glint of pleasure in his eye, leaned in closer to inspect Donald's head and neck. As he ran his fingers along his throat, a question arose in my mind: What particular lesson in anatomy would Donald be used to exhibit? I dreaded to think.

Hare and I had stepped back from the table almost instinctively as Dr. Knox undertook his inspection. I felt slightly unsteady on my feet, finding the entire process fascinating yet grotesque to witness. And here I was, as I imagined Nelly's accusatory eyes trained on me, a participant.

Such was my entry into the body business. I was keen to leave but had decided I was going nowhere without payment. I had come too far and invested too much. This very risky business required compensation.

I turned my attention to Hare, ever the dullard, as he peered up into the large empty theatre where the doctor's guttering candle was casting flickering shadows against the tiered seats and ceiling. Staring at him, I wondered, as I so often had, if he actually thought or felt anything. Had his thoughts, even for an instant, turned to Donald? He might as well be lying on that cold wooden slab instead of the old dead man, I thought to myself, there now being little difference in intelligence between them. I chortled inwardly.

As my mind continued to wander as I glanced around, I wondered if anyone — or perhaps any *thing* — lay hidden away somewhere in that still darkness, watching us. Unlike Nelly, I have never been a believer in spirits, but I sensed something in that room that evening, some presence.

I struggled to contain myself as I stood there, my scrotum tightening as the cancer reminded me of my own mortal condition, this mortal coil, as my beloved Hamlet referred to it. Donald was free of it all now, I thought. He was well beyond the treacheries of this world.

Or was he?

My mind turned again to thoughts of Donald's fate after we left. It wasn't the threat of no resurrection that unsettled me, although it once would have done, but that of being carved up like a roast lamb, although a bit more precisely and, thankfully, not for human consumption.

Violation was the word Nelly had used at the pub some months earlier when we discussed bodysnatching and the surgeons. I remembered thinking her concerns and reactions extreme. But now, as I imagined the room packed with an eager group of gawping students focused on a dead, unclothed body on the table, failing to recognise that this was once a living, breathing man with a voice and feelings, I understood better.

And yet, I thought, as I continued that debate internally, all of us fear death. We want to resist our final silencing and any type of desecration. But all will be returned to dust. *That which is born of the flesh is flesh.* Desecration, of one sort or another, will eventually overtake us all, rich and poor alike.

My thoughts ended abruptly as the doctor, his inspection complete, adjusted his monocle and turned to the practical details, details I thought would have been left to his assistant:

'The subject appears to be a good specimen. It looks very fresh.'

Despite this being said in a matter-of-fact way devoid of any suspicious tone, I was unsettled again. With my eyes glued on the body, I tried to see Donald through the Doctor's eyes, to reconsider him as a large piece of beef in a butcher shop, but to no avail. I could not reconcile the doctor's words with the man who lay before me looking as if he were only asleep.

After clearing his throat, the doctor set the candle down on the table and stated very matter-of-factly, 'We can offer seven-pound ten pence.'

Trying not to look surprised or pleased, I consulted Hare with my eyes. His eyes had opened much wider when he heard the doctor's words. And then his mouth fell open. And no wonder. To us two men who had undertaken gruelling physical labour for two or three pence a day our entire working lives, this amount of money was nothing short of staggering.

Looking as if he were actually about to speak and possibly jeopardise everything, I quickly cut Hare off and, as calmly as possible, confirmed the deal.

'Good,' Knox responded, as he stepped away from the table, seeming anxious to leave. Nodding to Paterson, he quickly added, 'We would be glad to see you again when you have another cadaver to dispose of.'

The word *cadaver* was entirely new to me and whether it was the way he said it or the foreignness of the word itself, I felt uncomfortable. With a single word, the dead Donald had been transformed. No longer was he a man but a *cadaver*, some sort of object that could be sold. This had the effect of making the whole business both unpalatable yet digestible.

Thinking carefully over Knox's words, the idea of Hare and I being involved with *disposal* cast our enterprise in an altogether different light. It did make me uncomfortable, a man known at the pub for a twisted sense of humour who appreciated a good pun. Constantine, my brother who lived in the Canongate, was one of more than a hundred street-sweepers, or *scavengers* as they were popularly known in Edinburgh, the vast majority of whom, as you well know, Mr. M—, are Irish. Those Irish, it is popularly said, are naturally born to the business, being regarded in Scotland as dirty, rotten scavengers themselves. Connie has long been employed in the disposal business, cleaning up everything from offal and dung, to rotting food and muck. I had never before considered corpses as a type of human *waste*. This was a new idea, one I needed more time to consider. I wondered, at this early point in the enterprise, if I could adjust to the good doctor's way of thinking.

Setting these ideas aside, I knew one thing for sure: the fact that the Mute and I could each make, between us, more than a full-year's wages in a single evening made us giddy with excitement. I now craved more whisky to toast our good fortune.

As we exited into the bracing night air, I reconsidered the challenge of crafting a credible lie for Nelly. With the exception of my mother, I had never known a woman so quick and observant. It was one of the reasons I was so drawn to her, had stayed by her these many years. She was as challenging as I was. It was also one of the reasons we were at each other's throats, fighting incessantly, especially when the liquor was flowing and possessive jealousies took hold. It was also why I sometimes hated her.

Keeping my story straight and staying mute about this business would also prove tricky for the other players involved: Hare was an ignorant braggart when drunk and Margaret had a penchant for gossip, coupled with an intense hatred of all women, especially Nelly, *a damnable Scotswoman*, as she frequently called her. I had a lot to negotiate if I was going to sign onto this enterprise long-term.

Knox had certainly captured my attention with his parting words: finding fresh dead bodies in a city that was churning them out by the hour couldn't be that difficult, I thought to myself. It was true that I had only come across a few unclaimed bodies over the course of my years in Scotland. Seeking them out might be considered work like any other, but find them, I was determined, we would. I said as much to Hare as we made our way back, excited over our good fortune, to our favourite pub in the West Port. Only to myself did I think, 'Otherwise, we may have to get creative.'

***

As luck would have it, about a month later, Joseph the miller, a regular tenant, fell seriously ill. Margaret urged *his expedient removal*, a phrase I knew she must have picked up elsewhere, Margaret not being particularly good with words. One night, after Nelly retired early, the two approached me with apparent worry about the possible infection of the other tenants. I pushed for calm and patience in the face of what I knew to be a ploy. These two missed their calling in the theatre, I thought briefly to myself, although I can see right through their superficial distress to the self-interest beneath.

'It's one thing to be ill,' I said, ignoring Hare and daring to look directly at Margaret, 'it's entirely another to be dead.'

Margaret's voice lowered, growing serious as she rounded back on me. 'I have my business to consider, Billy, and might I remind you that you and Nelly have been benefitting from that business for several months now. Indeed, you've been doing very well here if I do say so myself. If word gets out that we're harbouring a sick man, that's the death-knell for this lodging-house.'

I knew what Margaret was pushing for, so I insisted again on patience. 'Let's give it another day or two, Margaret. Nature might yet take its course and we may be spared any rough business.'

But Margaret was not a woman to wait once she got an idea into her head. The fact that the money we made off Donald was nearly depleted made her more impatient, so she renewed her appeal. 'Perhaps we should send Nelly up there to see what state he's in. She's pals with him, as she is with most of these sorry layabouts, and can probably weigh up the situation better than we can. He's paid up until Saturday, but he did nothing but vomit all last night. He can't have eaten in several days. I'd say he's not long for this world, but I have no guarantees, and you know me, Billy — I like guarantees.'

The mention of Nelly worried me. As was her way, Margaret wanted to involve Nelly in order to blame her if something went wrong.

'Not a word to Nelly, Margaret,' I snapped back, in warning. 'You know our deal. Should you breathe a word to her, I'm out.'

Besides, Nelly had been unwell lately, often sleeping long hours. She had also been vomiting in recent days, which was unusual for her. She was the type of woman who would work through anything, even the heavy bleeding she had every month. For a moment, I wondered if she had contracted Joseph's illness.

'I say let's make a quick shot of him,' Hare piped up, to which I feigned incomprehension.

'A cadaver,' said Hare, winking at me meaningfully. This time he spoke slowly and purposefully as if the tables were turned and I was slow in understanding. 'C'mon,' he said enticingly, in a manner unlike the usually mute Hare. 'Let's make a shot of him. The whisky's on me.'

'It's actually on him,' Margaret quipped, her responding snigger confirming my suspicion that they had discussed this idea in private and a plan was afoot. As usual, there was much they hadn't considered.

'And what about signs of foul play? Dr. Knox is an eagle eye as we've seen, and we'd swing for murder. No, I say let nature take its course. If he's deathly ill, it shouldn't take more than a couple of days. Then we'll make our way to Surgeons' Square.'

'No harm in helping nature along a wee bit,' Margaret immediately responded. 'Happens all the time, and no one's any the wiser.' Taking another swig of small beer, she added, 'Suffocation might be the best way. I heard tell of a woman who killed her husband that way once,' she said, looking meaningfully at Hare, 'and no one suspected a thing. He looked just as he did most nights when he came home drunk.'

This statement was as close to a confession as I would ever hear from Margaret, whose former husband Logue, the owner of the rooming house, had died suddenly and suspiciously the year before. Rumours had raged that she and Hare, a former lodger who had quarrelled with Logue and with whom Margaret was probably carrying on, killed him. These two, I thought to myself, are a ruthless couple of characters when they want something. Best to handle them with care, especially for Nelly's sake.

Still, there was no denying it: a payment of seven or eight pounds was the best prospect we had before us. After an hour's drinking and discussion, I agreed to *help make a shot of Joseph*. Barring his natural death beforehand, we determined upon doing it the next night and of using a heavy pillow and a lot of pressure. Suffocation, we thought, would be the least suspicious method. If he would drink a few drams first, we believed he would go down easily.

The minute after I'd signed on and a plan was arranged, Margaret went off for some gin and whisky. I headed off too, intending to make an early night of it. Instead, I shifted around restlessly as I thought through the plan, waking Nelly several times that night in my agitation. I got up twice and paced, and then had a couple of shots of laudanum. Finally, I went down.

The next day seemed to fly by, the time to act coming quickly upon us. As I left Nelly that night, I felt fearful as I wondered again whether Joseph's ailment might be contagious. Nelly, in her usual calming way, assured me that she was suffering from female troubles. I kissed her good night before I left, something I hadn't done in some time, our intimacy having diminished since my discovery of my illness. This was the other secret I had kept from her for months now. I couldn't bring myself to undress in front of her lest she see my red, swollen groin. Although I'd had pain for over a year, this was a new development. I couldn't bear to look at it myself. I drank to put it from my mind. There was a hardness in one sack and it was painful when touched. I flinched at the very thought of it. A doctor I'd visited had sold me a small sling for it to reduce the pain. I knew what Nelly would think: that I'd been with a whore again and contracted something possibly even deadly. Had I given the pox to her?

The answer was no but it took some time — and money — to confirm that. While I had been guilty of visiting whores in the past, that was several years ago. I had since put a stop to it as my pain was increasing. With some of the payment from Donald, I had visited a doctor who tried fixing me with a poultice using some ointment containing mercury. The swelling increased, suggesting I had something far more serious, something he called *scirrhous testicle*. At times I still desired Nelly, as much as I ever did. She had the rare ability when just kissing me to drive me into a frenzy of passion. No one could match her, but the stabbing pain and nausea that came with arousal was far too much to bear, and I knew once she touched me she would know something was wrong. So, without explanation, I had withdrawn from her in recent months. I worked hard to quell my desire and blunt the pain with whisky and yet there were times when stopping was not an option. I had managed to finish a few times in complete darkness, but I did so with a horrible mix of pleasure and agony, much more pain than pleasure. The sweet release often didn't come but when it did, it came at a cost.

It struck me as Hare and I made our way up to

Joseph's room, that I was harbouring an increasing number of secrets from Nelly. This was new for me and unwise as I knew how observant she was. It was only a matter of time before everything would be disclosed. Still, I reflected, turning my thoughts in a different direction, supplying Dr. Knox could change everything for us. I would buy her something new with the payment this time around — the silver luckenbooth brooch I had long promised, perhaps. This money could save us. I could find a doctor who might have a cure and we could leave the city and get a small cottage, just as Nelly had always dreamed, out in the countryside. Perhaps God did have a plan and he had led me to Margaret and Hare for a reason. Our troubles could soon be over.

Despite the sour smell of sick in the dark, unventilated room that accosted us as we entered, and Joseph's gaunt and chalky face, I wasn't convinced that it would only be a matter of time. He was too vocal and lucid. Perhaps these two greedy criminals had, with an eye to more drink and meat, exaggerated the state of affairs. While I lit up a new two-penny candle and propped Joseph up in his bed with the pillow I'd told him I'd brought for his comfort, we engaged in idle banter. Hare poured the drinks and I tried to catch his eye, thinking that perhaps we should rethink the plan. After all, Joseph seemed to perk up in our presence, telling us he'd been feeling better since he woke up mid-afternoon. He craved a full fry-up in the morning, he said, but for now, he said smiling, 'a few stiff drams might just do the trick.'

After a couple of hours of talking and drinking, Joseph started to fade before us, his speech slurring as he nodded off, so we decided to go about our business as planned. The alcohol had somewhat calmed my nerves and strengthened my resolve. Still, I was agitated, my heart beating wildly. Hare and I took a last drink before positioning ourselves at both ends of the bed. Telling Joseph we were going to shift him around for greater comfort, Hare pinned Joseph's legs to the bed while I squeezed the pillow firmly over his face to keep him from breathing. Despite being sick and drunk, he resisted, throwing his arms up violently and striking me in the face. Briefly removing the pillow, he turned his head, and desperately sucked in some air. He then tried calling for help, but I had recovered and secured the pillow, muffling his cry, rendering it audible only to us.

Realising our method wasn't working as planned as Joseph's flailing arms remained free, I ordered Hare to grab them as I tossed the pillow aside. Using one hand to seal Joseph's nose shut, I pushed his chin up to seal his mouth. Long unshaven, Joseph's prickly whiskers dug into my fingers. As I released them briefly to find a better position, he opened his mouth and bit my hand. I winced at the pain but made no sound as I sealed his mouth shut again. Once a strong man who spent years in the Carron Ironworks, Joseph struggled and resisted for several more minutes. When there was no more struggling, I instructed Hare to release his legs as I removed my hands from Joseph's face.

What we witnessed next shocked us both and remains etched in my memory. Although Joseph's eyes were closed, his body was convulsing, his chest rising and falling as he took some final deep breaths. The pale face of a few minutes earlier was now streaked with red as frothy blood and mucus drained from his nose and mouth onto the bedclothes. I stood staring at his bloodshot eyes and his body as it seemed to be emptying itself out — of air, urine, and, based on the smells that wafted around us, everything else.

Replaying the events later, I tried to process the fact that a person could be alive one minute and dead the next. What I saw that night taught me that death is a process rather than a moment. One doesn't just die. It's not a sudden thing. Death takes time, coming in stages. The last long deep breaths, I thought, are as precious as those we experience at birth. Just as the spirit enters the body, so must the spirit make its exit.

It might sound bizarre but a warm feeling of calm pervaded the room afterwards, a feeling so unlike my agitation as I, in keeping with the plan, helped Hare to strip Joseph naked. Afraid of being discovered, my arms and legs were trembling as we collected Joseph's other clothes, shoes, and boots from the room's small cupboard as Margaret had directed. In anticipation of the morning when we would take his body to the doctor's, we pulled the bedclothes over top of him before leaving. As quietly as possible, we descended the stairs.

***

I lay awake for hours afterwards trying to take in what had happened, what I had done — what *we* had done, I reminded myself — but I could find no rest. A former militia man who had never seen battle but had encountered some corpses in my time, I could not erase the images etched in my memory, the experience impressed on my hands.

Agitated, I rose well before Nelly and took a long, unsettled walk through the moonlit West Port, then up the Cowgate and back, trying to calm myself down before returning to the tramp hotel.

Only then, prior to getting back into bed, still agitated, did I realise I was wearing Joseph's shoes.

7.

Nelly

I didn't know what to expect as I headed, as directed, down the Main Road in Maddiston towards Jeannie Morris's cottage at the Western edge of the Muiravonside Wood where it met the North Glen burn.

'Everyone knows Old Jeannie's cottage,' Ann had assured me, 'in case you lose your way.'

Thankfully, I hadn't lost my way, although I did worry, as I walked, about my safety and where I would sleep that night if I went astray. I was relieved when I arrived.

Jeannie's stone cottage was tucked away in the forest backing onto the burn. She had a small pen a few yards off for her goats, pigs, and chickens, with a herb and vegetable garden in which she was working when I showed up. A stout woman with dark eyes and greying hair who looked to be at mid-life, Jeannie turned towards me with an open smile as I approached, almost as if she knew and expected me. I appreciated this warm welcome after I'd walked in an agitated state after leaving Ann. As Jeannie led me into her warm cottage where I was greeted with the smell of smoky peat, and chicken soup, I introduced myself and told her, 'My cousin Ann McDougal gave me your name and directions.'

Jeannie paused for a moment before saying, 'I only know of her, but I've met your Uncle Derek and remember him fondly. He helped build my henhouse, but that's going back many years now.'

Gesturing for me to sit down, she continued, 'It's nice to hear your family's getting on fine but,' she said, placing my sack on a nearby stool and focusing her attention on me, 'I can tell that you aren't. When girls come to me there is usually something wrong. I don't ask questions. I'm just here to help.'

To this point in my life, I'd had little interaction with complete strangers but, from the outset, I found it easy to talk to Jeannie whose demeanour invited me to confide in her. She felt familiar and sat quietly, listening attentively the whole while as I recounted some of the horrible details of my situation, some of which I'd initially decided to keep to myself. She punctuated my pauses with *I see*, held my hand, and drew me close whenever I was relaying an especially difficult episode. Never once did she interrupt. When I was done and had broken down sobbing, she said, 'Nelly, you have had some early and painful life lessons. Many men don't deserve the name. But you have nothing to fear. You have come to the right place. I can help you. But first, let's get some food in you as you've walked a long way and must be half starved.'

While I had built up a thirst walking, I hadn't thought about food, the packet Ann had made up for me remaining completely untouched. But Jeannie was right: after some hot tea and chicken soup, mashed turnip, and a slice of thick-cut bread and butter, I felt better and, more importantly, safe, out of harm's way. These are feelings I'll always associate with Jeannie.

She then handed me an old flannel bedgown of hers and told me to put it on while she prepared a hot toddy. I did as I was told, soon sitting up in her box-bed sipping the warm mixture as she covered me up with a few blankets.

'We'll see about it all tomorrow,' she said, stroking my hair and holding my hand as I drifted off. I tried to process all that had happened in a single day, but exhaustion fast overtook me. In this cottage, with a complete stranger, I felt as if I had been relieved of a great burden, one I'd failed to recognise I was carrying. As I lay enveloped by calm, I took the time to savour the moment. It was the first time since sleeping in my grandfather's house years earlier that I'd felt safe and at peace.

I believed then — as I believe now — that my mother was guiding and watching over me.

***

Some people you can't bear to be with for ten minutes, while others make ten years feel like a drop in the bucket and you welcome thirty more. So it was with Jeannie, so alike were we in temperament. She was a quiet, thoughtful woman who liked her space and respected that of others.

From the first to the last, she treated me like a daughter, and she was like the mother I had never known.

She was also the teacher I'd never had, instructing me about the natural world and all things practical, from sewing and cooking, to raising animals, growing food and herbs, and, perhaps most importantly, preparing herbal remedies. This last allowed her to help other women with a variety of female troubles over the years, and it was what she used to save me. My wish to learn more about my own body was answered by this wise, experienced, and caring woman. Regardless of their backgrounds, she treated every woman who entered her cottage — young or old — with respect. To Jeannie, everyone was someone from whom she could learn, and who could learn from her.

As I learned from her early on, Jeannie and I may have had different histories, but the end results were the same: unplanned and unwanted pregnancy. As she told me the next morning over hot porridge and tea, she had come inland with her father and sister from Mull to the outskirts of Glasgow some forty years earlier, after her mother died in childbirth. Her newborn brother died just a few days later from the jaundice. Her father had tried everything, but nothing could save him. Jeannie's little sister, Rosemary, was six and fell to the eleven-year-old Jeannie's care while her father, a weaver, worked all day and night at home. It was her father who'd trained her in the powers — both curative and destructive — of herbs. He often used his knowledge of traditional Scottish medicine taught him by his mother to help his poor neighbours who lacked money for a doctor. Over the years, Jeannie said, the village doctor scoffed at and denounced him, even sometimes warning people against her father's *devilish practises*. There had certainly been people he couldn't help, who were well beyond help, but his herbal remedies had saved many from terrible pain and sickness and, in some cases, death.

Eight years after they'd moved to Coatbridge, some ten miles East of Glasgow. When Jeannie was sixteen, she fell madly in love with a young lad named Iain who'd come in from Airdrie to apprentice with her father. They'd made plans to marry and live for a time with his parents, but when Jeannie revealed she was pregnant, he broke down and confessed that he'd been promised to another girl back home, a girl he'd known since childhood. He begged Jeannie not to tell her father she was with child as he only had another month left as an apprentice. He also begged her to be rid of the baby.

'You told me you know about these things,' he said. 'You have the medicine. You know what to do.'

While Jeannie stayed quiet until Iain's apprenticeship was done, she was deaf to his pleas to end the pregnancy. Ashamed and unable to tell her father what had happened, she decided to raise the child on her own. After Iain left, she set out for Maddiston. Her greatest sorrow was leaving her father and sister behind but she had no choice.

It was a long journey for a young woman expecting a child, but she hoped an Aunt would assist her. This Aunt became, in Jeannie's words, her saving grace. She and her husband took Jeannie in, helping her to birth and raise Ruth, her daughter. As fate would have it, Ruthie was a sickly child who never saw her second birthday. She died one autumn morning in her mother's grief-stricken arms.

'It was as it should have been,' Jeannie said at this point in her story. 'Some folk are not long for this world and I sensed when she was born that she was one of them.'

Craving her independence, Jeannie decided to move into the derelict cottage in Muiravonside Wood. While she continued to practise what she'd learned about her father's herbal medicine, she had also learned something of midwifery. She decided to dedicate herself to helping women with their female troubles. In combination with raising a few animals and tending a garden, by the time I arrived, she had assisted many dozens of women. Never once, if they were pregnant, had she judged or put pressure on them. Each woman, she said, must arrive at her own decision in her own good time, the raising of children not being, as she had learned from experience, for everyone, and never for the faint-of-heart.

Unlike some, I had made up my mind about the baby the minute I realised my situation. The prospect of seeing Rab's eyes in a baby's face sickened me beyond words. I couldn't even consider that child mine given what had been done to me. I also swore not to repeat my mother's history, and I was terrified, as Rab was my father, that the baby would be some sort of monster, deformed or mentally defective in some horrible way.

'I have to be rid of it,' I told her, my eyes looking down fearfully at my belly. 'I know that sounds horrible, but I have no choice.'

Jeannie asked no questions and set immediately to work after relating some details about the process and the pains I could expect.

'Thankfully,' she comforted me, 'you're not too far along, not even half-way. I am hoping it won't be too bad or take long. My only worry is you'll have a wee bit of tummy trouble with the medicine, but that's the worst there's been yet.'

I did do a lot of praying, and I was fortunate. In a week I was well enough to help Jeannie in the garden and with the animals, my small attempt to repay her. Unfortunately for Jeannie, but fortunately for me, my timing was right as Jeannie's back went out on her the day before I was set to return to Maddiston to find work as a housemaid. It took her months to recover, over which time I managed the place under her direction. I have never learned so much so quickly or worked as hard as I did then. Jeannie was a patient teacher and I was an earnest student. I surprised myself. I also felt I owed this wise woman my life.

Once Jeannie recovered, the issue of my staying on was never addressed. Everything had simply fallen into place. I was there for five years, over which time I learned about herbal medicine — how to identify and prepare such herbs as savin and the oddly named black hellebore that she had used to treat me. I became versed in the strengthening and soothing properties of yarrow and dandelion, meadowsweet and lady's mantle, and the stimulating effects of pennyroyal leaf.

Writing this from where I sit now, I am overcome by deep feelings, for I loved the pace of that life and its peace. Never before or since did I feel myself in touch with another person and the natural world. There was a harmony to my life that I had only known at times when I was alone in nature in childhood. On many occasions later in life, I wished I could have returned to Jeannie's cottage and that I had never left it, but some lives are plagued by bad timing.

Now, with some of my ailments, I couldn't live Jeannie's active life.

Then, in my early twenties, I couldn't stay. Something was missing.

Figuring out exactly what that was forever changed my relationship with Jeannie. But she was older and wiser, and she saw it coming.

***

What was missing from my life had a name. It was Ewan Alexander Morris. He had a job — master sawyer — and, after living in Glasgow for many years, a permanent cottage in Maddiston. He was also, unfortunately, twice my age, had a wife named Marian, several children, and a concerned aunt named Jeannie with whom he had recently become reacquainted.

I first met Ewan when I was nineteen and I remember everything — his tall frame clad handsomely in his dark workman's clothes, his muscular, freckled forearms, his caramel-coloured eyes, and most of all, his thick, wavy red hair that had a magical way of catching the sunlight no matter where he was standing. I didn't want to take my eyes off him. I *couldn't* take my eyes off him.

Better yet, although it took me a while to realise it, he couldn't take his eyes off me.

Never having been attracted to anyone before, I was slow to figure out my strange, new feelings — why I blushed around him, turning my eyes away when he looked directly at me, or why heat radiated up through my body when I pictured his face. I knew he was married and I shouldn't have these feelings, but I was helpless to control myself. And things only got worse after we talked because he acted as if I was worth listening to. No man, except for my grandfather, had ever given me that sense before.

It was Ewan's third visit. He'd come to repair Jeannie's chicken coop and she insisted he have breakfast with us beforehand. I found him so attractive I couldn't meet his eyes as we sat there eating, but I laughed at a few things and made a few comments. Just as we were finishing, he looked at me curiously and said, 'There's a lot going on in that head of yours. Most people — especially most people your age — don't think much about anything. They spend their lives trying not to.' He looked over at Jeannie as he said this, and she nodded in agreement.

'Work, drink, and sleep. That's all they want, all they care about,' Ewan continued. 'But that's not enough for me. That's never been enough. I suspect you're the same, Nelly. Just like Jeannie.'

I remained silent as Jeannie offered up a few extra words.

'You couldn't speak truer words, Ewan. Nelly has a mind of her own, and it's a sharp one. The world doesn't always appreciate that in a woman, but I've yet to find a problem she can't figure out and fix somehow. I was lucky she came along when she did. I am thankful to God.'

For a moment I feared Jeannie might reveal something of why I came to her, but my worries were in vain. She was, as ever, discreet, respectful, and protective of me.

After Ewan had gone home, when we were tidying up, Jeannie told me more about him. His wife Julia had lost her fourth child at birth a few years earlier and, although they moved away from Glasgow and closer to their families, things hadn't been right between them ever since. Ewan had relayed this information to Jeannie who then spoke to Julia about it. Julia now feared another pregnancy, but she rejected the methods Jeannie suggested, feeling she was going against God. Julia and Ewan continued to drift apart.

Jeannie's voice grew serious as she said, 'Nell, I can see you've taken a shine to him and he to you.'

Feeling embarrassed and flustered, I was preparing to protest when Jeannie put her arm around my shoulder and said, 'I've got eyes in my head. Never forget that.'

'I don't want to tell you what to do,' she continued, 'but I think it's best to leave such men alone. I've had ample opportunity myself over the years and I resisted, as tough as it was sometimes. But I know how these things are,' she said, returning to the washing-up.' I remember it well.' She sighed deeply, staring off into space, out the back door to the forest beyond.

After a few minutes, she turned back to me. 'Just promise me you'll be careful, Nell. We can often heal bodies, hen, but I have yet to find herbal remedies for the heart.'

***

Several weeks later, while Jeannie was away at the market in Maddiston, Ewan and I were intimate for the first time. He had come inside to get something before starting work and engaged me in conversation. It all felt strange, like I knew it would happen, that it had to happen. Still, I wasn't entirely prepared when it did. He told me he couldn't stop thinking about me the entire day after we'd had breakfast. He kept hearing my laughter in his head and had since carried on imaginary conversations with me about a whole range of things. There was so much he wanted to know, he said. I reminded him of the pleasures of companionship, made him hungry for them again.

In short, he told me, I had *wrecked his resolve.*

With no prompting from me that day, he talked about the loss of his fourth child and how, ever since, his wife had refused to let him touch her. He even felt she was repelled by him, blaming him for their baby's death. He'd come home late the night she went into labour. The baby came fast and by the time he had fetched the midwife, the wee boy lay dead, his face a ghostly whitish blue, his body curled up, the cord wound around him. That startling, horrible image, he told me, haunted him over the months that followed as he tried to cope with the loss. His wife's rejection made matters worse. He hoped she would eventually recover, but after a year, he realised that was wishful thinking. He tried, he said, but there was no talking to her. He felt judged and punished.

I felt Ewan's pain as he spoke, and knew he was reaching out for comfort. The next thing I knew, we were kissing. My head was repeating his wife's name but my body, which had only known violation, was repeating his. I craved the contact and when it came, it was soft and caring and loving, like nothing I had ever imagined. Ewan's caresses were a healing balm that brought me to life, setting off a fire I never knew existed. I have since cried bittersweet tears in the throes of the memory of those beautiful moments.

Over the course of the next few months, every Tuesday when Jeannie was away at the Maddiston market, Ewan and I met, offering each other a salve for our aching hearts.

One day, he showed up early with what I felt was a sense of purpose. Saying he felt uncomfortable in Jeannie's house, we went outside. Ewan pulled a heavy wool blanket from his cart and led me to a nearby copse of trees where we both lay down. It has been many years but I remember him like it was yesterday, this slow and gentle lover whose body seemed, naturally, to fit with, and respond instinctively to, mine. I was so much smaller and slighter than him. He handled me like I was breakable. And in certain ways, as I only discovered when it was far too late, I was.

I thought I had gone into things with my eyes open, but I was fast blinded. He had brought me to life, every aspect of me — my body, my mind, my heart — in ways I had not imagined possible, especially after how I was violated by Rab, a vile, repulsive man who had crushed all possibility out of me and made me hate my own body.

Every Tuesday when Ewan left, I craved him more. I wondered how I had lived without him. How had I, until now, managed without such affection and intimacy?

But it was not to last. And it was he who ended it, without a single word of explanation, apology, or goodbye. He just stopped coming to Jeannie's, not even dropping in to check on her.

Over the next few painful weeks, it became clear that Jeannie knew something was wrong. I was withdrawn and barely eating. Our conversations, once animated and frequent, died away. Although I sensed she knew the truth, out of respect for my privacy, she did not push me to talk.

Early one Tuesday morning after Jeannie had left for the market, I set about packing my few things. I lovingly made up the bed, laying a sprig of angelica across the pillow of the only mother I had ever known. I thought, as I did so, about how my life was a series of leave-takings. Tearing myself away from Ewan was painful, but leaving Jeannie caused me the greatest anguish. Here, in this beautiful place, I had found my truer, better self, a self at peace. I had also found a mother who nurtured me with a love I had never before known. She was, like my grandfather, a gift, a blessing, a rock. For me, to leave her was unthinkable — to choose to leave her was unbearable. But I felt it was time. I had no other choice.

I knew where I was going and the trip was overdue — Maddiston. But I wasn't going to look for Ewan and I decided that if I ever saw him again, I would ignore him as if he were a stranger. Like Rab, Ewan was dead to me, although I have since thought, with great sadness, of Ewan as my one, true, precious love.

As for Jeannie, I tucked her great love away — as I had my grandfather's — like a secret and sustaining treasure in the depths of my heart.

***

Trust me, if I could go back and redirect my steps and take another road, I would. I would go anywhere else, anywhere, even South into England where I vowed I'd never go, or over to Belfast by steam packet.

I didn't realise it at the time — how could I? — but it was in Maddiston that things went horribly wrong. It was there I met Billy and began drinking.

I had gone into the village in search of two things — a job and a school — and, luckily for me, the two came together: I cleaned the Muiravonside Parish School in the early evenings and, as arranged with the schoolteacher, was helped with some reading and writing during the day. It was part of my payment. What little money remained after paying my room and board went towards my new, ever-faithful companion — whisky. Often when I was sitting in my room late at night, nursing a dose — or several — I envisioned myself meeting Jeannie again and telling her that she was wrong — there *was* a remedy for a broken heart. It might be costly and result in nasty head and stomach aches the following morning, or blindly stumbling along the road like my mother once did, on those very rare occasions when I did go out in public, but at least it granted some temporary relief, some release from the crippling and tormenting pains of my life. But as everyone knows who has relied on it, the more you drink, the more your life falls apart, the bad decisions piling up like dead bodies around you while your daily need grows.

Since my arrival in Maddiston, I had avoided the market on Tuesdays, so I never saw Jeannie again.

A few years slipped quickly and quietly by on this schedule, a certain carelessness coming with the territory — my meals growing meagre, my clothes more unkempt. When I began to get sick more frequently, I drank more whisky and excused it as medicine. I remember feeling happy that my indulgences were private. As such, I fooled myself that they were more controlled and my drinking wasn't a problem.

By the time the navvies, both Scottish Highlanders and Irish, overran the village in 1818 to start work on the Union Canal, I was a die-hard secret drinker with a secondary penchant for laudanum. Although they indulged openly and raucously in a way that I — a woman intent on privacy — could not, I felt a strong kinship.

Say what you will about the navvies, one thing can't be denied: they are the hardest working, hardest living men on God's green earth. Given what Billy told me, that way of life — and death — comes with the territory: if you aren't as tough as nails when you start digging ditches, carrying loads, and cutting drains for canals, dams, and roadways for fourteen hours a day, you become that way over time. You have no choice. Such endless, back-breaking work beats the life — and the hope — out of you. Billy told me how angry he became once at a political rally when he heard the navvies described as *Scotland's engine of improvement*. He wondered who and what was being improved. The men he knew were reduced to walking cripples after sustaining injuries every other week. While they made their masters stinking rich, the navvies became misshapen shadows of their former, sturdier selves. To survive, they were forever self-medicating with whisky, gin, and other tinctures and medicines. If they survived past forty, they were good for little more than driving a horse and cart or becoming street hawkers. Driven like animals to do as much physical labour for the smallest wages possible, seasoned muckshifters dug enough in a single day, Billy told me, to bury themselves a hundred times over. Some of them did just that, the number of casualties enough to shock anyone who was paying any attention. But no one was.

There were some things that people did pay attention to, things that terrified them enough to be decried from the pulpit, like the fact that the navvies came armed with explosives and all manner of hand tools for their work — shovels, pickaxes, saws. That they did so in combination with drinking endless amounts of liquor horrified many an upright citizen.

'It's only a matter of time,' some ministers warned a year into the canal's construction, 'before they'll turn on their rate-paying masters. Mark my words. We'll see our Peterloo here in Scotland.'

On pay-days, the navvies were especially raucous, resulting in scores of brawls and injuries, and a rash of cases of the Irish flu with its morning-after vomiting and severe headache. Tramping through the countryside, sleeping wherever possible, often bathing naked in the canals at dusk and dawn, they either upset the locals or provided entertainment. People sometimes brought their children around to see them on a Saturday. Such a spectacle they were, a zoo of sorts, grown men treated like caged animals. And on a Sunday, entire congregations were sometimes marched down to their ramshackle huts to gawk at them from a distance, while their self-righteous ministers gesticulated fiercely, calling God's judgment down upon their wicked heads.

I saw things differently, recognising an opportunity. There was a lot of money to be made servicing them, so service them I did. My landlady, Lizzie, who worked at the baker's was an earnest assistant who was amply rewarded for every navvy she sent my way. Eager to attract a certain clientele and keen to conduct my business privately, I set up shop in my room as a palmist who, for a shilling, could read the past, present, and future from the lines on the hands. As only certain select male clients were informed, I also offered a palming of another sort on the side or, to be more exact, under the table. For that service I charged an additional two shillings.

My grandfather had taught me everything I knew about palm-reading and had said, since I was a child, that I possessed very rare and special abilities. The Irish were particularly drawn to fortune-telling, so I had chosen my service and my customers wisely. Within no time, I was running a steady business, the word spreading fast about my fortune-telling gifts.

My skills in the other department also came naturally and were nothing about which I felt uncomfortable. A woman, like a man, had to eat and drink, and everyone had their needs. As I saw it, I was safer than most married women, and had greater control over my life. I ensured pregnancy was avoided, certain forms of contact being strictly forbidden. I felt fully in control and Lizzie was always home and attentive to our secret signs for immediate assistance should anyone get out of hand. Kissing was strictly off limits, the touching of my bosom allowed, but no full exposure on my part. Most of my job involved stroking and tugging. The unmarried navvies being deprived of women for such lengthy periods of time, I was often surprised at how little stroking and tugging was needed to transfer their two shillings from their pockets to mine. I had several who, either overcome with guilt or embarrassment in front of a woman, broke down in tears, showed me their love tokens, telling me how much they missed their wives or girls back home to whom they were still sending money. Most had children and had sacrificed so much for them. Leaving their families behind felt as painful as an amputation. They had vowed either to return to Ireland or bring their families over to Scotland. Some spoke as fervently to me, their eyes filling up with tears, as if I was the woman they'd left behind. Regardless of their stories, I always exacted my full fee, female consolation coming, as I believed it should, at a cost.

The other women rumoured to be in my line of business had husbands or sweethearts who took most of their earnings. As I understood it, they allowed fornication where I refused. I marvelled at the power and profit of my independence, thinking how women are generally treated like dogs in this rough and tumble world, regularly kicked and beaten, all through no fault of their own, a woman's only option being — if they are fortunate and have an option — to exchange masters. I was, I thought proudly, charting a different course.

This was one of the rare periods in my life when I regularly attended Church and thanked God for my lot. The truth was, I had no one to thank but myself. Besides, I always nabbed a few customers among the pews, some navvies only interested in doing business with a church-going woman.

***

The night Billy first came to see me was a bad night. I was tired and irritable, suffering from the Irish flu.

It was Lizzie who had recommended me after Billy had declared the night before at the local pub that palm-reading was a load of superstitious nonsense. It also went against God's will and his word.

'Sorcerers, necromancers, and diviners are an abomination to the Lord,' Billy intoned, somewhat ironically, or so Lizzie thought. Didn't he realise he was speaking to the Irish?

Lizzie felt the need to issue a challenge. Just a few weeks earlier, she marvelled at a reading I'd done for her, so she waited until Billy was done speaking and approached him privately, urging him to visit me and put my skills to the test.

'There are certainly loads of charlatans out there, Lizzie said, who are clearly in it for the money. A shower of rogues,' she called them. 'But I know a woman, she said enticingly, who is sure to change your mind on the subject.' Despite Billy's responding laugh and open scepticism, a friendly conversation ensued that ended with Lizzie giving him directions to her cottage.

While initially keen on the meeting, I didn't know if, tonight, of all nights, I was up for the challenge. Hoping it might re-energise me, I took a few quick swigs of whisky just as Lizzie knocked at my door and introduced Billy before retreating to the front room.

I didn't know quite what or who to expect, but I certainly wasn't expecting such a handsome and friendly twenty-six-year-old man as William Burke. He wasn't as tall as some Irishmen are — they tend to run short or tall — but he was nicely dressed, having cleaned up for the occasion, and combed his thick wavy hair. Upon seeing him, I regretted not wearing my new print dress. I decided to wear it the next time, which was a very telling thought for me, a woman who had fairly recently sworn off men — I obviously hoped there would be a next time.

I tried not to appear too surprised when he said, looking at me with his intense blue eyes, that he was *a Christian and a sceptic but was willing to give it a go, just for fun.* 'Regardless of what I said,' he added, 'God's will would still be done.'

'Besides, he added, I do believe there are those who can tap into that will. Lizzie suggested you have that ability.'

Surprised by that description of my gifts, I responded immediately, 'I hope I live up to my billing.'

'Well, you're already living up to mine,' he said, getting comfortable on the neighbouring stool.

And then he said, very flirtatiously, 'Now that I'm seeing you, I'm even more intrigued.'

I'd be lying to say he didn't strike a chord with me from the start. And I loved that he was talkative. This one's a right, real charmer, I remember thinking. I felt my evening was looking up.

Pulling some money from his pocket, he said, 'Here's my shilling,' and lay the payment down on the table before me. 'Let's hear what the future holds.' Then he added the words, 'My future,' setting the tone and making things personal.

He then turned his attention to his hands and asked, 'What hand will it be?'

'Both,' I said, happy to focus on the reading as I could feel myself being seduced by Billy's charm and candour. Most of the navvies who visited my room were awkward and quiet and sometimes, given their strong Irish accents, even difficult to understand. The further south their origins, the more difficulty I had. But that wasn't the case with Billy. He also had charisma and with every sideways glance, I found myself smiling in spite of myself. I was also readily attracted by his intelligence, so I began with information about the hands.

'Each hand tells me different things,' I told him. 'The left hand tells me what you were born with — what traits you have from your parents and other family members.'

Billy turned his left hand over and examined it more closely.

'The right hand,' I continued, 'is always more interesting to me as it reveals what you've done with those things.'

He listened intently, his eyes narrowing as he looked over at me, trying to take it all in, me included.

'I'll say this,' he said. 'If it's rubbish, it's very complicated rubbish.' He turned both of his hands palm up and spread his fingers wide as if he were looking at them for the first time.

'I'm sorry,' he said, scrutinising them a bit more closely before daring to look at me directly. 'I tried my best to scrub all the grime off knowing I was coming here. It's hellishly caked into you by the end of the day with the work. I hope you can see what you're looking for, especially in this dim candlelight.'

I assured him I could and that I was used to it, most of my customers being navvies and most of my work being done at night. 'In fact,' I said further, 'given how the dirt settles into the lines, the hands are easier to read most of the time.'

So, I sat there, taking each of Billy's hands carefully in mine, one at a time. I scrutinised each for a few minutes before speaking, paying special attention to their shape, the length of his fingers, and the size of their various mounts. I brought them up close to see his major lines — life, heart, head, and fate. The whole time I was trying not to reveal that I was surprised by what I saw. The truth is, I had trouble making sense of them, both apart and together. Never before or since had I seen such very different hands. I would have sworn on a stack of Bibles and bet money, had they been shown to me separately, that they belonged to two different people. I remember thinking, then as now, this man Billy is nothing if not complicated.

After several more minutes examining them closely, I began the reading, letting him know some of what I was thinking.

'These are two of the most interesting hands I've ever read. I'll start with a few details.'

He looked at me intently as if bracing for something.

'The size of your palm and your life line tell me that you are noble and clever. You could live a long life. That's not to say that you will or won't, just that you were intended to. Whatever the case, your life will certainly be remarkable, your experiences intense. This doesn't mean that all of those experiences will be good, but they will be memorable for you and those around you.'

At this point, I pulled my stool back a bit and scrutinised Billy more closely, trying to get a better sense of who he was from his reaction. Unlike most of my customers, he proved a challenge to read.

'This area here on your forefinger,' I continued, pointing to the middle section that was longer than the other two, 'tells me that you are an ambitious person, a born leader with new ideas. Know that there can be dangers if you don't place some limits on yourself.'

As he adjusted himself on his stool, I noted his palm was sweaty. The room also began to feel warmer. I craved another dram of whisky as I continued.

'Now, let's look at your head line,' I said, running my finger along the long line in the middle of his hand to identify its location. 'This line tells me that you are a person who pays close attention and learns quickly.' As I said this, I felt uncomfortable. I could sense him looking intently at me. Out of the corner of my eye, I caught him staring at my lips, his face only a few inches from mine. When I turned and caught his eye, he looked away before leaning in again as if fascinated by the palm-reading.

'You could succeed at a variety of work,' I told him. 'You seem to thrive on variety. While change bothers others, you crave it. You like the challenges it brings and, unlike most people, you make the best of bad situations.'

During this entire reading, I was also busy scrutinising him, his reactions, his features. I especially liked the laugh lines around his eyes that bespoke an affable man. Catching myself at times doing more than palm-reading, I worked to refocus my attention on Billy's hands.

'Your head line also tells me you have ideals and vision, and work to change what you don't see to be right.'

I noticed Billy's eyes opened wide at this statement and he nodded, but said nothing. I found myself looking at his mouth, waiting for him to speak, and I couldn't help but notice that, unlike the many other navvies I'd met, he'd taken the time to shave. For the very first time I could ever recall, I didn't find his body odour offensive.

I checked myself and looked back to his hands.

'And now, let's look at your heart line,' I said, pointing to the long line across the top of his hand.

'Your heart line tells me that you are creative and feel deeply, but there is something missing. You are the life of the party but a loner at heart.'

Still receiving no response, I continued.

'I also see three children, here, in these lines under your pinky and two wives here as well. One of those relationships is more intense than the other, although your Mount of Venus suggests you like the ladies and may find commitment a challenge.'

As I spoke these last words, I could sense him shift around as if he were slightly uncomfortable. I noticed he smiled slightly and swallowed hard before placing himself in a more upright position.

'I don't know what you make of all of this,' I said, turning my attention from his hands to his face, 'but I will tell you that your right hand is showing me a person disappointed with life as you've known it so far, a survivor, a seeker who is still looking for something more — something to believe in.'

Billy smiled at me as if in agreement but, once again, he said nothing. As I continued, I realised I was finding him to be an even greater mystery than his palms suggested. Still hearing no comments from him, I offered some final insights.

'Here is the struggle I see: Your left hand shows a master, but your right hand shows me a master who will, by his own choices and because of his own character, fall into ruin. This doesn't have to be the case. Nothing is ever written in stone. As odd as it sounds, the lines on your right hand change over time.'

As I held both of his hands palm upwards in front of me, I noticed his facial expression had changed. He looked to be trying to process what I'd said.

'That was all very detailed,' he said. 'I'll have to think about everything. Right now, having been read like an open book, I just feel like I need a drink. I'll pay for it, of course.'

I got up and poured him a dram and watched as he quickly drained it off. He handed me tuppence. He looked as if he was still trying to digest all I'd told him and recover himself.

When I reminded him that the next customer was waiting in the front room, he asked, 'Would you mind if I come back tomorrow night? I have some more questions.'

I agreed and reminded him of my rate. 'It's the same rate for repeat customers,' I added as he stood up to leave.

Billy simply smiled and nodded.

'A woman after my own heart,' he said in a low voice as he held out the money to pay me. And then, much to my dismay, he left, closing the door behind him.

***

Billy came back twice that week and paid me each time even though I never performed another palm reading for him or any under-the-table palming either. During our second meeting the next night I thought that he, like most of the heart-sick navvies I'd met, just wanted female company. I soon realised it was more than that as the questions he asked were all about me — about my history and my family. He couldn't have picked a more resistant subject. I safeguarded my life history as if my life depended on it. I realised during my early meetings with Billy what little trust I had in anyone other than myself. Even after a few drams that second time out, I revealed precious little, telling him only that I had left home at fourteen and hadn't looked back but missed my grandfather so much it pained me.

Sensing my need for privacy, he didn't push. Instead, he took a different tack, one that transformed my room into a type of confessional and me, a Protestant by birth, into a father-confessor. By the end of that second night, he told me he was married in 1811 to a woman named Margaret Coleman. He had met her while in the regimental hospital in Ballina in County Mayo, and they had had two children together. He had written several letters since his arrival in Scotland some ten months earlier, urging her to join him, but he had received no response. He believed that the row he'd had with her father about property — a row that prompted his departure from Ireland — had turned Margaret irreversibly against him.

Whatever the case, Billy confessed to being relieved that she had refused. He said nothing about his children, a fact that both bothered and comforted me.

I was surprised by none of this, life being, as I had found it to be, a very messy affair with nothing in the way of certainty.

Before he left that second night, he put his hand on mine and squeezed it gently, but I immediately drew it away. I knew he wanted me and I had expected his advances, but I felt I still had a lot to think about — or needed a few more drinks. Billy was a charmer, and I knew where this could lead, especially if his wife were to change her mind. I had heard tell of women who came over from Ireland to be with their husbands who worked on the canal. The arrival of Margaret Coleman, children in tow, wasn't entirely an impossibility although it did seem unlikely given what he'd said.

But Billy wasn't put off by my resistance. If ever a man was persistent, that man was William Burke. In combination with his charm, this made him dangerous, more dangerous than I then realised.

The confession he made during his next visit took me by complete surprise. Looking back, it shouldn't have. I had read his palms.

Seating himself across the table from me that third night, Billy leaned over, took my hands in his, and said as he looked at me, 'I don't know how to read your palms, so I don't know if I appear anywhere in your life line — or what you called your heart line. I can only hope we fit together as your hands fit nicely into mine. I hope you will give me a chance to find out.'

This time, instead of pushing his hand away, I squeezed it lightly and then proceeded to run my hands along his palm with the tips of my fingers. I could no longer veil my feelings — even from myself. Despite everything I knew, I still wanted him. I can only put my reaction down to wilful blindness. That has been the story of my life with Billy.

It took another week of seduction, but I eventually succumbed. The truth was I had fallen hard for him during our very first meeting but my head urged resistance until I got to know more.

The night I reached my hand under the table to provide Billy with an unrequested palming of another order, I thought I was in control and knew what I was getting into. I couldn't have been more mistaken. In short order, he moved the table aside and, placing himself before me on his knees, began undressing me, fondling and caressing my breasts and neck with deep, wet kisses.

I knew trouble from the outset and Billy was trouble. Given our tremendous physical attraction coupled with his intelligence and charm, he was very welcome trouble at that point in my life. Given my heart line and his Mount of Venus, I also knew we should have stayed well clear of each other. For precisely the same reasons, we were fatally and explosively brought together.

8.

Billy

Like everything else, including sex, murder takes practise. Every body is different and the technique changes everything.

And my technique certainly left much to be desired that first time around, Joseph briefly fighting back and trying to raise the alarm in the house. So it was that the Mute and I were very nearly finished before we got started.

But, like the good doctor, once I got past the odious and disturbing aspects of my work, I began to develop a taste for it. I was keen to perfect a better technique, one that I practised and perfected on the next shot, an unnamed man from Cheshire who lodged at the tramp hotel over a few days. Having shown signs of jaundice thus endangering the guests, as Margaret facetiously called the other lodgers, she said he had to go. Here was a perfect opportunity not to be passed up.

Keen on making more money, and the man being, apparently, ill — something for which we had no confirmation — we had no trouble with him. His lack of resistance netted us an easy ten pounds. But by far the greatest outcome was the perfection of my method: I cast the pillow aside in favour of my hands positioned in a precise manner and it worked a charm. With Hare sprawled across the body so he could catch no air while pinning his arms, I stood at the top of the bed, pulling my thumbs up firmly under his chin and drawing my first two fingers firmly down over his nose. This left him no possibility of breathing and the job was readily done.

These early heady days were like my first drink of gin. Although I ended up as sick as a dog after each celebratory evening, most of the high was exuberant and blissful. I chose to focus on the rush, rising from bed the next day longing for another go around. Madame Geneva, being the skillful whore that she is, left me hungry and craving more. I told Margaret as much the night after we'd collected our second payment when I was soused beyond recall. While I had vowed at first not to touch any women, not to make any shots of them, I stupidly boasted after Nelly went to bed, that Hare and I could take two at once. Margaret flinched at the suggestion saying, cryptically, that she thought something could be arranged.

Enter Abigail Simpson, elderly matron from Gilmerton, only a couple of weeks later, who was decoyed into the house in the mid-afternoon when Margaret spied her wandering up the Cowgate. Abby, as she was known, had just obtained her weekly pension from her former master— a shilling and six pence, and a cup of kitchen fee. She was a bit tipsy after stopping for her regular tuppence pint when Margaret overtook her on the road, pretending to remember her from the old country. Before the old woman knew it, she was being escorted up towards the busy West Port on that frosty mid-February day, past the horses and carts and clusters of clamouring street-sellers, with the promise of a warm fire in the tramp hotel. Hare was ready with the drams and was soon caught up in another fantastical story designed to dupe the old woman — namely, that he was an eligible bachelor eager to meet and marry Abby's spinster daughter.

The party intensified after Nelly and I returned home an hour later, and ended very late that evening with Abby badly needing her bed, convinced there was no other option than to stay the night. Nelly seemed none the wiser as she went down to her bed early. As bad luck would have it, Abby woke up several hours later, vomiting. Margaret came to her aid, feigning concern, offering the old woman a home remedy in the form of porter and whisky. Abby resisted, whimpering and calling her daughter's name the whole wretched time. In response Margaret forced her mouth open and mercilessly poured the drink in. Within a few minutes, Abby was out cold, vomit everywhere.

Hare and I entered minutes later, drunk ourselves, to conduct the business. Given the old woman's state, I knew it would take no time. The Mute, unthinking as usual, did as before, laying across her chest while securing her arms. Fearful of leaving bruises or finger marks around her face, the tell-tale signs of foul play, I pinched her nose closed with one hand and pushed up on her jaw with my other to seal her mouth shut. Thankfully, Abby was too far gone to resist.

Or so I thought.

After some seconds and with no warning, the old woman's eyes shot open, all watery and blue as they stared up into mine. My heart leapt into my throat at how wide open they were. They were also not the colour I remembered them. And her face also seemed changed. Somehow, she looked *familiar*. As I wrestled to make sense of how I recognised her. Her eyebrows came together with such a beseeching look, as if she were about to cry, so intense and insistent. Shocked by this expression, I suddenly lifted my hands from her mouth and looked over at the Mute. But the idiot seemed to be asleep on top of the old woman, all his weight bearing down on her. I quickly stepped back from the bed, blinked hard a few times, and refocused my eyes to be sure I wasn't seeing things. Confused, Hare raised his head and barked over at me, 'What the hell's the matter?'

'Nothing,' I shot back, but I was fighting to compose myself.

'You look like you've just seen a ghost,' he said gruffly. 'Get on with it, man,' he commanded. 'We can't be up here all night.'

Not wanting to tell him what I'd seen, I grunted my assent, drew a deep breath, and moved back over to the bed.

As I repositioned my hands to get on with the business, Abby's sad eyes turned upwards again, accosting me. Theirs was an expression so compelling and so familiar it struck me dumb. I now recognised the face.

There on the bed lay my mother. Looking much older than when I last saw her, she lay staring up at me, her eyes pleading. Suddenly, tears streamed out and ran down her cheeks. Shocked by the recognition, I gasped so hard I choked. Through my coughing and unable to take my eyes off her, I touched her face to ensure I wasn't dreaming, to verify she was real.

And then she spoke, just a single word that paralysed me as I stood before her.

'Stop,' she said, helplessly.

'Stop, Billy,' she repeated again, this time addressing me personally. Although I was thrown off by its softness, the voice was unmistakably my mother's.

'Stop. I'm begging you.'

My eyes welled up with tears as, still in disbelief, I leaned in closer to be certain it was her. When I blinked to clear them, it was Abby's face that appeared again, her eyes now sealed shut as she lay there unconscious. I shook my head trying to process things, stunned again by the change.

The sound of Hare's angry voice roused me out of my trance.

'Did you hear me, man? What the hell's wrong

102

with you?'

When I failed to respond, Hare leaned forward off the bed and dealt a hard blow to my stomach. 'Damn you, Billy! We haven't got all night. Finish her up now!'

It took me a moment to regain my composure. I couldn't bear to look at Abby. I turned my head away after replacing my hands on her face and chin. Within a minute after applying the required pressure, I stood back watching as mucus and blood streamed from the old woman's nose and mouth and she began taking her long, last breaths.

'At one point, they die of themselves, really,' I said quietly to myself as I stood over her, watching in astonishment. Hare paid no heed. He had crawled off the bed, preparing to undress her.

As we jointly stripped the body, I cast one last look at Abby's eyes, terrified as to whose face I might see. If my mother had been there, she was nowhere to be seen now.

I looked back at her face again as we exited the room. Hare issued an angry whispered warning as we scrambled down the passageway, 'Don't dare do that again, you bastard. You hear me? Never again.'

Still in shock and not knowing what had just happened, I grunted my assent. In my mind's eye, I was still expecting Abby to rise from that bed, undead.

Like Hare, I wanted to get each job done quickly and quietly. I prayed I'd never have such a vision again, but I knew there were no guarantees.

As I crawled into bed beside Nelly that night after rapidly downing a few drams, I wondered if my mother was actually still alive in Ireland. Constantine and I hadn't heard from her, or about her, in some years.

I knew Hare would have thought me crazy if I told him what I saw. He'd consider me a liability, capable of doing or saying anything to Nelly … or a baillie. I certainly couldn't talk to Nelly about any of this. Ever.

So, what had just happened? I asked myself.

I mustn't have gotten enough sleep the night before, I said back to myself. I'd noticed nasty dizzy spells lately from a lack of sleep and a lot of drinking, but this was the first time I'd ever heard voices or had a vision, especially one so damnably real.

As I turned over onto my side to go to sleep, I prayed it would be the last.

***

An image of my mother's face — older, desperate, on the brink of death — haunted me as we made our way back to our pub in the West Port the next night. I spoke not a word the whole journey as I thought about this woman who had, for the duration of my childhood, lamented my existence. I couldn't get away from her fast enough even though I was told by so many growing up that, in my appearance, hard-headedness, and humour, I was just like her. That was why we clashed so much.

There was certainly no disputing our shared sense of humour. Never a quicker-witted woman graced the earth. Even Nelly couldn't hold a candle to her. As tough as she was, she loved to laugh and could make verbal mincemeat out of anyone who crossed her. My father, a farmer, was, by contrast, a ghost in our family, ruled over by this rough-and-ready, fleshly woman who could have raised us and farmed our small piece of land in the Parish of Urney, near Strabane, singlehandedly. Goodness knows how these two came together, but God knows they stayed together through everything, including the loss of three young children within a two-year span. My brother and I were the only survivors.

My mother beat my father into the ground with her tongue — although it rarely came to that — and directed his every move. Meanwhile, bless his cowardly heart, he never put up any fuss, readily obliging her every request. Looking back now, I think he was a man who needed direction. What I would have baulked at, he embraced. They were a perfect match.

My relationship with my mother, on the other hand, ran to the opposite extreme. In her view, my life was a series of mistakes. My first was to outlive my two older sisters, both of whom had died before their first birthdays. My mother never forgave me for it, it being her conviction that daughters will stay by you while your sons can never get far enough away. She had her own marriage to point to as proof that that was the way things worked. My father's family was in County Mayo while my mother's two sisters and her mother were just up the road.

Given my abilities with reading and writing, and my lack of interest in a cottier's life, at the age of twelve, I was taken into the service of a Presbyterian clergyman who later recommended me to a gentleman in Strabane. I liked the variety of the work and the fact that I could improve my writing skills while having access to their family library. While there could have been long-term prospects in both households, I'd set my sights since childhood on seeing the world. Now that I'd gained some education, I felt I was ready. My only prospect for leaving lay in joining the Militia, so that is what I did in 1809, my younger brother Constantine, my mother's favourite, eager to join me. The young officer I assisted had lured me in with talk of travel and a chance to savour all that the continent had to offer. This included its women and its wines. Although I couldn't have afforded much of either on my batman's salary, the possibility was enough to attract me at the time. As it turned out, never once in my seven years of service did I ever leave Ireland. As for wine, I have yet to taste it.

My mother asked me to stay and help my father on the farm but, although I felt sorry for him, I was deaf to her pleas.

'Are you trying to land me in an early grave, Billy?' she asked, incensed by my decision to leave. 'Worse yet, are you trying to land your father there too? It's one thing for you to leave but it's shameful to lure Connie away with you. He's still so young. Wouldn't it be smarter to see how you get on before he decides to join you?'

I stood there in silence, shifting uneasily from one foot to the other, while Constantine looked down at his boots.

'Connie's old enough to make up his own mind and he's done that,' I said, trying to remain firm. 'Look around you, Ma. There's nothing for us here but eking out a meagre living. Besides, it's not as if we'd be gone for good and you'd never see us again.'

'Tell me then,' my mother said, taking up the challenge, 'what exactly is out there?'

'I don't know,' I said. 'That's why I want to go see for myself.'

'You're still young and you know nothing, Billy. Don't believe everything everyone tells you. You'll soon long for what you're leaving, I can promise you. Such is the way of the world as I've found it to be.'

She could also see that I was going, firmly, to stand my ground. Since I was about eight years old, we were like two bulls facing off against each other, my mother and I, neither budging an inch. I loved her in my way, but she made it difficult.

She looked exasperated as she made a final attempt to convince me. 'I'll say this, but not in his hearing — your father might not say anything, but you're breaking his heart.'

This was a first for my mother. Never before had she mentioned my father or tried to use him to convince me to do anything. I knew what she said was true and there was no disputing it. My father needed allies in this house, and it must have been hard for him to see the only two he'd ever had heading out the door together. He was a man who enjoyed ritual and routine having grown up on a small farm. All he ever knew was work. Sadly, he'd fathered two sons who were afflicted with wanderlust, who yearned for adventure and change. He had never known that longing. He loved the land, the soil — *his* land, *his* soil. It, along with my mother and two sons were the ground beneath his feet. The thought of us leaving unsettled him. He had no one to take the farm on. His world was up-ending.

I remember him the following morning, as civil as ever as we prepared for an early departure. He embraced us heartily before handing us each a few shillings as we adjusted the packs on our backs. He told us to be strong and safe and to remember to write to our mother. He didn't want her to worry. He couldn't read but she could, being self-taught. 'You'll break her heart if she doesn't hear from you. She's not as strong as she looks.'

The funny thing is, thinking back, I don't remember a good-bye from her. What is etched in my memory is the image of my father, as calm as ever, the picture of pained sadness as he stood outside on that cold March morning looking out across the fields as we receded slowly from view.

That was the last time I ever saw my father. He died the following year while we were away. When my mother wrote to tell us of it, she said he died of a broken heart. I believe that to be true and I know my mother blamed me for it. I, on the other hand, blamed her, believing that, with Constantine and I away, she would have harangued him to death.

I tried not to think too much about my father's death. Like most things, I tried to drink it away. In the painful dreams that followed over the next few months, I saw his image across the field slowly fade and then disappear from view as I crossed toward him. Those were the only times I ever woke up in tears.

The next time I saw my mother, I had a pregnant wife in tow. Much to my surprise, she was pleasant when she met Margaret, happy about becoming a grandmother. Taking me aside before we left, she told me she hoped I'd come to my senses for the sake of our child and settle down. But I was set to make my next major mistake, which was to abandon my children in Ballina after a dispute with my wife's father over his property.

My father-in-law Coleman matched my mother in obstinacy. He despised me, in the first instance, because I'd gotten his daughter pregnant out of wedlock when he had his eyes set on another small land-owning suitor for her. In the second instance, I had my eye on inheriting his small plot of land as he had no living sons, even though I despised the cottier's life. I wrote to my mother about the matter and, ever practical, she counselled patience. 'Every man grows old,' she said, 'and mellows with age. They all need help from the young. As he gets older and loses his strength, he'll be thankful he has you to take over that land. Mark my words.'

I knew what she said was true, but I was impatient and regretted having written to her. As was my way, I paid her no heed, opting, after my dispute with Coleman, to leave the country to find work in Scotland and send money home with the understanding that Margaret and our children would join me later. For a time, I did send money, but never enough to bring them over. They never came.

The long and short of it was that my mother never spoke with me again, her last words being that *I'd already been the death of my father and I was sure to be the death of her.* It didn't help our relationship that Constantine later followed me to Scotland.

My mother wrote to my brother several times after that, but it was clear, because I'd lost touch with my wife and children, that she had written me off.

My mother's sudden appearance in Abby Simpson's death chamber convinced me that she was now dead and on the other side, wherever that was. I once thought I knew. What struck me so forcefully was how this dead mother was vastly different from the living mother with whom I'd had such conflict. Her voice was the same, but her tone had changed. She was meeker and milder, more loving, more motherly.

I, on the other hand, hadn't changed one bit. Although shocked to see her face and hear her voice, I ignored her. Sheerly out of habit rather than conviction, I focused my attention on prayer over the course of the following week, asking God fervently, who hadn't heard from me in a very long while, for her ghost to leave me alone.

It would seem that my prayers, issued at that point by an utterly faithless man, were answered. At least for a time.

***

Recovering from murder, like recovering from sex, takes practise. It's not much different than recovering from life actually, especially those days when you feel that life has you firmly and mercilessly by the throat or the bollocks, or both at the same time. The key is to find the crutch that dulls the pain without killing you so that you can build up some resistance. Thankfully, the world offers up an abundance of crutches. Unfortunately, when relied on to excess, they can prove fatal. I have seen so many faces of the drunken dead over the years. And that was before this body business. I count myself lucky — or I used to — not to be numbered among them. Over the last few years, as in my time with the Militia, I turned to innumerable bottles of whisky, laudanum and gin, and before my wasting disease of the past two years, I believed there was nothing that vigorous sex couldn't cure. Now, without the vigour, without the sex, I am fast wasting away. Only on my good days can I raise a glass and smile and drink to all that.

While it might seem unbelievable, before this body business, my crutch of choice was religion. I was a devout, church-going man, even as a soldier — Catholic, Methodist, Episcopalian, Presbyterian. Since coming to Edinburgh, I rejected the Catholic Church when a priest threatened me with excommunication for living, unmarried, with Nelly. I felt my calling was to become a lay preacher. Ask around in the West Port, Mr. M—. There are many still living who have heard me preach — both at their meetinghouses and in their pubs. I have always had a lot to say and been magnetically drawn to those who will listen. I can see them from a distance, their desperate need written on their faces. My words have been food for their hungry souls.

I have thought a lot about life and the world, my place in it, religion, God. The Big Questions. It is true that I always drank, but my discussions while drinking usually involved God. Whether drunk or sober, I could never seem to shake the subject, do what I can. If my mother is to be believed, I was born this way, asking and talking about God since I could first string sentences together. She never understood it, wondering what prompted the interest. It certainly wasn't her doing, or my father's. She must have breathed a sigh of relief when Connie came along, a boy whose needs were much more basic.

But I don't believe I'm different from other people. When everything else is stripped away, we all want something to believe in, something that will make sense of this world, of what we're doing here. There has to be some purpose to it all, we hope, some bigger picture. A Plan. We are all of us crippled children.

I read my catechism and prayer book every morning during my years in the Militia, attending masses, sermons, and prayer meetings whenever and wherever possible, both then and thereafter. Even with precious little money, I bought and read several religious books recommended to me — Isaac Ambrose's *Looking Unto Jesus*, Thomas Boston's *Human Nature in its Fourfold State*, John Bunyan's *Grace Abounding to the Chief of Sinners*, and Abraham Booth's *Reign of Grace*. The only work of literature I ever bought was one that I believed, mistakenly, to be a religious book — William Shakespeare's *Hamlet*. If ever a book asked the Big Questions and went some way towards answering them, I believe this is the book. I have read it religiously in my adult life, like a Bible in fact, several times a year. My copy has become so badly damaged with my thumbing through it, that I have had trouble making out the words on the page. I remember crying when the binding fell apart.

In 1824, all of my books were destroyed in the great fire in Edinburgh when Nelly and I were lodgers at Mikey Culzean's beggar's hotel. Thankfully, I had committed large sections of my books to memory, and could call them up for the lay preaching I did in the pubs. Reverend Dr. Dickson, one of the ministers of the parish with whom I regularly discussed issues and Biblical passages, soon found cheap replacement copies of my destroyed books after we moved to Brown's Close in the Grassmarket.

Shortly after that, I sold those books for food and drink. When you're on the cusp of starving to death, you prioritise differently, losing sight of spiritual salvation. The curious thing was — and I've never told anyone this — I'd been fast losing my faith in the years leading up to that fire. Ever since my time on the canal when I attended rallies about workers' rights and spoke with activists in the pubs, I wrestled with inner doubts, my thoughts turning increasingly to the here and now.

I thought perhaps the fire was a sign.

As I have grown more philosophical about this body business, I have asked some of the shots, during what they don't even realise is their last conversation, 'What does a man need more in the streets of Edinburgh: a Bible or shoes?' While the question always generates an immediate and impassioned reaction, most have disagreed with my answer. I can assure them, from this side of the grave, that there is absolutely no contest.

I repeat, I have seen, up close and personal, the hellishly, damnable drug that is religion that advises us to be meek and become as little children if we seek entry into the kingdom of grace. We are advised to be *lowly in heart, knowing ourselves utterly ignorant and helpless, relying wholly on our Father who art in heaven, to supply all our wants.* Like little children, we must bow to the authority and wisdom of God.

I have been struck by the fact that our earthly bosses adopt God's position, urging upon us the same devotion. It's a pity only the demoralised and destitute, weakened by starvation and sickness, rather than their powerful, comfortable bosses, pay any attention to God's commandments.

I have seen many little children, some as young as

three months of age, starving and sick, pass beyond the threshold of this life. Their breath diminishing, their faces ashen, their eyes sunken, their parents have prayed anxiously for assistance. But no God heard them, no boss paid any heed, and the parish only came to their aid once their children's wee bodies lay rigid and cold in a dark, dank hovel on a bed of straw and rags, covered by filthy pieces of cloth. My breaking point came with the death of Mikey Culzean's four-year-old son, who was the same age as my Daniel when I left Ireland. His death could have been avoided had there been help early on. Never have I seen such pain and suffering, him in the jaws of his sickness, his mother and father broken in their agony and helplessness. Never did I pray so hard to relieve a family. Never did I feel so powerless, my prayers futile.

It was then that I gave up on God. If He existed, I thought, He was despicable, not for his lack of assistance but for creating such defective, flawed, and careless creatures in the first place.

Nelly said at that time that I shouldn't have lost faith in God but, rather, in the people who failed to follow His tenets.

'If you are seeking divine intervention,' she said, 'you are never going to find it. That isn't how God works. That is how men, thinking in their limited way, expect God to work. With this expectation, they will always be angry and disappointed. These are the same men who push the fire and brimstone idea of God, the ones who can't see their own faults but are keen on judging, condemning, and punishing others.'

'You are looking through a glass darkly,' she counselled me. 'You have to seek God from the inside, from your heart, your spirit.'

But whatever spirit of mine remained, lay dried up from neglect over those many long years while I waited for a sign.

Given my experiences at that time, on this side of the grave, my Edinburgh Sermon on the Mount, proclaimed, in my mind's eye, from Arthur's Seat, overlooking that damnable Radical Road built from the shame and humiliation of our brothers, would have ended like this:

Believe me, my children, the meek shall never inherit the earth. Not as long as the powerful rich have any say in the matter. These are dangerous fairy tales we tell children and, if we remain as children, we will continue to believe them.

Here, we are enjoined to focus on our own personal sin and salvation, to focus on the next world rather than this world and the sins of others. We are told to abandon the possibility of change. Only death will bring change. At death, we will reap our rewards.

Some of us — just some — resist this advice and enter the real world, as shocking as that experience might be.

Some of us grow up. We reject childhood. We ask the hard questions and decide, come what may, to take matters into our own hands.

Let us take our counsel on this issue from the Good Book itself:

When I was a child, I spake as a child, I understood as a child, I thought as a child: but when I became a man, I put away childish things.

Amen.

9.

Nelly

Within a year after Billy's confession of love, we left Maddiston and made our way just outside the Callendar Estate in Falkirk. It was there that work had begun on the Black Hill Tunnel, which was to run through Prospect Hill skirting Callendar wood. In order to keep the unsightly Union Canal hidden from his family's large estate and gardens, William Forbes had successfully petitioned every Member of Parliament. His campaign had been the talk of the town. Billy told me the whole story. I was amazed by what could be done when a person had money, what power they could wield. In his usual manner of badmouthing the rich, Billy said there was no amazement in it. It was called corruption and until people stood up against it, it would continue.

In the meantime, he needed work. After a hellish year of muckshifting that had resulted in a badly injured back, Billy was chosen as one of the head spannermen in the tunnelling crew. It was his job to drill the holes where the tigers, the head men, determined the gunpowder charges should be placed in the rock face. Overnight, dozens of turf and wood huts were erected to house the navvies, and endless provisions of whisky, gin, and grub brought in by horse and cart. This shanty town soon had a small make-shift shop, chapel, and clinic. Many had better living accommodations and services than they had ever had.

I refused the work option taken by some of the

women, like Margaret Hare as I later learned, of donning a navvy's jacket and working alongside the men, spadeful for spadeful, although for far less pay. I knew my limitations. At best, I'd last an hour and be injured. I would certainly be exhausted. I decided to run my palmistry business at night, but I was still in need of daytime work. Billy thought taking in washing was the best option for steady money. I wasn't so sure given the cost of the materials required, including an axe, rope, a large kettle and washbasin, a washbat, endless laundry lye and ash. As Billy, like most men, was utterly unaware, it was also terribly hard work with all of the chopping and gathering of firewood, the hauling of water, and perpetual scrubbing and wringing. What I resented when he made the suggestion was the way he made me feel like a helpless, costly dependent in need of direction. Looking back now I can see that this was an indicator of things to come.

My first idea for work was to teach the navvies' children how to read and write, but I knew that no one would see enough value in that to pay me to do it. When I mentioned it to Billy, he just looked at me sideways and said, 'You're a real Scot, Nelly. Teaching them how to read people is a far better option. Can you do that? Even so, no one would pay you for that. That's something they'll learn themselves in good time, perhaps when it's too late and they find themselves locked up or on the gallows.'

Having no better idea at the time, I took Billy's suggestion of taking in washing, at least for the warmer months. What swayed my decision was our hut's proximity to the Glen burn and the ready availability of firewood, firewood that Billy, true to his word in those early days, helped to chop and haul each morning. Once the night drinking began, that soon ended, and I was on my own. To say that work exhausted me is an understatement. I did what I could so as not to feel I was a burden.

Everything changed for me after we moved out near Prospect Hill. What I remember most in the beginning was a sense of new-found freedom and release. From a solitary life in Lizzie's cottage, mine became a more sociable life in what would have been, without the navvies, a damningly remote and lonely place. The forest was peaceful when I was working, transporting me back to my time at Jeannie's, but it changed dramatically in the evenings in ways that I, now a more hardened drinker, welcomed. Each day was made up of extremes of hard work and even harder living.

No two nights were the same or predictable with Billy and the navvies who loved to sing, dance, play music, and tell jokes and stories. They said it was knowing they had the nights that got them through the days. That, and a lot of drink. It is said that for every mile of Union Canal completed, the navvies drank a thousand pounds sterling worth of alcohol. None of that mattered to me as they became my extended family, the family I'd never had. In their deep love of life, they were truly a nation unto themselves, a race apart. Although they lived like tinkers on the edge of society, they were a solid community. If a missus fell ill, other women readily picked up her children and cooked in order to help out. When one of the men was sick, they pooled their resources to assist each other as best they could. This made every bit of sense as being short even just a single man, especially if he was a muckshifter, as most were, set the whole of the tunnelling crew back in terms of the work schedule. When one man died, every man was affected, many to tears, some wakes running a full week, after work, at night, in the dark where they could let their feelings loose and be themselves. Anyone who undermined the community — who stole from or fought with his fellows or refused to do his share of the work — was driven out. An occasional drunken fight was acceptable, but anything more could result in a brawl, the navvies left to maintain order among themselves as the town wanted nothing to do with them. The worst nights involved clashes between the Irish navvies and their Highland counterparts who worked nearby. The locals stayed well clear of us, letting things be resolved by way of the fist and the dirk. I think nearly as many men lost their lives in those fights over the five years of the canal's construction as those who died working on it. Many dozens were buried along the way, up the hillside cresting the canal, small wooden crosses often marking the plots. Many more dozens, over the course of each month, became drunk and violent and were hauled off to gaol.

In later years, when the Irish navvies flooded into Edinburgh, it was painful to see them. Their sense of community had changed for the worst. In that heartless city, that rough and ruthless place where little work was to be had, they were a different, far more desperate and despised lot. Treated like a race apart, of another order, they became competitive and careless of each other's welfare. I could see the shift — while the sense of an Irish community persisted on the face of it, especially in opposition to the English and the Scots, it was every man for himself in reality. Even blood relatives were looked upon with suspicion, and theft became common among them.

Billy seemed to be of two minds about them, acting on one hand as if he was superior and they were entirely unrelated. On the other — with his dogged determination, survival instincts, and charm — he also called himself *a brother*. In all of my days with Billy, I'd never met the person he couldn't charm and I'd be willing to bet such a person didn't exist.

A quick-witted storyteller, he could talk about anything under the sun — religion, politics, history. He waxed especially poetic and philosophical about the Irish navvies, describing them during one of our early conversations as people with strong bonds who, with their humour and resourcefulness, could survive anything. Tragically, though, he remarked one evening, they were people forever in mourning. Having had to leave their homeland behind, and with their loved ones so far away — lost to them — every day was a wake, Billy said. Since coming to Scotland, he had watched and understood them intimately, as if from the outside but with the insider's sensitivity and desire to protect them.

I remember Billy's words from one of his pub sermons where he expressed these ideas.

'Life is like a big ceilidh to them,' he said, 'and death a bedfellow, as they fight to stay on this side of the grave. They laugh to keep from crying, drink to keep from dying. The drink helps to numb them from unbearable work and the hardships of this life. Tragically, there can never be enough drink. There is no endless bottle. They work to fill and drain the bottle, then fill and drain it again.'

After all of my experiences, I could relate to these people who had grown accustomed to hardship, survival, and leave-takings and, over the years that I lived with them, they showed me they could relate to me. For a time, fool that I was, I thought Billy, being one of them, could relate to me too. I certainly loved him more because of all the hardships he'd endured and for his survivor's spirit. In the beginning, I thought that we were well-matched: despite all of his protests, he was a navvy at heart, and I, for a time his precious Nel, was a navvy in spirit.

But everything changed when we got to Edinburgh where many, me especially, found that Billy, the charmer, had a treacherous manner of using our vulnerabilities, our needs, and our vices against us.

***

For a time, we were happy. Unlike so many of the wives and girlfriends of the other navvies who were generally ignored and regularly beaten, especially after excessive drinking on both sides, I was initially well treated, a woman envied, given the attention Billy paid me.

At the start, it was as if I could do no wrong, Billy frequently comparing me to his *disloyal wife Margaret who'd betrayed her marriage vows and honoured her father rather than her husband from whom she had also withheld their children.*

'I wish I would have met you first,' he would say to me, with such conviction, his eyes, filled with tears and gazing into mine, usually after one of our lengthy bouts of coupling. These statements were sometimes so overpowering I had to catch my breath. Frequently, I found myself astonished by him, in disbelief that he existed, that he actually stood there before me, made of real flesh and blood, a caring man of many powerful and well-chosen words.

Billy's statements bolstered my determination at the start to prove to him my total faithfulness, my difference from other women. I yearned to bear him children, as many as he would want. I gave no practical consideration to money or time. I assumed they would start arriving early as we used no barrier or withdrawal methods such as I had privately counselled the navvies' wives to use to give their bodies a break from childbearing. Sadly, while pregnant women and small children were everywhere around me, I remained barren, a situation to which I later attributed divine significance. Because I saw children as the confirmation of my bond with Billy, I cried at the first sign of blood every passing month. And many months passed, along with the shedding of much blood and many tears. After several years, I gave up hope, thinking pregnancy impossible. Something wasn't right and there was no use praying to change it. It was all in God's hands. On one memorable evening, a couple of years in, when he started to change, an extremely drunk and rowdy Billy spat out the theory that my infertility was due to *all of my whoring before I met him, along with that sinful abortion.*

'God knows and only rewards good women,' he said maliciously. 'He knows what he's about. We mustn't question His wisdom. His will be done.'

Looking back now, I can see that, because I followed his rules and supported him in everything during those early months, he showered me with attention and compliments. He never ever glanced at another woman. He shared his fears and hopes with me, along with his confidences. Who wouldn't have been attentive to him, given his special charms and bedtime attentions, especially after a lifetime deprived of love?

With Billy in my life then, I felt as if God had finally granted me His grace, His favour. At long last, I was reaping some earthly rewards, overdue but so very welcome. Or, perhaps, as I actually preferred to think given God's consistent neglect of me up until that time, it was the spirit of my mother working from the beyond, embracing me in the form of Billy. At least, that seemed to be the case until the Other Billy pried her hands away. After that, I found the need to remind myself on numerous occasions that I had had the opportunity to read Billy's palms and knew that there was much more to him than met the eye.

***

Over many long years, I have chosen to cling to the few good memories.

Some might find it impossible to believe given our horrific trials and sufferings, but even poor people have their red-letter days, days they can call up from memory to lift their spirits and sustain them during difficult times. My most significant red-letter day came on a gloriously sunny Sunday in August, a remarkably wind-free and cloudless day, when Billy insisted on a small mid-day picnic at the top of a hill just north of the canal. We had been living together for nearly four months and established a routine of working, drinking, and talking. I felt I had never been closer to another person, with the exception of my grandfather and Jeannie. I had certainly never opened up to another human being the way I had with Billy. I had started on that road with Ewan, but with Billy, I fast became an open book. I felt I had found my heart's safe harbour.

The picnic was Billy's idea and he had made a single ground rule for it: neither of us was allowed strong alcohol beforehand or during. As we had both repeatedly discovered, we were not good to each other with the drink in our systems. Or, to put it more clearly, he was horrible to me and I could return the favour in kind.

At the summit, we lay back on the small blanket we had brought, basking in the sunshine. Everything just felt right as Billy turned onto his side towards me, stroking my hair and face. When he started loosening my hair as he did just before intimacy, I touched his hand and stopped him.

'Billy, we can't do that here. We are not alone.'

Looking behind me and nuzzling my neck, Billy playfully asked me, 'Where? Are you seeing people I can't see again, Nelly?' Billy had heard me talk to my mother on the other side sometimes, which he teased me about, deeming it superstitious nonsense. I knew otherwise.

While it was true that we couldn't see any people down the hill, we knew that walkers had a way of appearing out of nowhere and when we least expected it.

'I don't want to upset you, so I won't,' he said reluctantly. Given my attraction to him, resisting Billy was always difficult. I decided simply to relax. I rolled onto my back and gazed up at the sky. I pretended not to notice as he reached into his jacket pocket and pulled out a small item that caught the sunlight. He leaned over and kissed me, placing it in my hand.

I squinted, trying to focus my eyes against the bright sunshine, as he explained, 'It's not the silver one I wanted for you, Nelly, but I hope you'll like it. I made it myself with your grandfather's cobbling tools.'

As I sat up and turned my back against the sun, I saw that I was holding a love token, a luckenbooth brooch made up of two interlocking hearts crafted out of tin, with a crown set over the top of them. Some weeks earlier I had told Billy what that token meant to me as my grandfather had gifted one to my grandmother.

Billy kept talking as he watched my reaction. 'I know I'm a married man, which means we can never be man and wife under Scottish law as I told you when we first met. You accepted me anyway. I want you to know that with this brooch, I am making you my wife in every sense, the laws of this country be damned.'

As always, Billy wooed me with his well-chosen words, and these words were the most powerful he'd ever uttered. My eyes welled up as he told me he'd crafted it just for me. I took his face in my hands then and kissed him full on the lips. He had been a right nasty bastard a few times recently, even slapping me hard across the face one night when I insisted he stop drinking and come to bed.

But I felt during this precious moment that this — this brooch and his powerful words — signalled a new path for us.

At that moment, I felt such gratitude, thankful for him and to him for loving me. I never saw him coming. I never thought anyone would come. Not for me.

'Thank you,' I repeated.

Thinking back, I remember that not a word of thanks was returned from him and, due to the changeable man that Billy was, my feelings of gratitude and hope were, tragically, short-lived.

***

Being unable, at first, to do anything wrong, within a few months, I could do nothing right. In that short space of time, it was as if the luckenbooth episode had never happened.

My fall from grace began with the occasional name-calling and criticism. After damaging a navvy's shirt while washing it one afternoon, a shirt that I then had to pay to replace leaving me out of pocket, Billy called me glaikit, our Scottish word for stupid that the navvies had picked up and frequently bandied about. I was upset when he said that in public, and those feelings grew over the course of that night as we drank. Laying together later that night, he cuddled close and said he hardly remembered the incident and I should forget it too. When I pressed him, he promised it would never happen again. But promises, they say, are made to be broken and this one was, and countless times, along with many others that followed. In fact, my life with Billy could be described as a string of broken promises. With every one came a slap at first, followed, as time went on, by a punch or a kick. It depended on the day and how much he had had to drink.

Some weeks later, Billy told my only friend about the episode, a woman who had, to that point, looked upon me with respect. I lost a full night's sleep after that, unable to process what had happened.

Then, about a month later, Billy walked in during a palm-reading session I was having with his friend Davey from Dromore. Seeing Davey's open hand resting on mine as we sat together and I did my reading, Billy shot me a look of disgust and called me outside, insisting that I immediately end the session. He made out to Davey that he was upset because I didn't yet have the supper ready, but I knew better. Not wanting to make a scene, I apologised and handed Davey back his money while he, in turn, offered endless apologies to Billy. It was clear Billy had been drinking. I should have been angry that he was spending so much money on drink, but he had turned the tables.

After Davey left, Billy looked at me repulsed and said, 'Don't think I didn't see the look on your face, Nelly. I know you better than you know yourself. You were just dying to put your hand under that table.'

I had expected some jealous words, but these stunned me into silence, as did the horrible look on his face that humiliated, embarrassed, and angered me. The fault, it would seem, did not lie with Billy and his insecurity, but with me and my devious ways, being a woman. I was put on the defensive, as became his usual mode, and no amount of protesting could convince him of my innocence.

Billy's decision directed everything that followed. It deprived me of the little bit of money I had and placed me more firmly under his control, something that I hadn't had to concern myself with as a single woman. He punished me for the small bit of freedom I still enjoyed.

A few days after the incident with Davey, Billy

returned home and announced, 'The palm reading is over, Nelly. It's too much of a temptation for you and too much of a liability for me.'

Not wanting to enrage him further, I bit my tongue, although doing so went against my instincts. I wouldn't remain silent during similar episodes in the months that followed, which made matters worse for me. Billy was unpredictable and uncontrollable. When he began slapping and manhandling me during his tirades, I became terrified to talk back for fear he might accidentally kill me.

In the years that followed, I have wondered if Billy was actually two people as his palms suggested, and the drink a trigger. Much depended on that and his laudanum, and what stage he was at in the process of getting drunk. The charming, humorous, story-telling Billy, the man who had gained my heart, could be overtaken by the brutal, bitterly cruel Billy who lurked beneath, ready to go off without warning once he'd passed a certain pint.

In the course of the frequent and endless arguments with the second Billy, I was lumped in with his wife Margaret and all of the women down through the ages for the havoc and hell we had wreaked on mankind. If ever a man could use the Bible against me, reciting passages at length, word for word, chapter and verse, to denounce the sins and seductions of wayward womankind, that man was William Burke. On countless occasions I heard the proclamation that I, Nelly McDougal, *the devil's gateway* and *first sinful defiler of divine law*, should be punished and shown no mercy. I started to wonder if Billy, who was usually logical, wasn't losing his mind. All of the insults he hurled at me made no sense.

It was then that Billy started to lay down laws about my life in a manner that tested me beyond measure. Soon, I could have no woman friends and, when we were out, I wasn't even allowed to dance. 'It might arouse the navvies,' he explained. 'You know yourself, Nelly. You always get carried away.'

The freedom of life with the navvies that I had eagerly embraced was, due to Billy's growing drive to control, stolen from me, as was my little bit of happiness. I discerned a pattern: I was criticised and insulted, after which came apologies and promises from him to change. This was often followed by sex and drunken sleep after Billy took a few drams while I, always shaken up and tense after a night of confrontation and turmoil, began to take double and triple doses of laudanum to numb myself to the pain.

A person could be forgiven for thinking they were going mad. I strongly suspected we were.

***

At one point — about a year in and during one of those memories I'd pay to be rid of — private criticisms and insults became public, and my humiliations grew. Railing against a woman's great sins and the impossibility of her spiritual salvation, Billy hauled me up onto my feet one night, presenting me to the pub's patrons as a woman he'd saved from a lifetime of whoring. Pushing him away saying I never needed saving was something I paid for later in private after we left the pub. On the worst nights, I was dragged by my own hair, which he gathered up tightly in one hand while wrenching me around and repeatedly walloping me with the other. During these horrible episodes, I was glad for the drink, as I was over the next days and weeks that followed given my pain and bruises.

Such episodes continued with the Other Billy. I excused and buried them all while wishing I could bury him, convincing myself that he was not in his

127

right mind. The navvies we drank with began to see these clashes as normal and, over time, I grew to resent them as well for always egging him on.

I came to realise that the navvies weren't much of a community where women were concerned.

And then, with the completion of the Union Canal came our dispersal and the end of our close-knit navvy society.

I remember the taverns in the various towns we tramped through for years afterwards — the excitement I felt when entering them, my thirst for liquor growing by the week, and the sickness and fear I felt when leaving them while being publicly shamed and abused by Billy who was always in some sort of jealous rage. I never knew what might set him off, but I soon recognised the fanatical look that came over his face just before he'd launch into me. He reminded me of my mother then as he didn't even see me, a veil falling over his eyes as he blindly grabbed me, hurling abuses and swinging at me.

From Redding to Polmont to Penicuik, Peebles, Linlithgow, and Leith, through Billy's various incarnations as a baker, weaver, and cobbler, when we moved around the countryside like tinkers sleeping wherever we could find a place — in cowsheds, haystacks, and workhouses — I was variously and regularly slapped, belted, kicked, and punched, the insults and curses being endlessly hurled. I longed for one kind word, but only managed to get those in the apology stage from a questionably remorseful, hung-over Billy who claimed to be as devoted to me as he believed I still was to him. At that stage in our battles, he would say he was driven, against his better judgement, into these violent rages. *He wasn't himself.* It was me — evil, loose woman that I was — who had set him off.

Drained after these harrowing rituals, I hated him

to the core but suppressed it. I have had the clothes torn from my back while being held down and kicked on the ground, while other men and women stood silently nearby, unwilling or afraid to interfere. Those who spoke would cheer Billy on with statements like, 'You teach her a lesson she'll never forget, Billy. Give her a good belting. She looks like a right bad bitch.'

Not a soul sought to help me and, in some ways, I was beyond help as I felt I could no longer help myself. Hadn't I committed myself to this madman who, as I could see so very clearly now, had a twisted idea of love?

Seeing such abuses going on around me over years with other navvies, I came to think it normal, the eventual outcome of all unions. Head-over-heels romance might begin with promise, but happiness could never last. Such was marriage, take it or leave it, as cursed as it seemed to be. Leaving was not an option, never an option. It didn't even cross my mind given the challenges of survival, especially as a woman alone.

I began to think of my Maddiston years with nostalgia then, but I knew there was no going back. Instead, I learned how to hate back — cursing and spewing out sick, retaliatory statements, fighting back to defend myself wherever and however I could. I still loved him as I believed he did me, somewhere deep down, all the while hating him in equal measure. I lived in hope he would connect with his better self, the Billy I had first met and fallen for. I knew what he could be and I prayed he might be transformed back. I became my own worst enemy — the sad, pathetic, yet hopeful woman who made excuses for him. In the meantime, his actions told a very different story, the Other Billy gaining the upper, more forceful and violent, hand.

And so we continued as we moved into Edinburgh

and the tramp hotel.

I remember thinking to myself one night in the pub that ours was unarguably a romance — a dark romance.

***

My love affair with Billy has long involved reaching back. Its very survival has required that I reach back to a time before lies and curses and beatings, when I thought he was honest and seemed to possess a heart. What has sustained me over our ten-plus years together are the good memories from our first few months and the luckenbooth story — and the deep-seated hope that he might, as in some fairy-tale, become the good Billy again.

Looking back, there were two Billies. There was the Billy I knew and could predict, a territory I had mapped out carefully, whose roads and rivers I had confidently traversed. Then there was the other, unpredictable Billy who often drank to excess and was unmappable, his terrain dangerous to navigate, much of it unknown. I tried to negotiate his highways and byways, but seemed doomed to failure — remembering rivers where there weren't any, while drowning in rivers unseen. When I tried a gentle, conciliatory approach, he berated and beat me for my weakness. When I met him head on, he punished me for my disrespect. There was no way of winning, either for him or for me. After every battle, our armies lay defeated, shattered ruins.

I shouldn't be so hard on myself where love was concerned, especially after the fact. Like most women, love was my laudanum. I took far less of the drop after meeting him. Billy became my drop then, energising me and sending my spirits soaring, making me feel womanly and wanted. We had endless conversations where I felt what I said mattered. But when things went wrong and love was lacking, and I found few sustaining memories to reach back to, I reached increasingly for the bottle — or bottles — of whatever was to be had. It was a bad combination all around — Billy and I and the endless drink. Everything seemed to get twisted up and confused where the three of us were concerned. He was a master at skewing my words, using them like weapons against me, patronising me as if I were ignorant. He took great pleasure in humiliating and demoralising me, putting me in my rightful woman's place, as he often described it.

Deep down, he hated me for loving him because he hated himself, and I fought, as if my very life depended on it, to confirm he was loved and worth loving. I can see now that I was repeatedly sacrificed at the altar of Billy's insecurities. And my own insecurities involved my believing that without him I couldn't exist, I was worthless, with no reason to live.

So, I was Billy's mirror image, his reflection, equally self-hating and insecure. How lucky for both of us that we'd found each other. What were the chances?

Adding in the drams and the drop pushed things to the point of madness. Such was the love between navvies as I had seen it — always lubricated, usually unbalanced, sometimes deadly.

And so it went on for a full ten years, our ferocious love, fuelled and soothed, in turn, by liquor and laudanum, through into our move to Margaret and Hare's lodging-house in Edinburgh when I found the first body.

And it ramped up after that.

At some point, I stopped conjuring up the luckenbooth story. It was quietly tucked away, like so much else in my life, in the dimly lit corridors of painful memories. I sometimes wondered whether those events actually took place. I had long wished they hadn't. That would have made leaving a possibility, opening a door that allowed daylight into the dark, unbearably stifling room that had become my life.

***

As hung-over as I was after our long day and night of drinking with Abby, I sensed something was wrong when I woke up and made my way into the front room. The place reeked of stale tobacco and spilled liquor, our empty glasses and Billy's pipe sitting on the small, stained table in the corner. And there on the low stool near the window lay something I wasn't expecting to see — Abby's mantle.

She must have stayed the night, I thought, which was a good thing, given how dangerous the West Port could be after hours, especially for an old, unaccompanied woman. Still, I was surprised that Margaret let her stay free of charge. She was probably saucing her up the whole afternoon to gain the tuppence for the room rental, although the cost of the whisky was far greater. I wondered what could have possibly motivated Margaret's generosity. The poor old soul told me she had precious little money. I hoped Margaret had been kind, although I had yet to see an ounce of kindness from that wicked, greedy soul.

Thinking that Abby must still be fast asleep and in need of some tea and a wee something from the baker's when she got up, I went round to Rymer's shop, just a couple of minutes away, then quietly returned to her room trying not to waken the household.

Nothing could have prepared me for what I found when I entered the only room I knew she could be in. The stench of vomit was so strong it made me gag and immediately step back outside. Upon re-entry, I breathed through my mouth and noticed that while a body was discernible beneath the blanket, it was totally covered up, including her face. The pillow was, oddly, on the floor beside the bed. She must have been horribly drunk, I thought, when she went to bed, and very sick afterwards. Thinking she must be suffocating, I pulled the cover down to give her some air, but the face I saw, all bloated and ghastly pale with her eyes shut, made me gasp and fall back. Dark ribbons of dried blood trailed down her face and neck. I knew from the minute I laid eyes on her that she was no longer of this world. I also knew that her death was unnatural. What upset me the most, as I pulled more of the cover away, was the fact that her breasts were exposed. Pulling the cover down even further, I discovered she was entirely naked. I shuddered as I wondered what had been done to Margaret. My stomach grew queasy. A quick search around the room revealed no drawers, not a single stitch of clothing. What in heaven's name had happened? Had this poor, vulnerable old woman suffered some horrible violation before being killed? She had been talking and laughing with me just hours before and now, here she lay, lifeless and rigid. Endless questions raced through my head — who had done this? What, exactly, had they done?

I had just met her, but the realisation of her possible violation and probable murder stunned me. She reminded me of my own mother whose corpse I had tenderly embraced those many years ago. I felt mixed emotions. Tears welled up as I sat down in shock at the foot of the bed, while anger rose up at this violation. I had to remind myself that I was still alive and to keep breathing. I was plagued by an onslaught of questions: What outrages had occurred? Who could have committed this wicked crime? I realised I was whispering to Abby's lifeless body, wishing she could speak and answer my many terrified questions. Someone might have killed her while she slept, I thought. But why?

My mind raced in all directions as I stared at her. A series of recent events began to make more sense as I stood there thinking, the pieces falling into place. I had overheard Hare and Margaret speaking of a dead man one night as we sat in the pub. I remembered thinking they must be speaking of some incident in the West Port, but I realised now it must have been closer to home. That couldn't be a coincidence, I thought to myself. I dreaded to think what Margaret and Hare, who I knew had been involved in Lucky's murder the year before, could be up to now.

I thought back over the recent deaths of Donald and Joseph and some unnamed English lodger from Cheshire, and the fact that Joseph's and the Englishman's dead bodies disappeared suddenly, no funerals being arranged that I could see. I had asked Margaret about them twice but was warned by Billy to leave matters alone. 'It's not our business,' he told me sternly, 'and it's certainly not yours,' he said, that familiar look of deep hatred for me taking over his face.

'The less said about it, the better, Nelly. Not a word now, mind. Bite your tongue.'

And then he leaned in close and finished things off with his signature flourish, saying, menacingly, 'Or I'll bite it for you.'

But here was something more terrifying than any threat — an old woman's bloody, dead, naked body in a bed in the tramp house. I thought then of the endless drink we'd been consuming lately and the ample quantities of food we could never before afford — smoked herring, stews — and endless tobacco. That had caused another row one night that ended with Billy telling me to mind my own damn business, to be thankful we weren't out there starving like every other desperate navvy — those hundreds without work and the basic means of survival — tramping and thieving across Edinburgh. The more sober morning after brought this different explanation — some sort of horrid goings-on involving Hare and Margaret, with Billy seeming to know something I didn't. I realised then and there that I would have to be more attentive to lodgers coming in and out because I knew no one would, willingly, tell me anything. Me. Nelly. *The bloody Scotswoman*, as Margaret so often referred to me.

There was a lot to take in, but this last thought jolted me back into the present moment: I was standing in shock in a rank-smelling room with a naked woman's dead body hidden and fast stiffening in a bed. Fearing discovery and with precious little time, I focused on my immediate duty, which was to the dead, not the living. I returned to our room where Billy lay snoring, fast asleep. Waking him was, thankfully, impossible after a night of heavy drinking, so I had no worries as I retrieved some of my grandfather's cobbling tools. Once back with Abby, I released the few remaining pins from her coarse salt and pepper hair, combing it out with my fingers across the small flat wooden board Billy and I used to fix shoes. With the aid of the knife, I took a hair cutting of several inches in length. I also cut some swatches from her thick, woollen mantle, which I tucked into my apron. I decided I would make a doll for her later, carefully and at my leisure, in private.

What couldn't wait was the sin-eating. Trembling as I removed the loaf I had brought for her breakfast and touching it to her cracked and bloated lips, I whispered the recitation I was taught by my grandfather:

'I give easement and rest now to you, Abby Simpson, that you walk not down lanes, or in meadows, or along pathways. And for your peace, I pawn my own soul. Amen.'

I moved the loaf slowly back and forth, about a foot above her body, from head to toe and back again. I repeated this action three times. After laying the bread down on her belly, I poured some of the ale I'd bought for myself into a glass. I spread a few drops onto her lips with my fingertips and then moved the glass above her body as I had done with the bread, from head to toe, while again reciting the prayer. I repeated the recitation three times.

Sitting down at the base of the bed, I ate some of the loaf and drank the ale over the next several minutes, thinking about how a small, surprise breakfast had become a meal of a very different sort. I thought about Abby's last unfortunate journey into the city to retrieve her pension money, a routine trip, as she had told me, that had come to such an abrupt and horrible end. Then I thought of her final journey, not home to her daughter as she had planned but beyond this world as she crossed into the next, the spirit world. I chewed the bread more intensely as I lamented that Abby would not be laid out in her own house by her own daughter, who could make her personal farewells while tenderly washing and lovingly preparing her mother's body, whole and intact, for the grave.

How many times can a person be robbed in this lifetime? I asked myself as I reached down to hold and stroke Abby's cold, wrinkled hand. *What, at the end of the day in this cold, cruel world can we keep that is precious to ourselves?*

The one thing I knew for certain was that I was meant to find and absolve her. Perhaps I was also hoping that I could absolve others of their horrible sin of killing this poor, innocent old soul. Who had perpetrated such a despicable act, failing to realise that they had desecrated their own souls? Jeannie always reminded me that we are as one, all of us connected, and that we must jointly keep God's covenant of love. Anything less destroys us all. Whoever had committed this horrible crime had breached that covenant and would pay in ways unknown.

Other plaguing questions assaulted me again. What exactly had happened here and where would Abby's body be taken? Something horrible seemed to be at work, and where the Mute and Margaret were involved, I knew that money must also be involved.

My disordered thoughts then turned to Billy just as my queasy belly released its contents into the bag that had held the bread and ale. I was overwhelmed by my confused thoughts and worries. Feeling sweaty and faint, I took several deep breaths, gathered up my things, and rearranged the blanket over the top of Abby, to cover her up one final time, with decency.

All the while, I wrestled with one burning, horrifying question: the man who had done this despicable thing to her and had made me the luckenbooth brooch — were they the same man?

I recoiled at the thought, preferring instead to place Margaret and Hare in that death chamber, that murder chamber. Besides, I thought I felt Billy come into bed shortly after me, which wouldn't have given him enough time to undertake this horrible, unforgivable deed. I thought I heard Abby being escorted upstairs *after* Billy came to bed. Whatever had happened, I knew there was a lot I had to keep quiet about, including the two new discoveries I had made that morning.

As I closed the door and descended the stairs, I wrestled with my thoughts and fears. I had my suspicions about the deaths of Donald and Joseph. And now I didn't know what shocked me more — finding Abby's dead body in the tramp-house bed or discovering, given my recent bouts of sickness in the mornings, that I had a baby in my belly.

In both cases, they were suspicions no longer.

10.

Billy

Irelied on Hare to get rid of the clothes in the morning down by the canal — Abby's shabby mantle and printed cotton shawl — before we jointly stuffed her naked body into a damaged wooden tea chest we managed to get for cheap up the road. I had spent another restless night with a two-penny candle and the drop. Finally, I drifted off to sleep, getting a couple of hours in before I was to walk Nelly up the High Street and then head off to Surgeons' Square to make arrangements for the body's — the *cadaver's* — disposal. I returned to the West Port afterwards, sleeping the rest of the day. My condition seemed to be growing worse. My cough certainly was, along with my fever. Worst and most painful of all was my constant and dreadful nausea and aching groin. No amount of sleep could grant me rest or release from the intensity of this pain. Whether I liked it or not, I had to get up and carry on with the business.

As arranged, a porter met us that evening at the base of the Castle off the King's Stables Lane. I noted my thrill of excitement during the exchange as we were handed ten pounds. I had never before seen so much money. Margaret took her regular pound off the top, a cut I greatly resented as she did none of the ghastly work. On that basis, I felt she had no claim to it. That money was rightfully mine — and Hare's who, by law, owned this rooming-house now as he was her husband. I relished the fact that this time, at least, Margaret was left to clean up the sick.

That night, as I sat staring across at Hare's repulsive, expressionless face in the pub, I thought about how easily he got off too, being able to close his eyes and lie there on top of the bodies, not having to see their faces or confront the reality of what we were doing. It was I who had the worst, most difficult job, the one for which I had to numb myself with endless drink and the drop. From what I could tell, Hare was sleeping soundly through the night while I was tossing, haunted by the sounds and sights of our victims. *This brute and brainless beast is like a dead man,* I thought to myself. And in response to my conversation with myself, I thought, *if only.*

There can never be adequate compensation for this type of work, I mused further. A little private business on the side might be in order if Nelly and I were ever to get out of Edinburgh to the countryside she loved so much. I knew I was a smart man, smarter than Hare. I didn't know if I could outsmart Margaret, but it'd be well worth a try, especially given how much I detested her. I would have to figure out where and how to commit the work on my own and how to transport the bodies to the doctor. I was sure that, with a little ingenuity and some help from an unsuspecting assistant hoisting the concealed bodies onto a cart for transportation, no one would be any the wiser.

Slipping into bed later that night, trying not to awaken Nelly, my foot touched something tucked in at the base, deep in the straw and rags. Reaching down, I pulled something up that was unidentifiable in the dark room, even after I ran my hands over it and held it up to my face to smell it. Carrying it out to the corridor, I lit the last of my two-penny candle from the night before and held it up. I couldn't believe at first, when my eyes finally focused, what I was holding. A shock ran through me as I realised it was the old woman's mantle. Here it was, evidence that that careless idiot Hare had fouled up. Even though he had so little to keep track of, he couldn't manage.

Returning to the room, I replaced it at the base of the bed and considered this new development. I could only come to a single undeniable conclusion: *Nelly knew*. I had no doubt. How else could she have had it? Unlike Hare, she was a quick study and capable of putting two and two together. What this meant only time would tell, but I felt angry and worried just thinking about it. I thought about the outcome if I were to tell Margaret about Hare's stupidity and this discovery. They had already suggested, jokingly, on a few occasions when we were out getting soused, that Nelly might be the next one we would send to the doctor's.

'You never can trust a Scotswoman,' Margaret had said to me one evening, looking over at Hare and winking. 'But you can always trust a dead one,' she followed up with a hearty laugh.

'You dare and you'll follow her,' I immediately shot back, looking her straight in the eyes with all of the hate I could muster, before cursing and spitting on the pub floor. Margaret's response was silence, her tell-tale smirk to Hare speaking to me in its usual infuriating, derisive way.

And there was something in the manner of their shared smiling and winking that evening that told me there had been a discussion about this. Serious and lengthy discussion. I knew they were not to be trusted and were waiting, eagerly, for a foul-up, any excuse to make a shot of Nelly. Mentioning the mishap with the mantle would only put her in danger. That must be avoided at all costs.

After the tremendous care I'd taken to conceal the body business, I now had the additional concern about what Nelly knew or conjectured, and what she might do with that knowledge. I felt a rage brewing at the Mute for his idiocy. Laying there immobile beside her in a state not conducive to sleep, I tried to breathe deeply and calm myself down, but my heart seemed to have a mind of its own and over the next several minutes, it skipped several beats. To calm myself, I changed tack and pictured Hare beneath me, prostrate on a bed, his eyes closed, face upwards. I fancied my hands perfectly positioned above his nose and mouth, ready to work their magic with the method I had painstakingly perfected. Just as he opened his eyes to see my smiling face, I imagined pushing up hard on his chin to seal his mouth shut while holding his nostrils shut. *Burking*, people have since called it, as you told me, Mr. M—. That is my dark legacy in this lifetime, you said. That wasn't something Nelly read during my palm reading, I thought to myself. And even Hare, I thought wryly, could be burked. I felt intense pleasure at this idea and smiled as I played out the fantasy.

I pictured myself leaning over him, whispering in his ear, loudly enough that he could hear me, 'It was only a matter of time until it was your turn, mate.'

I smiled to myself as I imagined uttering my final, excited word of farewell — 'Godspeed'.

I savoured the thought of permanently muting the Mute, of burking Hare, and chuckled quietly knowing how much Nelly would appreciate these jokes, if not the action.

Smiling to myself, I turned over and stretched my arm out across Nelly's back and drifted off to sleep.

***

Life is a death sentence. Think about it, Mr. M—, you and I are living under a death sentence right this very moment. We are dying by the minute, our time

142

limited. I have had the added benefit of feeling the very life ebb out of me over the course of this past year, infected as I am with the cancer. Just think: I, a rapidly dying man, have been doling out death to other desperate souls like me. You could say I'm a Grim Reaper of sorts here in Edinburgh, this kill-or-be-killed death manufactory, filled with so many others trying to stave off the inevitable. It seems fitting that the Reaper should be Irish given our wild, carousing wakes. We're the stuff of England's wildest nightmares, considered across this island as the scum of the earth. As my name becomes a household word, it'll be even truer now.

But death can't be staved off. Whether we wish to recognise it or not, we must each of us shake off this mortal coil, some sooner than others. Some suddenly. Some in a horribly prolonged and painful fashion. Rich or poor, happy or morose, death comes inevitably for us all. There is no escaping, although we can try for a time, and hope against hope that we are granted a long life. I see tremendous irony in my chronicling this history of the shots in such a matter-of-fact manner while suffering horribly from the cancer and preparing for the gallows.

The consummate irony is no one knows, until it happens, when their number is up. I like the exciting uncertainty of that. And no amount of money can buy you a pass or any answers in the death department, although those with money can buy the right medicines and a bit of time. I suppose the good doctor's researches, as he calls them, aim at granting longer life to those who can afford them. Even for them, death remains unavoidable, and while we can spin countless tales about what lies beyond the grave, it remains a right bloody mystery. *Hamlet* is best at capturing that, and it's all to my taste, lay philosopher that I am.

I once believed in a greater mystery, as I do now, but that was not true during those early stages of the killings.

I remember scrutinising the shots carefully in their final death throes but felt no closer to the truth. The impenetrable veil remained between me and *the undiscovered country from whose bourn no traveller returns,* as Hamlet beautifully describes it.

My gut told me then that there was nothing beyond the here and now. Still, the possibility of the unknown still haunted and taunted me. The one thing I knew for sure then was that this world is where we experience our heaven and our hell, and those with money and power play the biggest role in determining our fate. Making changes in this world is where we should focus our attention, I thought. Try as we might, we can't drink it away, although heaven knows I have tried thousands of times.

If I were to sum up my thinking then, it is this: duped fools and children have crafted the next world out of hope and fear. I began to come around to the good doctor's point of view: dissection shouldn't alarm us because there will be no resurrection. Position a thousand sentries in the churchyard to deter disinterment of your body. Place a padlock and a mortsafe over that coffin after you place it into the ground. The fact is that your body will rot and stink just like that of any dead animal in the woods. We want, desperately, to deny the flesh, to rise above it. But we are all delusional. In the end, we are but rotting flesh, a signpost of our moral rottenness.

John's gospel had it right — *That which is born of the flesh is flesh.*

We conceive of ourselves as God-born but our human flesh is weak, woman-born, corrupt and corruptible, down to the very bone.

Our flesh is but grass, as the Prince of Prophets,

Isaiah, ever a poet, tells us. Life is short, fragile, fleeting. Everything withers and dies.

It is only right, as I used to joke with Hare, that we should conduct our body business — our *flesh* trade — in the *Grass*market. That joke was surely lost on the Mute.

***

Being able to see clearly now and not through a glass darkly, I realise the joke was on me.

Death, like an aloof woman at a luxurious dinner party, has sat across from me this entire year staring me coldly and unflinchingly in the face. I have studied her gaunt and sickly countenance and, in my fitful dreams, taken hold of her gnarly, desiccated hands, begging her not to divest me of my life. But she has persisted, in her gravelly voice, to whisper my name. The truth is — and there is no denying it — death is a stinking, despicable whore up close. Like most women once you get to know them. A bitter bitch; her voice a death rattle.

I have felt myself a changed man over these past several years, inhabiting someone else's body, a body being slowly, humiliatingly divested of its strength and faculties. *Whose deteriorating body is this?* I have stopped and wondered to myself, for this one has betrayed me. I have awakened many mornings, after precious little sleep, with such deep, nauseating pain, chills, and weakness, wishing myself dead, wondering whose body I am inhabiting. Perhaps the better question is, who or what has possessed me?

I have been aware of the irony of this revelation while engaged in this body business. So very often at those cusp-of-the-grave moments — theirs and mine, although I am dying slowly and against my will while *they* go fairly fast and willingly — it has struck me

145

that many are too preoccupied with the next life when this one should be our focus.

For the longest time, I was delusional — like most people — living my life as if I might live forever. I trip over those words now: *live forever*. Who among us, except those living in the lap of luxury, would ever believe such a lie or make such a wish? Funny how the poor expect death by the minute, by the hour, by the day, while the rich sit comfortably, well-fed and secure, in total and utterly privileged denial.

My sick, tormented, and dying body has taught me many powerful, valuable lessons that I have transferred over to this body business.

You'd be doing me a disservice to think, Mr. M—, that I have mindlessly put people to death. At that most important moment of their lives, I have been nothing if not mindful. When called upon to do so and when Margaret wasn't involved, and it mattered most, I have been in possession of a gracious, caring bedside manner. I expect nothing less in return. Sometimes, I have wanted to trade places with the shots, for whom I have always shown the greatest care and concern. After all, I alone knew what was about to happen. Because Hare is entirely unaware and just does what he is told. Now, as I prepare for the scaffold, I hope my own prayers will be answered. After all, I believe that is what I've been seeking this entire time — that final, total, and complete blessing that will follow my inescapable pelting and haranguing by the mob, when I step up to the gallows before stepping beyond the veil where the greatest mystery will be solved.

My true enterprise, I have come to realise during this writing process, has been one of liberation, even if at first I didn't realise it because God had yet to show me the way and give me the signs. I have, over the past many months, freed people with concern. In killing the destitute, I have done them a sacred service, granting them a precious blessing — a quick and welcome escape from the hell that is this world, a hell created by their greedy, careless, wealthy brothers and sisters.

I have crowned them with oblivion, total freedom from pain and all worldly concerns.

Their eyes, and mine, have seen a different glory, and my greatest revelation is, I believe, yet to come.

***

If you ask me, it's a fear of death that drives all religion. None can escape it. Death levels all, both rich and poor. Read Psalm 49, *Every man 'seeth that wise men die, likewise the fool and brutish person.* I think, for some time, I took some solace from this idea of everyone being equal under God's law. So did others like Thomas Boston who wrote, *Man's life is a stream, running into death's devouring deeps.*

We all face the terrors of the unknown. Hamlet conveyed it best in his reminder that *in that sleep of death what dreams may come, when we have shuffled off this mortal coil, must give us pause.* Shakespeare understood these great truths and gave voice to them. I had the good fortune to see *Hamlet* performed several times. I returned to the theatre to learn and memorise many lines. To this day, I carry its insights with me, bringing it to bear on this body business. I have wondered if it is possible to make murder an art, a type of medical art that grants people escape from their unbearable, miserable lives. My brilliance and ingenuity, sadly overlooked in this dog-eat-dog hellhole of a world, found their rightful place here in the West Port.

I'm not very different from the good doctor, I think, only he is respected for his work — makes a name for himself — perfecting his techniques openly while under the admiring public gaze of his many ardent students. Here I am, his left hand, the person to whom he owes his growing reputation, barely scraping by, risking life, limb, and liberty to support his habit. Something is wrong with that. Like the fact that he, like his right-hand man, Paterson, and the Mute, aren't in here with me and won't also swing at the end. Four people kept this business going — five really, when we include that witch, Margaret — and yet I'm the only one who has lost my liberty, been labelled a criminal, and am about to meet my Maker. All of that, I note, without actual evidence of murder. Docherty could have died of natural causes. She consumed a lot of drink that day and night. I know because I kept refilling her glass. It's a funny thing, the justice system. Seems more like an injustice system to me, as I've often told Nelly.

For this, if for no other reason, I pray that the prophetic saint, Thomas Boston, is proven correct: *They who now live in palaces, must quit them, and go home to this house; and they who have nowhere to lay their heads, shall thus have a house at length.*

***

The formula for the shots is simple really, sheer bloody common sense, and has been painstakingly perfected right down to the precise manner and final moment of execution. I know this because I perfected it, contrary to suggestions in the press that Dr. Knox taught me my technique. What he did know was that we were doing something criminal, such freshly dead bodies being delivered every other week. He even participated in covering things up. You just have to hear what he did with Daft Jamie to know that. As for the method, it was I who perfected it with Hare merely taking direction. That is all Hare has ever been capable of — taking direction — and that is all he, and others like him, can ever do. The fine Dr. Knox and I are cut from a different cloth than the Hares of this world. We are of a visionary order.

Let me repeat, Mr. M—, while Hare has been vital to this operation since we started, I have ensured its success. You could say that I furnished the brains and Hare the brawn. At only fifteen, he worked as a bagman in Port Hopetoun, carrying the coals into peoples' houses. You wouldn't know, but that takes great strength, day in and day out, and Hare, a squat ogre of a specimen, was the perfect man for the business.

Hare's role is straightforward in my painstakingly perfected process; weight is everything as he lays across the victim's chest so they can't move and can barely breathe, while he pins their arms. Only Daft Jamie proved a true match for him — for us. It took both of us to take him down. As for my part, there's a lot that goes into suffocating a person so you don't leave marks on their faces. My job requires great skill and manoeuvring. It is not for the faint of heart. I have also striven, with every victim, to make things as comfortable, painless, and efficient as possible. Over time, I confess, I have come to enjoy the process, which is a good thing when a man has to eat. That is more than I can say for my mind-numbing work as a navvy.

I have, on occasion, fancied myself, like the good doctor, credited for my contributions to science, allowed to discuss my techniques with an admiring, eager and paying group of students in a crowded lecture hall. I can see them now, intrigued, to say the least, by the idea of identifying a precise and perfect moment of death, leaning in closer from their tiered benches overlooking the cadaver upon which I reveal my special method, the tricks of my trade, their eyes wide with fascinated horror as I disclose my safely guarded secrets.

I am purposeful and painstaking in my demonstration, using a few dramatic hand gestures and slightly modulating my voice to emphasise the key points in the process. I have long practised my presentations in my pub and street sermons.

Gentlemen, I say, addressing them boldly, ensuring that my voice is audible throughout the room as I lean over the naked shot laid out in front of me on the table. *I have learned that timing is everything in the process of shot-making.*

I give them a few moments to consider and digest the idea, before I clear my throat and continue.

And that is what it comes down to with the shots — a look in their eyes, a far-away look that suggests they're not here anymore. They are no longer present. They are already, somehow, out of their bodies. Make no mistake: the drink is key to the operation. It is vital that they be numbed, but not too much, as this helps them to see beyond themselves and this stinking, thankless graveyard of a world. Things are not up to me at that crucial moment. Little do they realise that they are actually making the call themselves. And you could say that answering that call is my special calling.

I would wax philosophical at this point, moving into discussion of the Big Questions.

The shots have been selected for a reason. They have shown up at the right time and the right place. God has placed them in my precious hands. How liberating it is for these chosen ones — all of them poor, desperate souls with little to live for, who have made no mark on this world because it strangled off every opportunity — to leave this hellhole behind while making one final, invaluable contribution to science and the progress of mankind. I turn now to the good doctor to explain and justify it to you just as he explained it to me, a man once blinded by ignorance.

Don't be fooled, Mr. M—, like Hare who's been clueless this entire time. It hasn't been easy being the chosen one. A tremendous burden comes with my job, a weight of responsibility as life and death are placed squarely and firmly in my expert hands. And this is where the gin comes in, Madame Geneva, a divine anaesthetic if ever there was one. I'm especially liberal with it with the ladies. And there have been many ladies. Indeed, there have been *mainly* ladies. I've kept count — twelve to be exact, because the lassies do go down a whole lot easier, and faster. If they're especially good girls, I lace their drinks with an additional drop or two of laudanum, my amber mistress. It works a charm and with a certainty, kicking in almost immediately, rendering them pliant in my hands and loose in the limbs. At this stage, I can even time her effects. In a matter of minutes, they begin to slur as their eyes glass over. Some of them, although they never could have afforded it, needed her every day just to survive. I'm willing to bet some of them would have pulled a trick or three for the Madame. It's only right that they should get it at the end from me, Billy, the charming Irishman, as I am known here in the West Port.

Don't you agree, Mr. M—, that death should be seductive when the time comes? What a gift for one to melt away, painlessly, into her final, divine embrace. So it is that I, the gift-giver, have spared no expense. On at least one occasion, I assumed the role of a long-lost lover, seeing past her age to the girl she used to be. I remember kissing that one, many times and passionately, with such deep and prolonged kisses she could barely breathe. I remember whispering, 'It's just you and me. Let yourself go.' And she did, my words working wonders as she went weak in the knees and wet in the drawers.

The men, on the other hand, are a different story, always needing prolonged dousing with whisky or gin, and ample beer, whatever Hare and I have going. And we always have plenty going in anticipation of the shot payment. In fact, as I've learned the hard way, the more drink the better — for them and for me. Throughout the entire operation, both when Hare and I worked together and when I worked alone, I only ever faced two problems. One was Daft Jamie Wilson who hardly touched a drop — damn stubborn fool of a lad that he was. His desire was for snuff, and a lot of it. As a result — and a more horrible result it almost became — he nearly finished us both off. It took a violent, panicked fight to put him away. The other challenge came in the form of the young deaf boy we had to lure into the bedroom where we had just delivered his drunk grandmother. We argued over whether to kill him at all. In the end, only after extraordinary mental effort on my part, because he was so very young and scared, did we manage to deliver him too. I did the dirty work, as usual — the tough, unbearable job of breaking his back. The expression of anguished suffering I saw on his face at that point has haunted me ever since. His was an ecstatic experience of deliverance into the hereafter. No amount of laudanum can ever erase that boy's suffering from my mind. Targeting him and his grandmother, who were lodging at the house, wasn't the smartest choice Margaret ever made. I could have killed the old cunt for it, and have since imagined doing so, with tremendous pleasure, dozens of times. She's the one who should have been rolled out of there in a herring barrel. I continue to fantasise.

But I digress, which is something I am wont to do in this dank, horrid little cell. So I ask you, Mr. M—, and the gentlemen who have questioned and condemned me, to grant me more understanding than I received in that courtroom last month. I ask you to fairly weigh the options as you read my words. Setting aside the deaths of Daft Jamie and the young deaf boy, what seems to you more humane — my method of murder, or the slow degrading and violent deaths that most working people experience here in Edinburgh and across this great nation and Empire? Who has more blood on their hands? Me or a thousand other employers and renegades who have more unrestricted power than should be legal? And why, when the poor and the desperate are being murdered by the day, and tens of thousands of children brutalised in mills, factories, and mines, trafficked in the streets, and even killed off by their own starving parents in need of insurance money, is there no one swinging for it? So many should swing, Mr. M—, God only knows. Thousands. I would call those wholesale crimes against the poor, if such a term existed. I would hang the lot of them if I had the chance. Instead, irony of ironies, they are hanging me.

And, gentlemen, I ask you because I feel I must — just how bad must this life be if being painlessly and promptly murdered is preferable to it? How bloody bad must it be? The answer comes in the form of two words — *truly horrific* — but there are really no words to convey the nightmare that is their lives. By the time these poor, desperate souls crossed the threshold into the lodging house, they have seen too many horrors in this lifetime and deserve my final, caring blessing.

I hope Edinburgh's most privileged sons can provide me with an answer that makes sense. Why would some poor folk willingly say, as did Job, and as I am saying now in the face of an unrelenting and vicious disease and imminent execution, *My soul chooseth strangling, and death rather than my life?*

Theirs, not mine, are the stories that should have been told, but all we hear in their wake is silence.

153

Dead silence.

11.

Nelly

Like someone possessed or mad, I felt for a time like I'd lived two lives with Billy, two very distinct lives, as unlike each other as day and night. Over the nightmare of years, I realise they were one and the same. He lured and manipulated me just as he did everyone else. The glass and the gill were our bonds.

I look back on everything like an observer who knows all of the lines and how the sequences end, but only vaguely remembers playing the part. And some might ask, what part exactly? After all, I did nothing, knowing nothing, never being part of the plan because Billy knew I would never agree to participate in hurting anyone. Not a soul. Not without provocation. And even then, no.

But I began to know and see things and had to stay quiet despite the need or the temptation. And this might be the greatest plague — knowing that something horrible is about to happen but not knowing to whom it's going to happen, or where, and not being able to stop it because that would involve risking your own life and a baby's and revealing that you know their dirty little secrets that are multiplying by the week.

Despite Billy's efforts to keep me away from the scenes of his crimes — that I initially hoped were not his — I began to listen and look, becoming the one who picked up the pieces.

Now, with him gone, I remain the bearer of those dark and dirty secrets, trapped in this, my post-Billy life. Its senselessness has become a crushing weight, like a coffin, containing his despicable lies and crimes, holding me down. How I managed to make the descent into this death chamber that has become my life is a question that torments me to this day. How our sweet love fast became entangled with pain, anger, bitter resentment, even hatred and repulsion, is an even greater mystery I have yet to solve.

What I do know is that death chambers never look like death chambers when you first enter them. There are no signs on the door. Sideways, seductive glances and the promise of some form of love and release lure you into a place where you believe you will be revitalised, born again. You can make yourself believe. I know now that you can make yourself believe anything. You go willingly, leading yourself in.

You learn the hard way, just as Billy's victims did, that there is a lot of pain behind those doors — and treachery. Who could have known? Certainly not me. But when I started to suspect things and became a witness, I resisted in the only ways I knew how and retreated with my carefully guarded secrets.

The one thing I know for sure is that Billy's greatest evil was not revealed in that courtroom in front of the well-heeled Edinburgh public. They may have thought it was, but I know better and while I too have done worse, it was always out of love or desperation. Over time, I opted to embrace the dream side of Billy, justifying and excusing the Other Billy. That was how I coped, how I dealt with his unpredictability and manipulation. It was how he wanted me to cope, how he trained me to cope.

But I can't and won't evade the truth now: I became his secret, complicit associate, even and especially in his crimes against me.

Shame on me.

And I began to live, more and more, in hopes of an occasional memorable evening when, with the help of many a glass and many a gill, I caught a glimpse of the Billy I first met, the one into whose arms I readily fell, madly and deeply. Those are my only fond memories towards the end, when he came to life in the pub after a day spent recovering from, or steeling himself against what, I now know, were many gruesome nights and mornings after. I feel sick when I think of Billy helping the heartless Doctor Knox, and how far removed he was becoming from me. I struggled against him to help the weak and damaged in their leave-taking of this horrible place, to do something for their souls.

Shame on him.

I feel equally sick about my sense of relief that there were others who sustained the same torment, victims who were abused instead of me.

Shame on me.

Shame. Guilt.

These are my mortsafes.

***

There came an evening in early April, a couple of months after my discovery of Abby's dead body, when all of my suspicions were confirmed. After a night of heavy drinking at the tramp-house with the whisky flowing freely, another woman's dead body appeared. Her name was Mary Haldane, a petty criminal and a fairly regular lodger, with whose family history I was well acquainted. She had two daughters, one of whom was married to a tinsmith and lived up the High Street, and another who had been transported to Australia for theft years earlier. Mary had never heard from that daughter again, the loss leaving a chasm where her heart used to be. That's the way she explained it to me. As was her way, after a few gills she would give us news about her Edinburgh daughter before launching nostalgically into stories about both of her girls when they were children. I recognised this as her way of coping, and I honoured that.

Mary lodged at various places in the city, but I never knew exactly how she survived nor did I — out of respect — inquire. There are, like me, thousands of such survivors on the streets of Edinburgh.

During our first drink together she told me she had experienced something harrowing like I had endured with Rab. Sharing those stories at the pub took a weight off me after a decade of silence. It was like talking to the sister for whom I had always yearned, a keeper of confidences. On an evening every other week over the course of a few years, Mary was that sister. I wonder now, looking back, if that is why Billy chose her. It was but another way to wound me — indirectly — to rob me of my only confidante. He seemed to take pleasure in stripping me of supports.

But he couldn't destroy or tarnish my memories of Mary, an unforgettable character and true friend who enjoyed drinking and what the Irish call craic. Stout and in possession of a loud and hearty laugh that showed off her single, large tooth that protruded out the front of her mouth, Mary was one of the best storytellers I have ever heard. She was clever with her jokes and wisecracks too, often catching the ear and the attention of people in the pub. I nearly peed myself laughing over the stories she told. Where Billy was a sermonising storyteller with a fine turn of phrase and an eye to a message about politics or faith, Mary brought her listeners inside her personal stories, always quick to see the humour and the tragedies of life. And strikingly unlike Billy, Mary could laugh at herself, as is a woman's way.

During her last visit, she started drinking and tale-telling in the late afternoon, laughing over some recent encounters. Despite the jokes, I sensed a sombreness about her. When I asked her privately if all was well, she said there was an issue with her daughter's husband and that Mary's man-friend was going to set him straight. I knew it must be a serious matter because that's the only time womenfolk get involved. Anyone who met her agreed that they wouldn't want to run afoul of Mary. She would be a formidable foe under any circumstances. While she could laugh and tell jokes with the best of them, she could also claw you blind if set off or pushed the wrong way.

Whether or not her daughter was the only thing bothering her that night, I will never know, but at one point, Mary left the pub saying she was going to have an early night. I found out afterwards that she'd paid to have her flask filled with whisky prior to leaving and then continued drinking, alone, back at the house. She made her way to the stables at some point, and that is where Hare found her upon our return. I overheard him whispering earnestly to Margaret after we got back. Knowing something was up, I quietly crept after them down the passage when they said they were off to bed. I sensed otherwise. Tucking myself into the dark alleyway across the lane with a view inside the stables, I watched as Margaret, Hare, and Billy, who arrived a few minutes later, lantern in hand, saw to her. When Mary didn't respond to her name, I watched, aghast, as Billy moved Margaret and Hare aside and then covered dear Mary's face with his hands before pushing her down firmly into the straw. From a distance, I saw the poor woman's hands frantically trying to fight him off. She then went into brief convulsions. I gasped, unable to move. Thankfully, no one saw or heard me. To make a sound would be to sign my own death warrant.

All three of them seemed intent on finishing the operation after which Margaret carelessly strolled away. Billy and Hare then undressed Mary, tossing her clothes to the back side of the stables. Hare left for a few minutes before returning with a thin blanket with which they covered and wrapped Mary's body, burying her deep in the straw before they returned to the tramp-house.

I knew they would have to remove her body in a matter of hours as that stable was used early in the morning.

I had strong suspicions as to where she would be taken next. I dreaded thinking about what would be done.

Seeing no one returning, I crossed the laneway to the house, my legs unsteady, my chest tight. I knew I would have to sneak out once everyone was in bed to get what was needed for her sin-eating. I also needed a strip of Mary's skirt and a few locks of her hair to craft her doll. I had recently completed three more — one for Donald, the other for Joseph, and the third for the unnamed Englishman. Although Donald had died of natural causes, Billy had hinted at his horrible fate. I was now convinced Joseph's death had been unnatural, like that of the unnamed Englishman whose body I saw leave the tramp-house very early one morning as I went off to hawk shoes. Given what I'd seen with Abby, the old unnamed woman, and Mary, I knew they too had been helped along.

When I thought of Mary's doll, I thought of her daughter. Mary may have been a drinker and a thief, but I knew, from what she had told me, that she was a good mother, as good as she could be under the circumstances, her life never being easy.

I then thought about my own mother who never had the chance to be my mother because Rab had poisoned her life. I was thankful she'd had a good sin-eating but I remember praying against that ritual for the return of my mother. I yearned for her to stay with me, love me, and be my mother. I prayed like my life depended on it, asking God to take me too if he couldn't bring her back.

With that memory at the forefront of my mind, I vowed to do a good sin-eating for Mary. I knew she would do the same for me — or, at the very least, pay for one.

I hoped, as I made my way to the shops, that I wouldn't need a sin-eating any time soon, but I knew there were no guarantees. I was sleeping in a tramp-house owned by murderers. I was also living with Billy, sleeping with a man I now knew to be a killer. I felt sick at the very thought of what I'd seen and heard that night.

And then, a more unsettling thought crept in — *we* were sleeping with Billy.

***

I have said there are memories I'd pay to be rid of, that I wish could be erased, memories that will haunt me to the grave. All of the incidents with Rab assume this cast, as do several that I witnessed in the course of the following weeks and months.

My next tragic discovery was little Effie, the young cinder gatherer. She regularly came around the lodging house to sell Billy small bits of leather for cobbling that she'd gathered from about the coachworks in Tanner's Lane where leather was prepared. While Billy had made his share of discoveries, Effie seemed to have the best luck when it came to finding the smoothest, choicest pieces.

I don't know how it was, but just setting eyes on Effie or hearing her name made me smile. Effie was well-named in my view because she had an effervescence rarely found in this dirty, desperate part of Edinburgh. As with Mary, I always had good laughs with her. No matter how low and hopeless I was feeling, or how sick, especially after late nights of overindulgence, she never failed to lift my spirits. There was a lightness to her that I envied. She was perhaps a bit simple and far too trusting, a double liability in these parts, but she emanated joy.

I had often worried about her, especially at night, because she had no one — no mate to protect her or mother to comfort her. She had a childlike trust, taking all manner of people at their word and, unlike Margaret and even myself sometimes, she never gossiped in a nasty or self-righteous way. She simply conveyed the news. It was thanks to Effie that I learned what was happening around the West Port — who had given birth, who had died, who had gone to the watch-house or been escorted to gaol. Effie had seen and heard it all as she wandered around at all hours of the night and day. I wondered if, when, and where she slept.

I don't believe she drank or, at least, I'd never seen her drink and my guess was, based on her size, that it wouldn't take much to put her away. How Billy managed to get her drinking, I'll never know, but drunk as a lord she was, as her bad luck would have it, when I found her asleep on the straw at the back side of Hare's stables. In the couple of weeks following the incident with Mary, I had regularly poked my head in at night, pushing my hands in through the straw, worried about other victims, always terrified I would find someone. I was plagued by questions and had suspicions as I had heard Billy mention some doctor to Margaret a few times recently. Billy didn't know any doctors.

So, when I found Effie late that night before leaving for the pub, I wasn't entirely surprised. While I expected a body, I was devastated to find wee Effie. She lay against a straw bale, her head propped up, a cloth eerily covering her face. Moving her head to the side and pulling the cloth away, shock overcame me with the recognition. That moment confirmed for me that no one was safe, not even me. Effie was well known in this neighbourhood. None of that had mattered to those who had hurt her. None of that had kept her safe. There was, quite clearly, something more important at play. Money must lie, I strongly suspected, at the bottom of the business.

At first, given the overpowering scent of gin on her, I hoped that she was just drunk. As I nudged her slightly trying to awaken her, I prayed she was in a heavy sleep after too much liquor. But she failed to respond and lay there immobile. My heart beat like a racehorse as I figured out what to do next. Holding my hand directly under her nose, I realised she wasn't breathing. When I touched my fingers to her face, she was still warm. If she was dead, she couldn't have been dead long.

I suspected she must have come up from King's Stables Lane while I was inside making Mary's doll and sorting out the rest of the group, trying to decide on the final resting place for that growing collection. It was becoming difficult to conceal them in our small room, and I couldn't risk Billy discovering them.

And here was another I needed to craft.

After several minutes of checking if Effie were alive or dead, I realised she was now beyond help. I also recognised that I was in danger sitting in those stables near her dead body. I certainly didn't want to end up in the same position, so I recited a quick prayer over her, kissed her forehead, and headed immediately over to the pub, fearing my absence would be a cause for concern.

I walked madly, my thoughts turning over the fact of the extra money that had recently been coming in. I had started paying more attention to where Billy was going at all hours of the day and night. It was the shoes that first made me put two and two together. Billy and I made very little money mending shoes, just enough to get by, and lately we rarely went into the street to do business — or, rather, I went out while he stayed back, which added resentment to my curiosity. I had also noticed new shoes in our collection that couldn't be accounted for, that Billy hadn't acquired or exchanged when we scavenged during our travels.

Money was always involved where the Mute and Margaret were concerned. I had heard so many schemes over the years about separating unsuspecting people from their money. Of those, few were actually attempted and even fewer were successful, Margaret and Hare not being known for their brilliance. Like many others, I was convinced that Margaret and the Mute had killed Lucky together, Margaret's former husband who owned the tramp hotel. Rumour had it he was poisoned so as to leave no marks on the body. Around that time, Margaret inquired about my knowledge of herbal medicine and those that could kill. I told her nothing, suspecting the worst. I regarded Margaret's treachery as monstrous. She and Lucky had come over from Ireland and spent several years together. Logue — his real name — was some years older than her, although he remained a vigorous man who worked on the canal beside her until construction was completed. Lucky may have been a rough man at times, but I'd never seen him manhandle her or anyone else for that matter. The idea of killing him seemed horrible to me.

Lucky's death struck many people as suspicious, as he had shown no previous signs of ill health. He could have bested most men in the pub, men half his age, but Billy and I figured that Margaret was careful not to carry on her shenanigans there. The poor man had, despite his brutality, a soft heart, helping people out

164

wherever he could. We had no doubt that Margaret had played on that — and his lust. Margaret always had a lot to say about a man's lust, offering advice on how to manipulate them by way of it.

Poor Lucky. The day he met Margaret, his luck ran out.

The same could be said for Abby and Mary. And Donald and Joseph and the Englishman. And now poor wee Effie.

The list was growing at an alarming rate, I thought as I walked.

When I arrived at the pub, I tried to sit down calmly across from three people I now knew to be murderers. I focused my thoughts on my duty — tending to Effie later that night. Her soul needed to be put to rest, especially after the horrible violence I suspected had been inflicted on her. She needed peace and a mother now, and I would offer her both.

***

And later that evening, I couldn't hold back. I couldn't help myself. It's the way I am. The way I've always been. I surprised myself when I spoke up because part of me was terrified, especially for my unborn child.

'Have you seen wee Effie, the cinder gatherer, lately?' I asked Billy, as we undressed and lay down together.

'No,' he said, 'It's been about a week since she's come around.'

'I came across her tonight,' I said.

Billy acted surprised.

'Tonight? Where? She wasn't at our pub. I don't even think she drinks.'

'I thought so too,' I said, 'but when I found her, she was drunk.' Then I added, 'Dead drunk,' emphasising the first word.

Billy silently shifted away from me and faced the wall.

'I know,' I said, staring at his back.

Before I could stop myself, the next statement was out. 'I know what you've all been up to.' My trembling voice became a hoarse whisper. I feared his reaction.

'Billy. I know your secrets … the three of you. And I know there have been others,' I said.

In response, Billy suddenly rolled over and grabbed me firmly by the arm. I couldn't see him in the dark, but his voice was menacing.

'Listen, Nelly, you're playing with fire. You're going to get us both killed if you don't keep your nose out of this business.'

Then he offered more information. 'Here is all you need to know. Donald died with a debt owing to Margaret. She harped on about it. You know how she gets. We did something — the Mute and I — to shut her up. They forced me into going along with a scheme — it involves a doctor — and while it's gotten out of hand, it's become a business and we've made a fair bit of money at it.'

He squeezed his fingers into my arm to reaffirm his point. 'You'd better pay heed, Nelly, because they threatened to kill you if I refused to go along with it. They warned me you'd be the next to go to the doctor. They laughed about how a dead Scotswoman can tell no tales.'

I said nothing in response to this horrible idea, but it confirmed my worst fears. A doctor was involved.

I could tell Billy was agitated as he adjusted himself in the bed. I was the one now silent.

Although he was facing away from me, his next words were clear. 'These are not people to play around with, Nelly. You know them as well as I do. They mean business, and now we have other business to attend to.'

166

I swallowed before saying, in a terrified whisper, 'Well, you'd have to protect me. And you should know this — now's as good a time as any to tell you, Billy — if they killed me, they'd be killing two.'

This last statement was followed by an unusually long silence before he added, 'If you're telling me what I think you're telling me, Nelly, you're a damn liar. You can't have children. It's been ten bloody, barren years. Besides, we haven't been together in months.'

To this last statement, I answered defensively, 'But I'm only a few months out now, Billy. I ignored the signs. Had you been with me lately, you would have noticed the changes.'

But Billy would have none of it.

'It sounds like a miracle, Nelly. And you know I don't believe in miracles anymore. It's certainly not an immaculate conception. You forget that I know your history and I've watched you in the pubs with other men.'

I didn't expect his next, crushing words.

'I don't know what we can do at this late stage, Nelly, but you'll have to figure something out. Like Jeannie did.'

Such were Billy's last words to me before he lay back down to sleep.

I had grown used, over the years, to being worried about myself, but now I realised I had more to worry about. I lay down and cried quietly.

I suspect Billy heard me but he said and did nothing. I listened as his breathing took on a rhythm and he started to snore.

In my mind's eye, things happened differently: Billy rolled over and held me from behind, like he did during our early days, only this time, he explored my changing body, stroking the baby in my rounded belly and massaging my full, heavy breasts, lightly kissing the back of my neck and comforting me.

This took place in my mind's eye.

But in my mind, after Billy's response and explanation, I was starting to consider my options and what I might do to stop him — or them — from hurting me, hurting us. I knew one thing — I wouldn't repeat what I'd done years earlier with Jeannie's assistance. While I might not care about myself anymore, my baby was a very different story.

***

I never gave nor took advice. Margaret's advice to me, which she only offered once, was to the point, as was everything she ever said to me. 'Men are simple. Give it to 'em regular — food, sex, drink — and they'll follow you like a lovesick dog to the ends o' the earth. They're all dogs really, as I found out at a very young age — as most women find out. Until you realise that, you're in for a heap o' trouble. Set out strict rules and keep to 'em. Don't give in. You've got more power than you realise. We women always have the power — only most of us don't recognise it. Just remember that and always keep the chain short.'

Over the course of a few years, she had made more than a few slighting comments about my infertility and how it might prove to be a liability with Billy.

'He's told us many a time he wants children. He left his other two behind. She wouldn't bring them over. That was heart-breaking for him. Why he chose you, Nelly, I'll never understand. You've done precious little for him.'

I looked that old harridan straight in the eye when she said that, but that was all I could do. I have vowed never to give her any opportunity to attack me physically. I know she would do me a great deal of damage. I take great pleasure in knowing that Hare, as Billy has told me many times, keeps a lot of secrets from her, she who thinks she's smart and in control. *Think again, Margaret,* I want to say to her, looking her dead in the eye with a smile on my face. Instead, I always bite my tongue and walk away. My statements rattle around in my head.

Who am I to laugh now when Billy's been keeping secrets from me? Margaret must be pleased to know that, especially given her hatred for all Scots, me in particular. But here, she's far more hated than I am. Scots here in Edinburgh make fun of her accent, treating her as if she is stupid and disease-ridden, along with all her other brethren living here in Little Ireland. Regardless of the secrets Billy kept from me, I still laughed at her, although only privately.

Billy befriended her and the barbaric looking Mute because we were desperate. He was lured into doing things he would have thought despicable just months earlier. Billy helping a doctor? 'And what have the doctors ever done for us?' I can hear him roaring that question aloud at the pub when we first started hearing rumours about the bodysnatchers. 'The doctors never help anyone but themselves,' Billy would chime in, responding to his own question. If they could fix his cancer — the cancer he doesn't think I know about — that might have been seen as a fair exchange, but that would never happen.

All of these thoughts ran through my head as I crept out of bed in the very early morning to return to Effie who lay fast stiffening in the stable.

And this, I inwardly questioned Billy, is what you call caring for the poor? This? Wee Effie would never hurt a soul, not even if she was paid money. That was the God's honest truth and everyone knew it. Something about how she looked laying there made me decide that today would be the day I would make my way up the Radical Road and bury the commemorative dead, my precious wee dolls. I worried by the day that Billy would find them where I'd carefully tucked them into my small travelling box. Countless times I'd wrapped them up tight in their cotton and worsted clothes, bathed them with a few tears, prayed over and stroked them lovingly while asking God to put an end to this nightmare. I had, more recently, carved sombre expressions into some of their tiny faces, restitched and glued some of their clothes, and decorated their coffins, their last wee box beds, with some of the tin metal I sometimes used for shoe buckles. I carefully cut small sections into shapes, gluing them firmly onto the wood. It was the least I could do for my precious menagerie to make them feel more loved. After all, they had been stripped of everything else — life, hope, decency. This was the least I could do to ensure their possible resurrection beyond the grave.

Perhaps, somehow, in painstakingly crafting these precious creations with an eye to their salvation, I was trying to secure my own.

12.

Billy

Ilove women or, to be more precise, women love me. It's been that way as long as I can remember and, in my defence, I can't be blamed for it. These are gifts, as my mother always said, that are God-given. My gift of the gab, my seductive smile, and my positive, infectious humour attracts them instantly. They come like moths to a flame or, as I've seen over the past year, like lambs to the slaughter. Especially the older ones and especially when they're drunk. My apologies, Mr. M—. I can't help myself with the dark humour. It's the Irishman in me and it is well-lubricated by the drop.

The same could be said for Nelly — she too came like a moth to a flame — although I wouldn't be the one to say it, and especially not to her face, because she hates to be lumped in with other women for any reason or in any way. She fell fast and hard, and once we had our pleasures in the bedroom — and she responded with such keenness, I can tell you, because my gifts extend to the private quarters — I could see that, for her, there was no going back. Even after all we have been through, she has remained committed. Even when I suspected she knew about the business — and she certainly knows now — she still loved me. Even after being put on trial and publicly humiliated, she is still my wife in name if not in law.

In my own way, I have loved her, although once I started looking at everything and everyone through the cancer — even Nelly — there were shades of hatred and bitter resentment for my being short-changed on this side of the grave.

And, as always, I looked at the world through degrees of drunkenness. Nelly and I both. Sobriety has been virtually unknown to us, a country rarely visited during our time together. The same may be said for all of us in the West Port, Mr. M—, whose world you wouldn't dare enter. Ours is a shadowy den of inebriates, a den of iniquity. And they are dens, truly. Just as we are treated like animals, we live like them. I hasten to correct that statement as I have corrected others throughout this sorrowful tale: *we have been made to live like animals*. There was a time, and it seems so long ago now, that I would recite Psalm 141, asking God to set a watch before my mouth; keep the door of my lips. Incline not my heart to any evil thing, to practise wicked works with men that work iniquity: and let me not eat of their dainties.

When I consider what happened to me, what brought me into disgrace in innumerable temples of low men, I can only come up with two things: desperation and a need for the bottle. Just as I was treated like a disposable object in this place of desperation due to the greed of others, so did I treat other people. I want to put it on the record here and now and say to your *Courant* readers as if they were ranged before me — or whoever will get to read this, because I don't know your intentions — that there's a cancer out here, a horrible disease, one for which we in the West Port are not responsible, to which we are all — some sooner than others — fast succumbing. There are different ways of killing people. While my mode was up close and personal, some people specialise in killing at a distance.

And my own cancer — the very thought of it — demanded further denial, the drop and the whisky becoming necessary to me every day. I needed both to get out of bed, to stay out of bed, to conduct the business. I needed them simply to face what came to be seen as the everyday horrors of my life. You haven't seen it face-to-face yet, Mr. M—, but death has a way of truly unsettling a person, making one desperate and unpredictable. Trust me, you'll take all the drugs and drink you can get as your time approaches. At least the shots were spared such long, drawn-out trauma. As I see it now, I offered them a kindness, the only kindness I knew how to give — a brief but exhilarating inebriation and a final, speedy release from the nightmare of this life. I acknowledge that only a few were already at death's threshold, but all were on their way in this hostile, unpredictable town. It may seem an inconvenient truth, but we all must die at some point and from where I sit, I envy my shots their lot. As I've said in my earlier confession, I regret my crime of selling them to a doctor for dissection, but at least my victims went quickly. And here is where my compassion should be commended: they didn't even see death coming. With only two exceptions, it happened quickly. There was no time for fear. Trust me, Mr. M—, that is a special gift. You would choose that over the cancer any day. Or night. And night time is the best time for our soul's departure — if you have to choose — just as you are laying yourself down to sleep, praying the Lord your soul to keep. Once I got used to the operation and practised a few times, perfecting my technique, I always recited that prayer in my head while sending the shots off. It became part of my ritual, a sacred farewell, a blessing.

My last moments, in stark, undeniable contrast, will be spent in the early morning hours before an angry, jeering mob baying for my blood. I dread the sobriety and starkness of it. Trust me, if I could trade a second completed notebook for a bottle of whisky smuggled in on that last morning, I would. I will need to take the edge off — that sordid and blunted edge of reality that has ruined this life for me. Never once has it done me in quickly; every torturous thing happened slowly and painfully.

And to think — because it makes me laugh to do so — that my final harrowing moments will be followed by an even greater degradation with anatomical instruments wielded by the butcher, Doctor Monro, shows that even the final joke will be on me. By Doctor Knox's account, as conveyed to me by Paterson, Monro is a barbarian. His reputation precedes him. He handles bodies like a butcher does his meat. He is certain to abuse my corpse for the fun and publicity of it. I can just imagine how many good, upstanding Edinburgh Christians will file past my mincemeat remains, laid and arranged like those of kine freshly slaughtered and portioned out. Apparently, the doctors are keen to see my skull — for the interests of science, they say, but I know better having long studied the minds of men. While the cadavers of the shots I provided were used to teach people, mine will be used *to teach people a lesson*. I predict, just as Nelly used to predict by palm-reading, that *they will miss the point*. Copies of my story should be sold, under the title *Confessions of an Irish Laudanum Drinker*, so the truth may be told, once and for all.

But I believe I was talking about Nelly. We undoubtedly have two different stories, she and I, two divergent tales of our time together — one before and one after the arrival of the cancer. I don't recall much of the one before. Whether it was the drink that obliterated my history, old age, or a lack of care on my part, I will never know. What I do know is that I've been too busy with the daily business while trying to deny my own dying body.

And then there was the baby who came at a very bad time. I can see now that there never was a good time for her arrival. I ask you, is there ever a good time for poor people to have children in this body- and spirit-crushing world? It sucks the very breath out of them, and what remains, it eviscerates.

Nelly doesn't know, but I kept the pair of Maeve's baby shoes, the only pair I ever — and in secret — cobbled for her. *Her wee pit boots for the coal mine,* as Nelly's grandfather would have called them.

I can barely bring myself to say her name. I choke every time. It's the only thing that ever unnerves me, even though I was harsh to Nelly when it came to the baby. You wonder where all of my pain lies? No, you actually don't think or care a wit about me, which makes sense now under these circumstances, but it was ever true before. I will answer my question nevertheless: all of my pain lies buried with her, wherever she may be. Where is she, I wonder? Is she awaiting me on the other side?

She would have been a year old come June … had she survived.

***

While I remember, with bitter regret, suffocating the young deaf-mute and will forever hate Margaret for putting him and his granny in harm's way, I think of the second Mary — Mary Patterson — with a deep, gutting sorrow. For a brief couple of hours, I sat close to her, the object of her attention as I fixated on her moist full lips and coy smile. I envisioned myself a young man again, unencumbered, that day, with the ability to start over, my passion for life renewed. Nelly's confession just weeks earlier about her knowledge of the business and of carrying that bastard child added to the weight of my misery. I cursed her for it and burked another old woman, simply out of spite, leaving ample evidence — including her pathetic, stinking clothes — in the same bed where Abby met her fate.

Mary Paterson, in contrast, offered the prospect of a lightness I hadn't known in many a long year, perhaps had never known. I felt that she — and she alone — could transform the last dreadful months of my unbearable life into something more meaningful. For a few short hours, I envisioned my whole twisted, sordid life as a rocky uphill road that plateaued and gained clearer direction only after I met her. You could say she was my Radical Road, Mr. M—. It took endless pain, punishment, and misery to get to her. She was a welcome sight, a beautiful, longed-for blessing.

Sadly, she was my road not taken.

I know she was only half my age, but there are some people who catch your attention and you feel an instant connection. There's no explaining it. It just breaks in on you with no rhyme or reason. Such it was that early morning when I made my way to William Swanston's, a spirit-dealer in the Canongate, around the corner from my brother Con's lodgings at Gibb's Close. My intention was to tell Con about the baby and ask his advice, but I ended up at Swanston's just as Mary entered. Over the past year, I'd spotted her several times in that neighbourhood, and knew her name to be Mary. I'd never much noticed her friend but knew them to be inseparable. *And everywhere that Mary went, that lamb was sure to go*, I playfully thought to myself every time I saw them. They had just passed a hard night in the local watch-house, agitated because they were dry without drink. Careless of the time, both were keen to make up for their lost evening, to put the watch-house behind them.

Ours was a curious exchange in Swanston's for *they* introduced themselves to *me*. I stood drinking rum and bitters with the publican when they entered from out of the drizzling rain and ordered their gills. Overhearing us, they began interjecting comments and jokes. I was quickly taken — as any man would be, given the saucy boldness of them — immediately ordering three more gills of rum and bitters at my expense. They'd brought a spirit of my youth in the door. The banter and laughter continued over the next hour with Mary drinking rapidly and growing increasingly flirtatious. I responded in kind despite Janet's presence, at one point answering Mary's questions about the source of my money with the lie that, if she played her cards right, I had a substantial pension and could maintain her handsomely, making her comfortable for life. 'It would be my great pleasure,' I said, thereafter repeating the words slowly and with emphasis. It was bait she readily took, immediately inquiring as to the amount of her future clothing allowance. While she preferred herself better with her clothes off, she provocatively told me, she said she had a passion for finery wherever she might find it. I answered with some seriousness, basing my rough calculations around providing two shots monthly to Dr. Knox, and envisioned setting her up in the Canongate where she would serve me — and only me — privately, knowing nothing about my business, or Nelly, or any brutality ever again.

To that point in our conversation, she had mentioned her rough life as an orphan in Edinburgh. I could tell it pained her to mention it, and for a moment I thought of Nelly first sharing with me the account of her brutal encounters with Rab. Then as now, I felt the desire to assist and protect. Such has always been my way, Mr. M—. I have shown much natural charity, especially where the promise of sex was concerned.

I know I can tell you — because you look like a man who can well understand — the other irrepressible feeling I had about Mary in Swanston's that morning. You've seen the drawings of her in the anatomy lab in her full resplendent natural glory, as God made her, and I can assure you she was irresistible. Despite the drinking and the early hour, I also felt the urgency of another, extremely familiar desire not felt in some time. What was odd was the absence of the accompanying pain to which I'd grown so accustomed over the past year. Perhaps, I thought to myself, there is hope for my recovery yet. Perhaps the last poultice, laced with mercury, had done the trick and I was finally on the mend. I decided I had plans for the extremely pliant Mary if I could get rid of the ever-resisting, suspicious Janet. So, I invited them to breakfast at my brother Constantine's house, buying us a bottle of whisky from Swanston's prior to leaving.

But some things never go as planned. What is it Rabbie Burns wrote? It's one of my favourite lines, about which I heard a whole sermon once, one applicable to my life. *The best-laid schemes o' mice an' men gang aft agley.* You could say Mary chose her own fate that day, ending up dead drunk after her long, dry evening. With Nelly showing up at Constantine's house mid-morning after he had gone off to work, furiously jealous and fit to be tied after we'd all breakfasted like kings — although Mary sat slumped at the table fast asleep after, drunk on whisky — and Connie's wife, Alice, desperately running off to retrieve Hare, my dreams ended early on. Events just assumed a life of their own. I couldn't risk Connie and Alice finding out what we were up to, so there was no other way out. Just like me, she was not a lucky one, that Mary. In that, we were well-matched. After life as an orphan before becoming a streetwalker, she was fated for an early death. She chose her time and I, reluctant but understanding, obliged. Little did she realise that morning that I came in answer to her prayers.

Some may claim to have lain with her. I'm sure there are dozens in Edinburgh who can make that claim. I note, in passing, that they had to pay her. I was hoping to claim to have been with her last, but Janet foiled that plan, leaving me to escort her out to get some air while Mary lay sleeping on Connie's truckle bed. Janet and I then had pints and porter across the road, an additional expense. I never felt so strongly about having to be paid for my trouble before. When a man makes an investment in the form of a fair quantity of drink, tea, bread, eggs, and smoked Finnan haddocks, he needs to see it pay off.

And, given the money I got for her, she paid me, and handsomely. Sadly, I had to split the payment with Hare who showed up after I had the unsuspecting Alice go out and purchase a tea chest into which the Mute and I later stuffed the voluptuous, naked Mary Paterson with due ceremony. Such a sad and pathetic state she was in and such a truly sorry and heart-breaking waste it was. I nearly shed tears thinking how my investment didn't pay out as planned.

I can assure you, Mr. M—, that dead or alive, she was an outstanding specimen. Perhaps better dead than alive, as some men say about some women. Mary was the best woman as ever I saw, a true Scottish Venus. She was worth double the money I got for her, probably more. I found out later about the sketches made of her and I'm willing to bet good money that the last tricks she turned were conducted on the dissection table without her consent. I know Knox pickled her in whisky for three months. No need to wonder why.

***

I suspected, based on a comment made by Paterson when we dropped Mary into Surgeons' Square, that Hare had been up to some private business of his own. I thought he might play me a bad turn after we'd moved from the tramp hotel but, as it turns out, he couldn't wait. What gave him away was Paterson's greeting of surprise when he addressed the Mute saying, 'Back so soon?'

My surprised response was side-lined when the other assistant, looking shocked once we'd opened the tea chest and carefully removed Mary's naked body and placed it on the table, leaned over and whispered a few hasty words in Paterson's ear. Paterson immediately left the room, returning with a pair of metal scissors, which he held out to me with explicit instructions.

'Cut off all her hair. Cut it as short as you can. My fellow here says he recognised her immediately and fears others will too.'

I stood struggling — physically and emotionally — with the cutting of Mary's thick, curly auburn hair. This was not the type of intimacy I was hoping for that day; I can assure you. The Mute just stood there, looking mindless as usual, examining his feet. Paterson continued, 'Where, we are wondering, did you find her?'

I was one step ahead of them. I had worried that Mary might be recognised, so I didn't miss a beat in my response.

'She apparently drank herself to death. You can smell it on her.'

'Apparently,' repeated Paterson, almost in a questioning manner as he eyed her body from top to bottom. 'She's certainly dead now,' he said, and his assistant sniggered as Paterson followed up, 'More's the pity.'

I agreed with that sentiment, as would all men who saw her laying there in all her fleshly, womanly glory. I still felt the need to offer up more details and quell suspicion. It was a good thing I'd practised my statements on our journey over.

'An old beggar found her drunk in the churchyard and flagged me down just as I was returning from my brother's house in the Canongate.'

'Lucky for you,' Paterson said, barely holding any scepticism back, 'that you happened to be passing at just the right time.'

And then he added a surprising comment that suddenly sobered me up, 'It's a pity she isn't carrying a baby.'

'What was that?' I inquired, thrown off, as I turned her head to the side and removed more hair. The reference unfortunately brought me back to my plaguing thoughts about Nelly and the baby she claimed to be carrying.

'I said, it's a pity she isn't with child.'

'Why?' I asked, still confused and finding the reference unusual given my recent concerns.

'We pay much more for them that way.'

He followed up to clarify, 'We pay more for the mother and the baby. The small subjects, as the doctor calls them, are especially hard to get hold of these days. We know there are many illegal burials happening in Edinburgh to avoid the bodysnatchers, so we have a hard time finding them — the small subjects, I mean. It would seem you people — you Irish — are especially careful about them. Something about the resurrection and the next life, or some such thing. I suppose it's a Christian prejudice, really, not just a Catholic one. We hold no such ideas here; I can assure you. Or, at least, I don't. And it's obvious neither of you do either,' he said, casting a glance over at the Mute, who also looked to be paying close attention to the conversation, a thing unusual for him.

Paterson added, in what seemed an afterthought, 'That's a good thing. Not all of your brethren are of the same mind.' And then he advised us, as if he were making a request for delivery, 'So just keep your eyes open as you do your rounds — wherever you do your rounds. You people will insist on having children you can ill afford, so keep it in mind. You could say we'd like some big ones and some little ones.'

While I flinch now, as I did then, in response to his insulting remark about my people, my mind was preoccupied, careless about the large or the small subjects. Standing there, staring at Mary's beautiful dead body, her full breasts and nipples beckoning to be mouthed in that cold, clinical room, the swollen lips of her sex peeking out from beneath her fine, downy body hair, beckoning to be slowly stroked and fingered, I felt the beginning of a throbbing erection.

If ever I felt regret over selling a body, Mr. M—, this was it. The thought of the delectable pleasures I had missed rendering me angry and irritated. I needed to leave that room, be out of sight of the enticements of that, now breathless, body.

My plan for the evening was to fall fast into the arms of Madame Geneva in order to obliterate the memory of this buxom beauty and this golden opportunity lost.

And Nelly, I thought, now with child, had best watch herself.

13.

Nelly

Over the next couple of weeks, Billy didn't speak to me, with the exception of once when he said, quietly and cryptically, he was *busy making plans*. When I asked *what plans*, he snapped back, 'For the move,' as if I were a mind-reader and should have known what he was thinking. 'A move is necessary,' he added in his serious voice. 'The sooner, the better.'

Luckily, he had found a place not far away, he told me, we would be better off there, alone together.

'Just you and me. We would be safer. Especially you, Nelly.'

He said he didn't trust the Mute and Margaret. We both knew they were unpredictable and, apparently, he had fallen afoul of them in some business transaction and they had suggested that it *might be my time*. They were, he told me, encouraging him to *send me to the doctor*.

I heard a very different story the second time we spoke about the move as we returned late one night from the pub. I was drinking little then as it wasn't agreeing with me. Billy, on the other hand, was making up for my abstinence. That night he was drunk hours before closing. By the time we left, he was railing at me, saying it was he who didn't trust me anymore, not Margaret and the Mute. I was the one who couldn't be trusted, especially when I was drunk. I knew too much and could endanger us both. I knew not to laugh then given the state of him as he spoke in staggered phrases while stumbling up the close to the tramp-house. To laugh would infuriate him so, as had become second nature, I bit my tongue.

I noticed he hadn't mentioned the baby. I could endanger *us both*, he had said. There was no mention of *her*. For him, she didn't exist. I noticed that he hadn't mentioned her since I had disclosed my situation. He hadn't said a word, which worried me. I knew he was upset and busy mulling things over, especially the very idea of her. I knew he believed the baby wasn't his, but I knew the truth. I had been with no one else and my guess was he even forgot the times we had coupled despite his pain. Even had I wanted to go with someone else, I wouldn't have dared, although I had my share of opportunities. There were times when I was sitting alone in the pub and men would come over to speak with me. I was always quick to discourage them, for their own sake and mine, telling them my man was just across the pub, had his eye on me, and had a vicious temper they wouldn't want to mess with. Billy, ever jealous and watchful despite how drunk he was, saw all of this, and would suggest to me later, during the slapping and the punching, that I really wanted to go with them, that I could hardly hold myself back, whore that I was.

Rab's voice, from years earlier, echoed in his words.

Just like the mornings after those nights of jealous railings, he had been brooding since my news about the baby and, in my experience, it was never safe to be around a brooding Billy. He was liable to snap suddenly and give me the back of his hand or a punch in the belly, along with a nasty piece of his mind. Anything could set him off, so it wasn't safe to be near him, especially now that there were two of us to protect.

Although I didn't acknowledge it to myself, I was the one who felt unsafe. My sleeping was off because

I was afraid of something happening while I lay there vulnerable. I was afraid of something unpredictably being done. To us. The baby and I were, I felt, in jeopardy in the tramp house. I was a light sleeper at the best of times, but I had started listening for any unusual sounds in the dead of night. The West Port being a very busy, noisy place at all hours, my sleep was often disrupted. Finding myself lying there, sick and sleepless, I thought about what needed to be done before the move.

The opportunity to take care of some business finally came in early April. Billy had risen just before dawn to go see his brother, Connie, in the Canongate. He had told me the night before that he had a bit of business to discuss with him. Besides, he hadn't seen him in a while. A visit was overdue. My job tomorrow, he directed me, was to sell the pairs of shoes he had sequestered away in a potato sack in the corner of the room. Having guessed at their origin, I dreaded the job. He said there was no place to put them where we were going, and I must sell them all, even for a bargain if need be. We had to be rid of them.

I didn't tell Billy, but I was also faced with demands of my own.

Billy's early departure was my cue. About a half-hour after he left, having settled my belly with some tea and covered myself well as it was raining lightly, I packed up the dolls in the deep flap-pocket of my apron, arranged my cape, and started on my journey. My goal was to find them a secure and proper burial spot before Billy discovered and destroyed them. This was a sacred mission, one for which I had to prepare myself — my heart and my spirit. I knew exactly where I was going — the Salisbury Crags, an area close to Arthur's Seat, after which mission I would walk down to Constantine's to visit him and Alice, his wife. I knew Billy would be surprised and angry to see me, if he was still there when I arrived. While he had told me his plans the night before, I wondered at them as I had the same disquieting feeling I always had when I knew there was a body in the house or the stables. I suspected he was up to something. As he was always on his best behaviour in front of Constantine, I felt no worries about showing up unexpectedly. Now would be the best time to tell Alice I was with child. It was becoming increasingly difficult to hide. Just recently, I had to let out the waistband of a couple of dresses in order to accommodate the baby. Along with my belly, my breasts had grown fuller and firmer too, fitting much more snugly into my shift.

I no longer wanted to keep the baby a secret. In a matter of months, I'd be holding her for all the world to see. To my private delight, she had recently started kicking. This little flutter of movement deep inside me, especially when I was at rest, gave me a thrill of pleasure. It put a secret smile on my face. Billy caught me with that look one day and wondered at it, although he said nothing. In time, I think he saw I was happy about the baby and it irritated him. He had worked hard over the years to empty me of my happiness, to deaden my spirit. I revelled in this small private rebellion.

What gave me even greater joy was the fact that she and I had what I called conversations. Privately and quietly, I talked to her, and when I pressed my finger firmly into my navel, she responded by kicking back, full of life. Whatever and whoever she was, I felt she was the spirit I once possessed. Such thoughts were mainly painful, sometimes bittersweet.

Despite these moments where I reacted, naturally and with some excitement, to being with child, my true feelings about her were mixed; a combination of happiness and fear given what I knew the life of girls to be. It didn't help that this brutal place, this Edinburgh, contained Billy and the terrifying situation into which he had gotten himself with no means of turning back. 'I'm too deep into this thing to get out, Nelly,' he had said in recent days, his voice desperate, his words breaking off. 'The doctor relies on us,' he said, as if trying to justify his involvement. Billy's statements, and the tone in which they were said, plagued my thoughts.

With very good reason, I worried about bringing a baby into this world.

The thought of my having a boy was even more unsettling as I knew I would associate him with Billy. I imagined Little Billy, a child I knew would grow to hate me over time — his own mother. Raised in this place and by this father, he would soon come to hate all women. In between half-hearted prayers to God to take the child before her first breath — a painful but liberating blessing in disguise — I prayed for a daughter rather than a son; a strong, fierce daughter who would steal her father's heart and, unlike her mother had, wouldn't put up with mistreatment. I had been through enough. I couldn't bear the thought of her traversing the same road.

Only as I started walking that morning, mulling over these muddled thoughts as the rain tapered off, did I realise how long it had been since I'd been out of the West Port. Only once I was up on the busy High Street, my step directed toward Holyrood Palace, did I feel I left that stifling enclave behind, filled as it was with desperate people, such horrid, foul stenches, and endless noise. It had fast become a world for me of bitter, bad memories, a prison I felt was inescapable.

What came over me that morning as I walked away from the West Port was an unexpected lightness. I should have kept on walking once I laid the dolls to rest that morning. I should have left everything behind and returned to Jeannie. Despite my shame and reluctance to contact her, I knew she would help me, as she had those many years earlier. She had been my one true friend; the cherished mother I'd never had. As Billy well knew, I had long wanted to get back to the countryside, the city never being a comfortable place for me. But that plan, sadly, didn't enter my mind that early April morning as I turned off the High Street heading towards the Radical Road skirting the Salisbury Crags, feeling with every step that I was leaving my cares behind. I began to think, as my steps assumed a steady rhythm, about what I wanted for my baby. I dared, on my walk that day, to dream about a shared future. This was the power of the baby that I mistrusted and resisted. With her, the hope and dreams that had long ago been extinguished from my life returned, and with hope, I knew, came risk.

Looking over the sprawling town of Edinburgh as I followed the Radical Road, I felt for the dolls in their wee wooden boxes, carefully tucked away in my deep apron pocket. Billy and I had crafted a number of those coffined figures in advance of my giving them each a face, some clothes, and a name. I remember his remarking, when he first saw the little wooden soldiers, about them all looking the same.

'That's how we were seen in the Militia,' he'd said. 'Disposable and with no identity. It doesn't pay to be a soldier.'

It was he who had taught me how to use the right cobbling tools for each process. Little did he realise then what he was doing. While I didn't know what lay in the future either, I must have had a sense of something to come. It was curious how life had brought dead people together with the new and unborn. Life had put me — death's midwife — in touch with the troubled dead. A door had been opened between this world and the next. Since I began making the dolls, I had felt a deep connection, like an umbilical cord that could not be severed, with the other side. It seems strange to describe it as a lifeline, but that is exactly what it was. By way of the dolls, I regularly spoke to and comforted Billy's many victims who found themselves adrift, their lives so casually and brutally cut short. They had each become my children, and as I walked, I cradled them protectively against the baby in my belly while humming a sombre lullaby.

With no one nearby, I let the tears fall that wet, grey morning, my feet moving at a steady pace along the wide pathway sloping up the Cragside. This was to be a ritual I would undertake on several later occasions. As I mounted the Radical Road and contemplated the fortress-like cliff face of the Crags, casting my eyes across Edinburgh to Castle Hill and the West Port, I prayed for release for Abby, Joseph, Effie, Donald, Mary, the unnamed old woman, and the Englishman from Cheshire, who had lost their lives in that damnable tramp house. I prayed for their release from the pain and the last bloody violations each had suffered at the hands of the doctor, and the horrible crimes perpetrated against them by the man I loved. With every breath as I walked, I pictured an end to each of their agonies, each innocent, vulnerable spirit being released and rising above and away from me, looking down from above the Radical Road, above Arthur's Seat and this magnificent but treacherous city called Edinburgh where they had lost their lives. In my mind's eye, there was exultation as each was delivered from shock and pain into a quiet, weightless state of peace as they ascended above me, spiritually unburdened.

Leaving the Road and following a rugged footpath up and across the gorse- and stone-covered hills, I looked around for the secluded spot where Billy and I had discovered a small hollow at waist height in the rocks. Wary of the baby and not wanting to lose

189

my footing, it took me some time to reach it, but I eventually found it and the natural shelf inside where I could lay each of the seven small coffins in a row, one alongside the other. I kissed and blessed each doll individually before reaching in and arranging them tenderly in their wee box-beds as carefully and comfortably as possible. I was relieved that the rain had stopped so as to avoid their getting wet. All the while, I sang a coronach taught to me by a Highland neighbour when I was a child. I sang this song of mourning softly and slowly, in a language I didn't understand, repeating, over and again, the few lines I knew. That melancholy song suited the mood of the moment, purging me of sadness in the form of many tears. In singing, I rid myself of their pain and mine.

Once finished with my arrangements, I took a few pieces of slatestone found nearby and placed them in an upright position in front of the hollow — now, a natural sepulchre — to shield its contents and shelter it from the elements. Knowing a few of the victims to be devout believers, I recited the Our Father after everything was done, praying as well for those I felt might yet be missing and for whom I had not yet made an eternal bed. I prayed ardently for the end of the business, as Billy called it. Having completed this ritual — my mission — I set my sights on returning down the cliffside footpath to the Radical Road, from whence I would make my way back towards the High Street.

As this was the place where Billy and I had walked several times after first arriving in Edinburgh, it held bittersweet memories for me. I was reminded that our lives hadn't been all arguments, anger, beatings, and resentment brought on by excessive drinking and lack of work. We had shared a few fond sober afternoons of walking here following our initial arrival. There were many hundreds like us at that time, desperate migrant labourers in a new town, who had just come off years of backbreaking work on the Union Canal. I remembered experiencing a renewed sense of hope with Billy then. A magical connection had returned to us and there was a greater sharing of intimacies. I hated to face myself now as a person uncared for, although I well knew that had long been my state.

I bitterly cursed those memorable moments of pleasure and passion. *What is left*, I asked myself, *these many years later, after all is said and done?* All hope has exploded and disappeared. In those few brief minutes of contemplation, I moved from memories of joy to a gutted feeling of grief, returning from the heights of my blessed mission to confront the dregs of my life that had been shattered and empty of hope. Such feelings of bitter loss, I thought to myself, suited my location given what Billy had told me about the origins of this Radical Road, a place that enraged him. I had heard the children sing about it many times but it was Billy, the avid history-teller, who had explained their song to me.

Round and round the Radical Road, the radical rascal ran...

With venom rising in his voice, I remembered him telling me the story of 1820 during our first walk here. How a group of weavers from the West of Scotland — Stirling, Paisley, Dumbarton, Ayr, and other towns — had protested brutal and unfair working and living conditions in what was called the Radical Rising. It was Scotland's Peterloo, Billy told me, which was dreaded and predicted by several ministers when we lived in Falkirk during the construction of the Union Canal. Political reform was demanded, along with a Scottish Parliament. This was accompanied by a General Strike where greater freedom was demanded for Scotland. He recounted how the army was then called in, followed by dozens of treason trials, many imprisonments, several executions, and a score of transportations. 'The law,' Billy said, 'is a tyrant as are those in control of it.' He had, he said, along with his radical brothers, read his Thomas Paine, the working-man's champion who had written in support of them and their natural rights.

Unemployed weavers were then used to build this road when Scotland's most famous writer and celebrated son, Sir Walter Scott, had suggested it as a work project after the King's visit in 1822. 'They want work?' he had said. 'Well, here's plenty for them.'

As a Scot, I was ashamed when I heard that damnable story. It was heartless and cruel and reminded me of the brutalised navvies, although they, at least, had received some money in exchange for their precarious labour. The working man had entered a new and different world in 1820, Billy said, one on which he wished he could turn his back. I too wished to go back to that time, only a handful of years after I had met Billy. I yearned once again for its great promise before my hopes had been crushed. As I walked, I prayed that we could all — me, Billy, and the radicals — start again anew. My heart grew light and relieved for a moment as I also imagined Billy's unsuspecting victims in 1820 still alive and breathing. It was painful to return from the heights of my imagination to this road constructed of crushed stone and broken promises.

For Billy, this Radical Road was paved in the blood, sweat, and tears of bitter humiliation. I remember trying to convince him otherwise, as we walked and talked. Those who had built it, I said, probably had time to reconsider things and to count themselves lucky and thankful to be alive. So many others, as he had told me, had either been transported to Botany Bay or executed. At least these men hadn't been forced to leave Scotland.

'But this became a country worth leaving,' Billy responded, bitterly. 'A place marked by shame and defeat. When a man can't speak his mind freely in his own country or find respectable work to feed his family, what do you have? A country with no future, which amounts to no country at all.'

I could picture the radicals differently and better this morning as I walked alone, Billy's sad words running through my head. I felt the shadows of men walking upright beside me with their picks, shovels, and blasting powder slung over their shoulders, their caps sheltering them from hours beneath a hostile sun or pelting rain. I could imagine hours upon hours working high up that hillside, the overseers haranguing me. The drink must have been plentiful, I thought, with that backbreaking work and the harsh heat. I then reconsidered my consoling statements to Billy. Those men must have, on some days, wished themselves thousands of miles away — or even dead. I knew the feeling. In my mind's eye that morning, I pictured those men walking beside me, firm in their conviction despite their abuse and the relentless physical pain they'd suffered. I had seen hundreds of their kind just a handful of years earlier in the navvies, the necessary but disposable men. Them, and their wives, had become like family to me. I had befriended and helped to heal, and even bury, some of them.

Round and round the Radical Road, the radical rascal ran.

The children's song rang through my head again as I thought about Billy, once a staunch supporter of radicals, an upright man of conviction I once admired. No longer. Damn his lofty, seductive words, I thought. Try as I might sometimes to defy him, fear and concern now lived with me every day, my heart heavy with misery and regret.

And what of our child-to-be? He was a funny

man, that Billy. He had precious little now to do with children, which was odd because children, like everyone else who ever met him, were drawn to him, his humour, his playfulness. Once upon a time, they liked him more than they liked me, and at the parties we would hold in the house, he would play the hurdy-gurdy for the children and hand out sweetmeats. He had done that as a navvy too. Those were the days. And that, I reminded myself, was another Billy, the Billy to be trusted, the Billy to be loved. Now, despite my loyalty to, and love for him, I would have to be on my guard for the children and what he might do to mine — to ours.

I realised as I walked that I had to face, with no denial and no drink, the New Billy and our new reality, the one where my flashes of hating him beat out the love. I had to declare that romance with the dream Billy to be over, dead and buried. He would never return. *How*, I thought to myself, *can I manage that in the state I am in?* To which, my inner voice responded, *That's women all over. With the help of fantasy and false promises, they're always digging their own graves.*

But I lack the strength, I returned, speaking back, *despite knowing I am stronger than him in many ways. I will work at being strong for her — and for myself. What other choice do I have?*

While I had missed my opportunity that day, I decided that next time I would lay the dream Billy to rest. Fashioning him as a soldier in one of my little box-bed coffins, I would bury him up on high, secure the protective pieces of slatestone, walk away, and never look back.

***

Only as I made my way back down the High Street

towards Gibb's Close, just minutes from Holyrood, did I remember that I was supposed to be out hawking shoes that morning. I knew Billy would be livid when he saw me, if he was still at Constantine's. He had impressed upon me that we couldn't take the shoes with us and I had assured him they would all soon be sold. Meanwhile, they sat idle, in a sack, back at the tramp hotel. With any luck, I thought, Alice will be home and I can inform her about my situation and arrange for help once I go into labour. I figured it was only a matter of weeks and, as I well knew, babies had a habit of coming unexpectedly, plans or no plans. From my experiences at Jeannie's, I also knew how quickly things could go wrong during a birth and I feared being alone and possibly in danger with no one around to help. Heaven knows, I couldn't rely on Billy who, like most men, was clueless and could unintentionally put us in harm's way.

Connie's place consisted of a single room entered along a dark passage and down a narrow wooden staircase. While small and poorly furnished with tattered curtains and a few tawdry prints tacked to the wall, there were a number of chairs and a table where they held many a small party. One seemed to be in progress as I knocked on the door that late morning, which I thought was odd given the hour. A few voices and laughter could be heard from the passageway, so I knocked loudly a few more times to make sure I had been heard. A strong smell of tobacco and whisky accosted me as the door swung open.

I could tell that Connie's wife, wee Alice, was surprised to see me. She spoke with some agitation as she invited me in and told me that Connie had gone off early to work, after they had all breakfasted. They were just discussing, she said, what was left of the whisky.

I saw immediately that *they* not only included

Alice and Billy but two dishevelled young women, one of whom, with dark hair, was seated directly next to Billy at the table strewn with several empty bottles and whisky jars. The other woman lay drunk and asleep, sprawled across the truckle bed in the far corner of the room, her face hidden by her arm and a wild profusion of auburn hair.

Unhooking my cape and preparing to seat myself, I saw Alice and the other woman, with some surprise, notice my belly. Billy stood up and glared at me, his eyes angry as he blocked my path to the chair. The young woman at the table, deep in her cups, looked up at him, confused, and asked who I was. When he offered no response, Alice awkwardly blurted out, 'This is the gentleman's wife,' to which the girl surprised me with an apology, saying she 'had no idea he was married' or, she added, looking at my belly, 'that his wife was with child. He had never said so.'

I had no reason to disbelieve her. Although my voice was shaking, I told her, 'I have no dispute with you. My business is with Billy.'

He wasted no time responding in his typically nasty way.

'Well, I've no business with you, Nelly, and you've no right being here. No one invited you in. You're supposed to be up the Canongate hawking shoes.'

He then added, sarcastically, for effect, as if I wasn't even there, directing his attention to Alice, 'And I don't know who she's been having business with on the side, ladies, but I can assure you that that wee unborn bastard isn't mine.'

I'd be lying to say his words, designed to sting, didn't throw me off my guard. Having had years of practise, Billy knew exactly what he was doing, and I had become an expert at blocking pain. I bit my lip hard so as not to cry. A jumble of new thoughts arose at the scene before me. I realised what was possibly

196

underway. I wondered if this was the process every time and if it involved coupling beforehand. What, exactly was going on and what was Alice doing here? None of it made sense. Based on what I knew of them, I couldn't imagine Alice and Connie being even slightly involved. No, I said to myself, they must be in the dark. Connie isn't here and there must be a plan to dupe Alice. She doesn't know why she is going to fetch Hare.

Just as I wondered if the other girl was meant for Hare, Alice, who was growing agitated by the minute, stepped towards the door and announced that she was on her way out, as Billy had requested, to fetch Hare. Sensing my distress and ever considerate of me, she inquired if it wouldn't be best if I accompanied her back to the West Port.

Thinking quickly on my feet and fearing the two young women might be in mortal danger, I rejected Alice's offer and tried to think how I could raise some alarm. It was obvious Billy wanted to be rid of me and his temper was up. He was always unpredictable when drinking. Ignoring me, he returned to his chair in the corner while I moved towards the table and addressed the young woman seated there:

'I'd be careful if I were you. You now know he's already lied to you. I've spent the better part of ten years with him and he's not to be trusted. Watch yourself and your friend,' I said, nodding over in the other's direction.

No sooner was the last word out of my mouth than Billy threw his drinking glass at me. Despite moving my head quickly to avoid the collision, the glass grazed my face, cutting me above my left eye. I'd just narrowly missed being blinded. I felt the stinging pain from the nasty strike first, before the blood started. Alice, always a friend, reacted quickly and stepped back into the room. She dampened a rag with some of

197

the remaining whisky instructing me to hold it against my eye. That the drunken Billy remained unmoved through this entire scene upset me more. Fearing more violence, Alice told me to step outside to speak to her. As we exited, Billy followed, pushing the door fast shut behind us. As Alice and I stood, both of us shaken, in the passage, we heard some commotion inside over the next few minutes. Suddenly, Billy opened the door and escorted the petrified young woman out past us. I shouted after her as she scrambled up the stairs.

'I wouldn't leave my friend behind with him if I were you. Just look at what he's capable of.'

But she neither responded nor turned back. Billy did turn back though and, tightly grabbing my arm, said, angrily, 'You're embarrassing yourself publicly again, Nelly, and if you don't shut your bloody mouth, I'll shut it for you.'

He snarled as he spat out his last words. 'You're putting yourself — and your bastard — in harm's way, Nelly. I'd watch myself.'

Ignoring these threats, I turned my attention instead to the vulnerable young woman in Constantine's room who was at Billy's mercy. I also wondered where the dark-haired girl had just scrambled off to. I hoped she'd escaped and would not return.

Knowing I'd be putting myself in harm's way if I dared re-enter, I convinced Alice to remain at home, promising her I'd go fetch Hare. Pretending to be upset and jealous over what had happened, I urged her to keep watch over Billy and the drunk woman until Hare arrived. On the heels of this chaotic drama whose conclusion I hoped to have altered, I exited, shaken and speechless, into the busy noise and drizzle of the Canongate.

***

I dreaded Billy's return home from Constantine's that night — or wherever he would be until the wee hours. While I had managed, after going around to Hare's and finding a clean, soft patch for my eye, to sell three pairs of shoes over the course of a few hours, I knew Billy wouldn't be thinking about shoes or sales.

When he came in, I lay as motionless as possible, pretending to be asleep.

As he got into bed, he said, 'I hope you're lying there, terrified, Nelly. Another move like that one today and I won't be held accountable for my actions.'

A few minutes later, he said, 'You need a plan for that bloody baby. We can ill afford it and I won't acknowledge the bastard. You want to think long and hard about that. I know you have ways to be rid of it. If you can't figure it out, I can help you. I have a few good ideas.'

An enraged Billy continued with his drunken threats. 'Just remember from now on that what I say goes, and if you don't do as I say, you both go and that will be the end of it.'

He finished off, 'Trust me. As you well know, I am not a man to mess with.'

I lay paralysed with fear as I processed these threats. I had always trusted Billy's threats. He was forever true to them and never true to me.

But the baby, as was her way whenever I lay down, started kicking and paid no heed.

14.

Billy

Just after Whitsunday, Nelly and I took a room two closes over from the tramp house, between Weaver's Close and Grindlay's, with the carter, Brogan, and his family. It was three pounds for the year and I had the money, so I paid it up front. I knew Brogan had wondered at the source of my money so I had to be careful. But it was also true that he had enjoyed the benefits of proximity. He'd had many a free dram at the pub and the tramp hotel with me over the past few months, sharing in what I told him were the proceeds of my successful sideline selling small still whisky.

This move signalled a break for me from Margaret and the Mute, which I heartily welcomed at that time as I weighed up the possibilities of branching out on my own. I also flirted with leaving Edinburgh, but soon realised my folly. Without my perceiving it, Edinburgh had gotten under my skin, into my blood, holding me fast and tight in her dark harlot's embrace.

It was at this point that something changed in me, something profound. I recall this not with a sickening feeling but a perverse sort of pleasure, another sign of how much had happened in a mere matter of months. Beyond the horrible events with the young deaf boy and those with Daft Jamie, it is the thing I have never, to this point, acknowledged. Not to anyone. Even myself. The fact is that my need had also changed. I no longer engaged in the body business just to satisfy my desire for drink, or the drop, or good tobacco, or even to further perfect my technique, which I had practised so well and so often I could perform it in my sleep. I didn't even do it just for the meat and endless drams, to which I had fast grown accustomed over many months. You must know that craving, Mr. M—, being a meat man yourself? Well, I can confirm, once a meatless man tastes meat, *there is no going back*. It's the one thing I've truly missed since I've been locked up here and shackled to this gad.

This new need seems to have grown in me unawares — it involved predation, of going out and finding someone, the next someone, the *chosen* someone. This undeniable hunger overtook me and had to be satisfied every fortnight or so. While I had developed a taste for meat, the drop, liquor, and fine tobacco, I had also — and especially — developed a taste for the hunt and what I began to call *the release*, an exhilarating moment that I felt relieved both my suffering and theirs.

When the need came upon me, it was fierce and unrelenting, rendering me agitated and feverish until I had the next chosen shot in my sights. It was, as I excitedly remembered it, like the drive for sex in my younger years. That desire became an incessant voice in my head that haunted and goaded me as I walked through the Grassmarket, closely eyeing the passers-by, weighing them up as possibilities. I didn't ask questions when this gnawing craving came upon me full force, as it did regularly. Try as I might, it could not be ignored. A wild, ravenous animal lay caged inside my skin, tormenting and exciting me with its need and the prospect of that ecstatic moment of release. When this drive consumed me, my energy changed, my whole body was affected. My heart raced, my focus intensified, and my skin tingled in readiness. All feelings of my illness and any pain fell away as a fierce alertness overtook me. At the blissful moment of their release, I experienced an odd combination of sensations: exalted and unshackled, I lost control and sometimes even, as I noted afterwards, all memory of the events themselves. While I could have, as I said before, performed my part of the operation in my sleep, I realised I fell into an intense trance while I was engaged in it.

It is that trance — whose source I came to understand later — and the exultation, that I remember most keenly now from inside these prison walls, alongside my newfound sense of purpose. I felt the need, as I'm sure the good doctor can understand, to continue my experiments, but I had also been gaining a growing sense of purpose and mission to bring salvation to the destitute and with it, came a newfound faith in God. I had begun, once again, to pray every night upon my return to my room after heavy drinking. With my candle burning on the low stool beside my bed, alongside my bottle of laudanum, my mother also began to visit me. Kneeling beside me as I lay there, she would stroke my forehead and sing me to sleep, just as she had done with Connie and I throughout our childhood. No longer was I subjected to the tormenting visions of her anguished face and desperate voice during our victims' final moments. Instead, she watched over me during what often became night time agonies and rough mornings-after when hangovers and flashbacks to the harrowing last words and moments of the dying would rise up, goblin-like, to torment me.

Thank God, I thought to myself at those plaguing moments, she was there to soothe and lull me because, heaven knows, Nelly was nowhere to be found. A wall of impenetrable silence had fast developed between us and we avoided each other like the plague. I believe she began to hate me around that time, worried for the baby I then didn't believe was mine, and mistrusting everything I told her. I withdrew further into myself and my night time rituals, hating her in return.

It was my mother, during those long, drawn-out mornings when I wished myself dead, who assured me of God's grace, telling me to watch for the signs. She assured me of her protection and my salvation — that just as I thought I was lost, I'd been found, and where I thought I was forsaken, I was sanctified. My initial response was disbelief, but I grew into her way of thinking as the weeks drew on. Estranged from her over the course of my childhood, this was a welcome reconciliation, one that occurred as much with God as with my mother.

It also confounded me. How had it happened that, just as I had felt myself unseen, unworthy, and forsaken, and was thinking of abandoning the body business and leaving Edinburgh, after my endless battles with Margaret and the Mute — the harridan's puppet-husband — that God had shone His blessed light upon me, entering my life and guiding my hand?

The more I turned this question over in my mind, the more a light was illuminated inside me and everything began to make sense. It was, as I came to see it, in keeping with the accounts I had read of the chosen ones. God's hand, my mother assured me one night, was in everything. 'Never forget that the Lord works in the most mysterious of ways,' she said, quietly singing to me and stroking my back as I drifted off to sleep.

I knew I couldn't talk to Nelly about all of these changes, although I longed to speak with someone as I wrestled with doubt. What, I tormented myself during each early morning, if the voices in my head were entirely my own, born of too much laudanum and whisky? What if the body business, and the anguish I suffered long after the bodies were sold and dissected, was making me lose my mind? I knew Nelly would have some answers — she always did —

but I knew I couldn't speak with her, that her answers might contradict my mother's, might try to divert me from my chosen path. I couldn't run the risk of giving her any power over me and my decisions.

I told myself that she would mock me, especially as I had — often fiercely, just months earlier — disparaged God. 'Not only had He abandoned me,' as I had told her and anyone in the pub who would listen, 'He had abandoned all of my Irish and Scottish brothers.' Now, my narrative was of another order.

In the face of my confusion, I prayed for His guidance and heeded my mother's words that I should await the signs, although signs, I knew, could sometimes be more misleading. I knew the evil one could confound the senses, so I had to be vigilant and on my guard.

I ushered these doubts aside at the time, believing my walks through the West Port to be directed by a hidden hand. God must know my intentions, I thought, how carefully I worked to take the victims down with ease, to deliver the shots from their lifetimes of suffering.

Sitting down to my regular pints at the White Hart one night, I had a further revelation. I no longer cared about this world anyway. I had long ago untethered myself from it and risen above the vicious scramble to survive. It was, I remember saying to myself, dead to me, nothing but a stepping-stone to a higher and better world. My calling, which was the only thing I should attend to, was to assist the chosen ones into the next world. They, and I, should seek one thing, and one thing only — God's redemptive glory. That alone should be my concern, especially if I hoped to follow them.

While I intended to withhold this truth until the end of this account, Mr. M—, I am prompted to disclose it to you now. I have received indications that my own death — that I knew then to be imminent given the intensifying physical pains involved with my cancer — would mark my final triumph. I have been assured, in repeated and vivid dreams revealed to me after the death of my sacred and secret beloved, Mary Paterson, that I will be gifted by God. The Almighty has granted me — through the power of the visionary dream — the promise of eternal glory. Sadly, I have received no assurances about Nelly, but I have come to understand and accept God's judgement given her lifelong acts of fornication and her unforgivable sin of abortion.

Say what you will, Mr. M—, my record and conscience are pure and clear as I sit here today in Calton Hill Jail. My earlier confession —like most — was not undertaken, as you well know, with true contrition or for my benefit. I did as I was told in composing it, taking great pains, as directed, to make my ability to read and write appear rudimentary. I realised the importance of denying my intelligence and of printing it as a warning to those who one day may still — praise God — rise up, but I know its truth: it was a pamphlet of lies designed to deceive.

I can make my solemn declaration to you, here and now, that I always targeted the sick, the lame, the elderly, the faithless, the whores. Never once did I kill a working man with a family to feed. Never once, as God is my witness.

And God has assured me, repeatedly and when I least expected it, that He was calling all of my victims — those whom I was called upon to save — home to Him. He has consistently sent me, His earnest and devout messenger, the signs of my salvation and theirs. Over these last many solitary weeks, I have become an expert and attentive sign-reader. I have shaken off all of my uncertainties and slept with assurance.

And while I have, so far, maintained my great

secret, you should know, Mr. M—, that He is calling me now. It will be my turn in just a matter of days. This world's system of injustice has failed to see me and my labouring brethren for what and who we really are, to see our true value. It has also failed to see my mission for what it truly is: make no mistake, I have wiped away all tears from their eyes and will die, in the eyes of God — like my Radical brethren before me — a martyr.

I am a man of tremendous conviction, a man of no weak and fragile faith. You can have my damned body after the fact. Take it and do with it what you will. Dissect it down to its minutest parts and hang my skeleton up as a sideshow, as some of these gaol-guards have taunted me will be done. Saw off the top of my skull to study my brain. Examine its cavities and peer into my eye sockets. My eyes shall still see the glory.

***

My first move towards martyrdom had come many months earlier. I recall exactly when it happened. Moving into Brogan's changed everything, just as I had hoped it would. After I discovered that Hare had been conducting some business of his own (the public doesn't know the full extent of his crimes, I can promise you, Mr. M—), I too decided to branch out. I relied on my own devices at the tramp house, but was caught, Hare and his harridan keeping a sharp eye out to make sure I wasn't turning any tricks of my own. I tried to outsmart them, killing an old woman at an unusual time of day, but I was discovered and made to give them half my payment, in addition to Margaret's extortionate one-pound rental rate. An argument ensued as I protested I'd been short-changed since the business began. I revealed how the doctor's assistant accidentally let me know of Hare's private business. This would explain his new clothes, ready money, and his means of getting things out of pawn. Did they take me for an idiot? I asked. Without me, they would have nothing, I reminded them. Despite the evidence, they denied everything and refused to hand over a shilling.

'There should be a fee paid for the use of my technique,' I challenged them, to which Margaret simply laughed, saying I was mad, and should see to myself. I cursed them both, then and there, and called them what they were — damned liars in league with the father of lies.

'We will see who finds you out,' I said ominously as I hastily left the tramp hotel, although I knew we were all in this business together and if one went down, we would all fall together.

Angry and dispirited, I had no choice but to move Nelly and I out and pursue my own private business. God knows, I desperately needed the money. The baby they didn't know about — that I hoped they would never find out about — was on the verge of being born, and I had made no plans for it yet. I couldn't even bring myself to mention the creature. Soon, I would be burdened with two hangers-on. It was time for me to make my move.

My plan was simple and perfect, as are all of my plans: moving under the pretence of protecting Nelly, I would make sure she would pay her way.

***

I received the first sign of my election and God's hand in the business early one afternoon soon after our move into Brogan's.

Coming off the Vennel steps, I ran into two familiar constables escorting an old woman along the road. I could tell she was drunk and I knew she was Irish, her broad accent betraying her as she insisted, while trying to escape them, to leave her alone, that she was fine and knew where she was going. One sniggered as he drew her back. 'You have no clue, grannie,' he said. 'You'll be at the watch-house in a minute.'

Sizing up the situation at a glance, I recognised the gift that had landed in my lap. Reading the signs, I wasted no time. I approached them with a familiar smile, as if I were seeking someone.

'Why, Auntie,' I said in the thickest Irish accent I could manage and sounding breathless, 'Here you are. Nelly and I have been all over the Grassmarket looking for you. You've had us worried sick.'

I gave each of the constables a smile of relief before saying, 'I'm so glad these two fine constables found you, given the state of you. You were supposed to return to the tramp house after you left the pub.'

Eager to escape the officers and avoid the watch-house, the astonished old woman smiled up at me while taking the hand I held out to her.

'I hope she didn't cause you any trouble,' I said. 'She obviously lost her way back, the poor old soul. She's not been long in Edinburgh, having just arrived a few nights ago to visit the family.'

'She'll soon be needing a place to lie down,' one offered, winking at me as he released her into my care.

'Eh, Missus,' said the other. 'You'd best watch yourself around these parts, especially the West Port. You can never be too careful. Edinburgh's a far cry from the Irish countryside.'

'Never were truer words spoken,' I responded, genially. 'Thanks so much again, officers,' I said. She stumbled a bit as we walked away, but I held her up, the stink of drink off her strong enough to knock a man down.

Out of their hearing, she thanked me for my assistance.

'That was quick thinking, Billy,' she said. I was stunned by her addressing me by my first name. This must be a sign, I thought to myself, mulling over the circumstances as we walked towards Brogan's.

'We Irish have to stick together,' she added, each word garbled and slurred as she spat it out. It was hard to put a sentence together in a state like hers, as I knew from experience. It would soon be even harder to stand up. I knew what had to be done and why we had crossed paths.

The next part came easily. I asked her name, and then feigned a distant relationship by way of my mother. Whether she believed me or not didn't matter. What did was that she was willing to come with me and was keen on drinking more. We had much to celebrate, I told her, thanks to our family reunion and the fact that she wasn't headed for the watch-house.

I then escorted this woman, whose name I have since forgotten although she spent her last precious hours with me, home to my new room where we shared a couple of drams. It didn't take much to put her away. In fact, no other shot ever went down so easily, a fine sign for the first bit of business conducted on my own. I remember also thinking, as we entered the dark passage to the room, how perfect this new place was. The tea chest was delivered an hour later, secured in the shadowy passage before being secretly removed, once I transferred her remains, in exchange for ten pounds.

Suspicious of the chest, Brogan riddled me with questions after returning home early from work. I lay his concerns to rest with a few drams, a small price to pay given the money involved.

I suspect Brogan later snuck back to the chest and nosed around. Something mustn't have sat right with him as he and his family left without a word the very next day, taking my annual rent monies with them.

I looked out for him in the West Port afterwards as I worried he might spread rumours about my affairs, but I never did see or hear from them again. I was thankful that he'd left behind his youngest son, John, who was keen to run errands for me when needed.

Brogan's sudden disappearance, along with my rent money, brought to mind the constable's stark warning, which I knew, from my experiences in Edinburgh, should be taken to heart.

You have to watch yourself in the West Port. You can never be too careful.

15.

Nelly

The first thing I did the afternoon after the hateful incident with Billy and the young women at Constantine's was to craft a doll and name it Billy. I cried and cursed as I did this, hating him for what he did to me and what measures I now had to take. As was Billy's way, he had left me no choice.

I fitted and stitched the doll's small clothes from one of Billy's old shirts that I'd used to wrap and conceal the other dolls and their wooden coffin cases. Its traditional baptism began with some of my tears falling down over its face followed by cutting it, precisely and painstakingly, above the left eye, just as he had done to me the day before at Connie's. For that purpose, I used the square needle from our cobbling tools. For effect, I cut myself slightly with the needle afterwards, dripping the small droplets of my blood onto the doll's face, rubbing them in before smearing them down across the front of his clothes.

'There you go, you bastard,' I whispered, defiantly, looking straight into its face as I held it up in front of me.

'Bastard,' I repeated, with relish. 'That will now be your unspoken middle name. I will whisper it, but only to myself, every time I see you.'

'I baptise you in the name of your father, the devil, and all of his fallen angels. '

'To lure and hurt women is a despicable act. Bastard.'

'To lure and hurt me is even more despicable,

especially after I trusted you with my horrible secrets about Rab. Bastard.'

'May whatever you have done — and will do from this moment on — come back to haunt and hurt you a thousandfold. Bastard.'

'In the name of the Father.' I banged Billy hard against the table.

'And of the Son,' I banged him again.

'And of the Holy Spirit.' I finished off with a couple of good hard, memorable bangs.

My prayer over, I pushed the square needle as deep into Billy's wooden belly as I could without breaking it. I did the same above his left eye again, gouging out a little bit of wood from his upper cheek. I then smeared more blood over top.

'Although you may seek forgiveness,' I said, before putting everything away, 'you will never be absolved of your sins.'

And with that I smacked Billy's head against the edge of the bed, just as I had once done with Rab's doll.

'Amen,' I said, quietly.

The ritual was a small but necessary pleasure. I had little else to hold on to and relished the fact that there was no possibility of Billy retaliating.

'Bastard,' I added again, for effect, hitting him off the bed one final time for good measure, before tucking and securing him away, suffocating him hard and fast under the covers.

***

Billy said we moved to keep me safe, but I know better. He must have taken me for a fool.

I had hoped he moved here to end the business, but I know now I was dreaming. True to form, he has never lived up to his promises or my expectations.

Worried about what his plans were for the baby, I appealed to him with the idea of family, the one we had spoken about those many years earlier. In response, Billy told me to be quiet, not to breathe a word to anyone about it.

'Soon, everyone will know anyway,' I said, brazenly, knowing I was bound to set him off with every word. I knew it was a flimsy challenge but a challenge it was.

Billy said nothing in response. He just left the room, while signalling to Little John, Brogan's idiot son, to watch the door.

That I was with child wasn't noticeable with my cape on. Margaret and the Mute had no idea, and while I was happy to keep that secret, I worried and wondered at the requirement. Billy had threatened me, saying the doctor wanted babies. I let him know I would die before he ever got mine. I'd kill myself first. And that would put an end to her.

Or then I would kill the doctor, I told him. 'If you — or anyone — dares to touch my wean, Billy, you will live to regret it.'

Billy gestured for me to calm down, but I felt the need to make my point clear. Plus, he had me riled up.

'You'll get her over my dead body,' I said, faintly, my words fading fast away as I thought about her loss. I had no qualms about doing away with myself, but she was an entirely different matter.

At one point over the next week, Billy stopped letting me leave the room. Without ever mentioning the baby, he said he was worried about me. I was *in no fit state to be wandering about the High Street selling shoes*. I still had many to sell but *his* plans, which he assumed were always *my* plans, seem to have changed.

He had paid young John, he said, who was off work with an injury, to make sure I didn't leave the house when Billy wasn't home.

I knew I was utterly at his mercy. In combination with my natural exhaustion with the baby growing, Billy's declaration alarmed and unsettled me. As a result, I slept a lot and prayed Alice would come and visit me as she had promised. Once the waters broke, things could happen quickly as I had seen at Jeannie's cottage. Bad things.

What I did know was that it wasn't right to trap me in a room, especially when I could go into labour at any moment. I had told young John a few times that if he heard screaming, he must open the door or else he'd have blood on his hands.

I'm fairly certain John knew nothing of my condition. He just did as he was told by Billy to whom he looked up and admired. The truth was John was not very bright and would do anything for the money. Billy also paid him well.

It had been a couple of weeks since I'd seen daylight. Sometimes, I'd spy a bit through the small upper window at the back of the house, where the room was located, but that was the extent of my contact with the outside world. Being pent-up indoors caused me, and the baby, distress, which I knew wasn't good. I slept a lot over that time, always humming to her and gently stroking my belly. I tried to remain calm and to act as if everything was normal. The truth is, I enjoyed the quiet but I hated being closed in against my will. The channelling I'd perfected when at the mercy of Rab also had other uses. When things got really bad and I panicked with claustrophobia, I could think myself out of that room, back with Jeannie, out in the comfort of the country.

As he'd done for months, Billy lived a night life, rising only in the late afternoon or the early evening just before supper. He consumed a lot of laudanum in order to deal with his pains in the wake of brutal years of canal building, and only came to life when he was drinking. Now, I just saw the wearying aftermath of that heavy drinking, as he would check in on me once a day, always looking hellish and unkempt, leaving soon after waking in the adjacent room and heading directly to the pub. He had Little John bring me food and drink from Rymer's while he was out and I'm happy to say, John never once forgot me.

Billy and I rarely spoke but I know he heard me crying some nights. As I neared what I thought was my due date, I reminded him once again that Alice would soon be needed, that he'd be risking mine and the baby's lives if he didn't make arrangements.

'It won't be long now,' I warned. 'Alice said she would help and bring a midwife. We will need water and a lot of rags and some good swaddling clothes. You would do well to prepare and gather them now, Billy,' I said. 'Please listen.'

But my words fell on deaf ears.

There once was a time when I would talk and fight back, and even provoke Billy for the hell of it. But now was a very different time. Between us sat another whose life and death hung in the balance.

I listened as Billy came and went over days. No supplies. No Alice. No mention of a midwife. Nothing.

Until one night, when he made a threat that worried me like never before.

'You can't just leave me here — leave us here — possibly, to die,' I said to him, desperately, when he came in to check on me before leaving for the pub. 'Or is that the plan?'

Billy seemed taken aback by the suggestion.

'There is no evil plan,' he said, smirking back at me. 'Why would I keep feeding you? I want to see how you come through the birth.'

While I didn't know exactly how to read Billy's statement, I knew that underneath it lay a dark threat. What if I didn't *come through*? What if I came through and she didn't?

As I contemplated potential outcomes, Billy added, 'And when that time does come, Nelly, I will go and fetch Margaret to help.'

My heart skipped a beat when he said that. Billy knew how disturbing that statement was and he delighted in my torment.

'You know she is the last person I'd call into my childbed, Billy.' In fact, I thought to myself, the words 'help' and 'Margaret' were as opposite as good and evil.

'It's Alice I want, and Alice I need,' I said, in earnest. 'This is not the time to upset me, Billy. I've been through enough.'

As a last attempt to rouse some feeling in him, I added, 'Remember, this is your baby too.'

But this appeal to the Billy I first loved failed to provoke a response. I worried about his next steps. Whatever they were, I knew I would do anything to protect my baby just as I had always done everything to protect him.

For the time being, I knew I could do nothing, imprisoned in this small, rancid, sour-smelling room with its filthy bedcovers and marred walls. It dawned on me that I was not only at risk of losing my mind but of losing the baby if Billy persisted in ignoring my pleas. This marked the beginning of my vivid, unrelenting nightmares of an endlessly crying child who could never be found and soothed.

Left to drown in worry and provoked at times by Billy's strategically chosen and tormenting words, my nightmares, like my belly, grew.

***

One afternoon, just a few days later, in mid-June, my suspicions proved correct. Billy came home without warning. He was not alone. He had a portly old woman with him in skirts too heavy for the weather who, despite being drunk, was chortling away happily to herself. She stank of stale piss and manure, as if she'd been sleeping in a stable. At first, her Irish brogue being so thick, I couldn't make out much other than her name — Maggie. The old soul was rubbing Billy's hands as he brought her in and repeatedly saying something about her luck. I soon realised he'd used one of Margaret's old tricks and convinced her they were related. Acknowledging me for the first time in days, Billy told me he'd saved her from the watch-house. Could I go out and buy a bottle of whisky so we could share in a wee celebration?

Sensing what was afoot, I held back, giving Billy an anxious, inquisitive look. What, in God's name, was this man planning just as I was about to give birth? But his eyes refused to meet mine as he stood there, and his actions showed impatience. In part paralysed by dread, I knew I wasn't moving fast enough for Billy's taste. As he handed me the money, he shot me a look so ferocious I knew I had to remain silent and obey. I knew I was in the worst position a person could find themselves in in the West Port — entirely at William Burke's mercy.

As the old woman made herself comfortable, Billy escorted me to the passageway out of her hearing, patted me lightly on the belly, and said, in the blunt, nasty voice he used during his worst, most tyrannical moments, 'We need the money, Nelly, for you and your brat. Goodness knows, you're bringing nothing in, and you won't be for some time. Run along now. The old soul will need a last drink or two for a good send-off. We owe her that, at the very least.'

Billy knew he would especially unsettle me by suggesting my complicity with murder. Terrified of his retaliation and feeling I had no choice, I did as I was told.

After weeks of being locked indoors, it felt good to get outside, even if just for a short while. I was worried about running into someone who knew me and would see my condition, despite my wearing a cape in early June. For those few minutes outside, I tried to forget about everything around me and my horrid circumstances. I breathed in every moment of freedom as I walked to the shop and back — a trip I used to take every day — praying that he would be kind to the poor old woman and kinder to me and our unborn child.

When I returned, I walked as quietly as I could up the passage. Initially, I heard no voices, which frightened me. Had he already done away with her in the front room? As I approached, Billy opened the door wide. There she sat, the old soul, a lovely smile on her haggard face as she blessed me for bringing more drink.

Glasses were filled and then refilled as she and Billy drank and talked and laughed over the next half an hour. I just sat, an onlooker, marvelling at how charming he could be, how funny and engaging, even when planning murder. He is utterly soulless, I thought to myself, watching his empty, icy blue eyes as he sat across from me during the entire transaction.

Fearing I might spoil his carefully laid plans and seeing I was unwilling to drink or participate, Billy signalled for me to leave. I did so promptly, desperate to get away and return to my prison-cell of a room.

Had the old woman thought about where she was going to sleep tonight? Had she any idea this night would be her last? How could someone not be careful and place themselves, especially when drunk, in harm's way? How could so many be charmed by him? But I knew I could ask the same questions of hundreds of others here in Edinburgh, myself included. And the answers were easy to find, especially where the drink was concerned. We were lured by the comforts and the escape it offered, in combination with the fellowship. Who was I, I thought to myself, to act baffled and ask such questions?

And just as I began contemplating my own situation and when the baby might arrive, just as I was nodding off in my own bed, trying to imagine myself elsewhere — anywhere else — the door was suddenly thrown open and Billy entered unexpectedly. As he propped up the heavy old woman who was barely able to stand, he stumbled forward and released her. She flopped down next to me onto the bed. This intrusion was shocking to me and was rendered even more distressing by an extremely agitated Billy who now instructed me to move over and lay myself across her body. The truth was I could barely move. Angling my pregnant body proved next to impossible as I lay there, especially with a stout woman directly beside me. When I didn't respond immediately, Billy leaned over and slapped me hard across the face, telling me to do as I was told. If I couldn't move on top of her, I had to hold her legs down, he said. I manoeuvred myself onto my side and did as I was told while the old woman groaned and cried out for help. I then watched as Billy carefully arranged his hands before placing them over her nose and face. In my mind's eye, I begged him to let her go. I cried out, telling him there were other ways for us to manage. We had always managed before. He must give up this horrible business.

But my mouth remained closed. I said — and could say — nothing. Things happened so fast and my words, I felt, would come too late. I'd also be putting the baby at risk. Some minutes later, I watched as Billy released his hands. Horrible, noisy exhalations overtook her and bloody drool fast leaked out of her mouth. By the time she stopped moving, and I had got myself up and onto my feet, the old soul was gone from this world, laying there unmoving, her bloodshot blue eyes staring straight up past Billy towards the ceiling. I stood, in shock, as Billy leaned down and closed her eyelids.

'I can't stand when they look at me like that,' he said. 'It's the eyes that unnerve me every time.'

I stood staring at her body, the bloody spittle trailing down her mouth and neck, her last expression a death mask horrible to see. And Billy just laughed as I looked towards him, my face in shock, and said, 'You should see yourself, Nelly. It's only a dead body, only a dead bloody woman.'

And as I stood gasping, trying to calm my agitated breathing, he added, 'And if your bastard is to be fed, there'll be many more.'

'Don't worry,' he said, as if trying to calm me. 'I know the first one is a shock. You'll get used to it in time.'

But I was trying to process the fact that someone — a woman I didn't even know until a couple of hours ago — lay dead on my bed, and that I had participated in taking her life.

Who was this Billy? I asked myself

And the question that followed on its heels was even more unsettling for me to answer, *Who was this Nelly?*

And as I struggled with the horror of my situation, I heard a loud *splish* and felt a slick wetness course down my legs, leaking onto the floor. At first, I thought the old woman's bodily fluids must have spilled out from somewhere. But I knew that was impossible as there hadn't been any wounds. Besides, the sound wasn't right.

I then realised what was happening.

With my recent walk, Billy's shocking entrance

with Maggie, and my sudden, awkward movements on and around the bed, my waters had broken. My thoughts shifted quickly from the dead woman to myself and the baby. I knew time was of the essence. With my hands placed underneath the baby in my belly, I made my way, as gingerly as I could, crouching and shuffling, into the front room, where I sank down onto Billy's bed and shouted for him to go get Alice.

***

Billy proved, as I knew he would, utterly useless. Worse, he was careless of me and his own child, as his lack of preparation showed. His act of ignoring my words and warnings spoke volumes, placing me and the baby in danger. I believe he was also secretly praying for me to die along with her so that he could cart us both off to the doctor where he could claim that we died of natural causes. So many women — as I well knew from my time with Jeannie and the navvies — died in childbirth, the child along with them. Besides, the baby and I were worth more to Billy dead than alive, especially her, as he had told me many times. Our deaths would solve all of his problems.

Left on my own, the next few hours saw me listening to and working with my heaving, panting body through waves of unstoppable contractions while I prayed to God that both of us — she and I — would come through without harm. My first concern was if her head was down and the second that I would open wide enough so she could get through without injury to me. I knew I needed patience, along with some massage in preparation, then good strong breathing and precise bearing down when the right time came. Following that would come what Jeannie called the third phase of birthing when, with its contractions, I had to make sure everything was expelled — the cord and the afterbirth. All of it. I had seen far too many women seeking assistance at Jeannie's after horrible blood loss. Others had been infected as a result of doctors not knowing what they were doing, and some of them died.

I had to block out what happened earlier that evening. I had to forget that a dead woman that I had helped to kill lay stretched out, never to move again, in the room next to me. I had to protect myself and Maeve, for that was what I'd decided to call the baby, after my mother.

No Alice came because no Billy left the house. The birth happened faster than I expected for a first child. That Billy was more afraid of natural childbirth than the unnaturalness of murder made me laugh privately to myself just before the contractions picked up. When they came fast, I tried to slow things down to ensure the baby wouldn't be harmed and I would remain intact, without splitting and bleeding.

Billy stayed out of the room the entire time, checking in only to see if I needed anything after he heard her first cries several hours later — food, drink, water, rags.

I felt exhausted after the first wracking contractions of her birth. Listening to my body, I rested between them. They came in slow waves at first, then mounted. It felt as if I had done this before given how many births I'd assisted at with Jeannie. I remembered the intense and powerful ritual of it. Rhythmically and in stages, the series of contractions came on. And just as rhythmically, I held my breath, pushing hard for as long as possible before breaking for breath. In my mind's eye, the ghost of Jeannie was there with me. Just as she had directed dozens of labouring women, she was now directing me.

When Maeve finally slid out, all rubbery and slimy, I whispered words of thanks to God and, with tears in my eyes and a grateful thanks to Jeannie's great teaching, I cut the cord with the clean knife I got from Billy. I then cleared her nose by suctioning it with my mouth so that she could breathe. Holding her up carefully in some of the softest, cleanest rags Billy had given me, I heard her cry for the first time. That boisterous wail was a holy sound to me, like nothing I've heard before or since. With it, she declared herself safely on this side, and I, the woman who promised with all my heart to be her devoted and attentive mother, was blessed to witness the miracle. I marvelled again at the great, god-like powers of women, their body's divine capacity for creation. Taking great care to wipe and clean Maeve more thoroughly, I removed all of the creamy bloody mixture to reveal her beautiful soft skin and face. Here she lay, the gift that God had unveiled and given to me. *My* gift. *My* tiny miracle.

I tenderly wrapped and swaddled her, making sure she was warm and protected. In my heart, I thanked Jeannie once again, the surrogate mother who had taught me so many valuable lessons in love and caring for the small, vulnerable, fragile things of this world. Here I was now, unexpectedly after years of trying and waiting, a mother myself. Nor could I yet say that precious word aloud. It was so sacred to me. I feared I could never live up to its power. *Mother*. To this day, no word contains as much magic for me or as much terror. Beyond God's love, there is no greater force. I worried about fulfilling the expectations I'd attached to it.

As Maeve lay fast asleep, swaddled in my arms, my pinky in her mouth to soothe her, I lay utterly exhausted in Billy's bed, a bed I'd never before slept in. Overwhelmed by the calming warmth of a love I'd forgotten existed, I wrestled with tormenting thoughts:

How, I asked myself, *could I have lost sight of myself, I, who was once a small and vulnerable thing? How did*

I end up here, still loving a man I continued to try to fix while he was breaking me?

My only answer came in the form of a single, complicated word. *Love.*

But all of my love for Billy has been stifled, my inner voice responded. *How is it that love can become a menace and a madness in the wrong, uncaring hands?*

My first words to Maeve emerged out of this collision of painful thoughts. I repeated a promise, a word-charm to love, care for, and protect this precious, vulnerable little one despite my horrible situation with Billy. Then, I bathed her in my grateful yet terrified tears.

And with that bittersweet baptism, I blocked out the fact of the dead woman lying in the room next to mine, cradled my newborn, swaddled daughter close to my breast, and fell fast asleep.

16.

Billy

Nelly told me once that she thought women were closer to God because they, like Mary, have babies. Women, she thinks, can tap into the divine spirit more readily, and are more in touch with God and the world beyond.

I have wondered on occasion if Nelly's steady intake of whisky and laudanum has turned her head. I have wondered what I will do with a madwoman once she permanently crosses the line. As I know from my inquiries, the Edinburgh Lunatic Asylum does not accept paupers, only rich, mad people whose desperate families can pay their own way. We, the poor and despised vermin of the West Port, are in no such position. Only the streets remain where Nelly may be turned out. I must remain stoic.

'The men of God,' I tell her, as if I am speaking with an imbecile, 'have reminded us repeatedly that women are not to be trusted. They — women — got us into this accursed mess of suffering in the first place. Read all the books, I tell her. I know you've read some. They all point to the same inescapable problem. Women were whores then, and they're whores now. Call it palming or what you will, it's whoring, and there's not an ounce of anything spiritual about it.'

She has wondered aloud how such a radical as I claim myself to be doesn't recognise that women are the hardest done by and face the greatest hardships and prejudices.

'What of Mary Magdalene or Esther or Ruth?' she

asked, challenging me, as she is always wont to do. 'They were women who fought back, courageous women who resisted their oppressors and stood up to fight for what they believed in. You told me their stories, Billy, and I listened attentively, with respect and awe. What of them?'

Then she added her own personal flourish, and I chuckle recalling the memory, 'I've told you about my own life. Did you never wonder how I managed to sustain myself and survive?'

'No,' I said calmly before launching into my theory, 'because I believe, like most women, you've been prone to exaggeration. You're no heroine, and certainly no Biblical one. It's blasphemous for you to compare yourself to Esther, Ruth, or Mary Magdalene. You're a fallen woman through and through with a bastard now to prove it. God has cursed you and others like you, and I fear there may be no true and full redemption for any of you. I've always had trouble believing that the God-given glories of this world will be granted to you, even at the Resurrection.'

'Well, we shall see what we shall see. All will be revealed when the time comes, she shot back. We are closer to the divine. If you had ever witnessed a child's birth, you would know better. Always remember — without us, you couldn't be born.'

Then she added, 'And I often think, with few exceptions, that the world would be a far better place.'

Difficult as it was, I resisted the temptation to respond and walked away. It wasn't worth the effort. Nelly and I had a number of these disputes over the years, including one in the pub many moons earlier where I told her, 'You lot are all the same in the dark. Nothing but holes to be filled, and useless without a man. Am I wrong?' I asked aloud, questioning the nearby pub patrons who were laughing and carousing, leaning in paying close attention to our latest wrangle.

Such was always my way. When she asked for it, I happily held Nelly up to public ridicule. She would make a spectacle of herself and I was always willing to assist. I enjoyed every single insulting minute of it — the attention, the laughter, and especially, her humiliation.

***

Peggy — Peggy Haldane — was my second gift, my second sign.

She had come looking for her mother or, as she told me over a few pints, that was one of the reasons she made her way into the West Port that afternoon. She had recognised me as Nelly's man and, as she was alone, she agreed to sit down with me and share a few drinks.

I was surprised, once I realised who she was, that she hadn't come sooner. But that's life in Edinburgh for the dregs of society. There is no time in this desperate netherworld to do anything beyond what must be done to survive. And so, Peggy, Mary Haldane's daughter, had survived through the spring into the summer, after the disappearance of her mother. She drank and thieved and was twice arrested, she told me proudly, for vagrancy and *infesting* the New Town — or such was the vicious description of her doings advanced by the Justice of the Peace.

'Life must go on, the drinking along with it,' she said with a wry smile as we toasted her work of infestation and took another swig, her slurred speech increasing by the dram.

'Still, I am desperate to find my mother. I know if I was the one who'd gone missing, she'd be frantic looking for me. And I know she wouldn't stop until she found me.'

It wasn't long after that statement that she stumbled

outside to pee, and I knew it was time to move the party elsewhere. She was staying alone near Hare's tramp-house, she said, but could sleep wherever her legs could carry her. *Did I happen to see her mother the last time she was in the West Port?*

She knew Nelly and her mother were good pals and hoped Nelly could give her some information, possibly shed some light on her disappearance. 'Where is Nelly tonight'? she asked, concerned. 'It's rare to see you alone. You two are always here together.'

I immediately offered my well-rehearsed response, 'Nelly hasn't been well,' I said. 'She's back at home, sleeping.'

'Female troubles,' I added. 'I've long suffered,' I said, laughing, 'from a similar problem. Troubles with women. Every man's plague. Let's make a final toast to that, Peggy,' I said, holding my glass aloft.

Then, with an eye to my own interests, I offered Peggy some of the peace she'd been seeking. I moved the conversation onto the track of good memories, telling her that her mother had spent some time talking with Nelly and sharing some laughs when she last saw her in the West Port.

And as I was telling Peggy how her mother shared some fine craic with Nelly that night, I realised what was also needed. Peggy Haldane had as much right to comfort as anyone, and I intended to help her.

What peace is available, Mr. M—, to those agitated souls whose bodies are wracked with the pains of poverty and want? No wonder we sign on readily to all of your God-forsaken churches. Heaven and heavenly peace appeal mightily to our battered hearts and souls. They are a welcome, necessary balm. We readily embrace the idea of an afterlife in a place of comfort and security, the blessed hope of entry into a world of comfort and a carelessness we have never known. It is right, I now know, that we look to God to relieve us, but we must never forget to hold man accountable for denying us our rights on earth.

As I thought through these ideas as we drank, it dawned on me that it was only right to reunite Peggy and her mother, a woman I'd released from life's dark agonies months earlier. Otherwise, peace would continue to elude her in this damnable place where she was regarded *as a pestilence*. I realised there was a reason why God had brought her to me, and we had crossed paths.

More than any other shot I've ever met, Peggy had the sincere look of yearning for the other side, a desperate look I've come to know well, to which it is my calling to respond. I heard God whisper to me as I sat there listening to her. And then there were His signs. How else could I account for our encounter in this pub in the mid-afternoon when I normally wouldn't even be out of doors? How else, if it wasn't meant to be?

And I must minister to other interests as well, both human and divine. Peggy would serve my purposes, I decided, just as I would serve hers. Her need was palpable and I was available, with Madame Geneva handily at my side to fulfill the request.

I received eight pounds for Peggy the next day, reluctantly splitting the proceeds with Hare as I needed help with her transportation. Doing away with her in my new lodgings allowed me at least to dodge the rental rate.

Another damaged tea chest came in empty and went out filled.

But I can tell you this, Mr. M—, and it brings a smile to my face to remember it, pleasure being something I've been lacking in this infernal place. What Mary Paterson couldn't give me, I received instead and in full measure, much to my surprise, from Peggy Haldane. Ignorant of the fact that Nelly lay sleeping in the next room, Peggy was as willing and as able as I was. We came together in our joint need and, as drunk as we both were, it was a profound and memorable send off. The pleasure — and the payoff — were all mine.

***

Although I didn't recognise it at the time, Brogan's rental theft and sudden disappearance was another sign of God's grace. With his departure, another room with another straw bed became available, along with some old furniture, offering me space for the expansion of my business.

The truth was I also needed the time and space to figure out my next move. With a brat occasionally crying in the next room, its mother assailing me for items needed from outside, I was glad to have more time alone.

Thankfully, the young John Brogan had remained behind as my assistant. He was as handy and helpful a servant as one could find. He wasn't the strongest or the smartest lad, but he was reliable. There was no one better at taking direction, as long as he undertook one request at a time. He beat Hare, hands down, and was well worth the little I paid him. I briefly flirted with the possibility of initiating him into the body business, thinking it might soon be time to replace Hare. I had even calculated the savings. John had proven himself trustworthy when I needed privacy and required discretion. I knew this because I had tested him. Besides, I liked the idea of a permanent servant. A man could get used to making demands and having them satisfied by a ready underling. I could see its attractions for my so-called superiors.

And besides, depending on what happened with Nelly, I realised I might need a servant long-term.

17.

Nelly

In an instant, despite the sudden shock that led up to it, Maeve's birth changed everything. She became real to me in the flesh, separated from me. With her arrival, my world collapsed down to a single function — sustaining her. She was all that existed, all that mattered, all that I lived for. Except when Billy came in with food, drink, rags, and swaddling sheets, and removed the soiled cloths and garbage, we remained securely in our own little room with no disturbances, sleeping and eating when necessary. I was, after the unsettling events of a week earlier, returning to a peace and calm I had long forgotten. Like a person after a lengthy illness, I felt myself returning to life, stronger, healthier, and renewed. This rebirth was entirely unexpected as was the sense of energy that accompanied it. I lost sight of our captivity during this brief but memorable period of bonding.

Over that first week, I fell in love with the tiny preciousness of her, the seeds of a mother's fierce care and protectiveness fast growing within me.

On the first day, I memorised Maeve's face and wondered at the fragility of her, committing every delicate feature to memory. Her tapering, miniature fingers, tiny, perfectly formed fingernails, fair blush of cheek, and long, dark lashes mesmerised me. Her almond-shaped black eyes were certainly mine, my mother's; her smooth, fine, sandy-coloured fuzz of hair, Billy's. To think, I thought to myself, teary-eyed, that I had been granted this miraculous gift at such a late stage in my life, humbled me beyond words. I regretted, bitterly and sincerely, with acute pain in my heart, that she had not come sooner, before all of my sweet love for Billy had turned sour. Before the West Port. Before Billy's 'body business.'

By the second day, I cradled her naturally as if she had always existed, cupping her head to my breast as she suckled, keeping her warm, secure, and swaddled. How it was she nestled into me so perfectly, her body so precisely configured to contour against mine, I didn't know and didn't question. I had been so alone, untouched, and unloved for so long. Only now could I see that my life had been a desert and Maeve an offering of fresh water. Our connection was a revelation, perhaps some form of reward. For what, I didn't know, and didn't care to know, but she signalled a new stage in my life, infusing me with hope of a future. Perhaps, I dared to think, children are sent to us for a reason, and at particular times, to save us from our dreary, depressed lives, to save us from ourselves. Would she give me the strength to leave Billy? Would she remind both of us of our early days and possibly redeem us through love?

By the third day, my fears set in again, monstrous and fully formed. Could I be trusted to protect her? Did I have what was necessary? The task was immense, overwhelming, terrifying. My worries outweighed my joys. She was so very vulnerable, as was I. Holding her protectively against me as she breastfed, my salty tears falling down across her face, mixing in with my milk, I thought of how this little bundle of life, so delicate, small, and defenceless, rendered me more vulnerable to Billy.

Would Billy come around to loving and protecting her? What if the answer was no?

On the fourth day, I trusted to God's will and followed my heart, with the hope that Billy would follow suit. What a priceless gift had been given us. She made me make sense. My breasts, always an encumbrance, seemed natural. They existed for one reason and one little creature — to feed and nourish her. Maeve. And she gave my life purpose. I would do everything — and anything — for her from here to the end of my days.

On day five, I panicked, thinking, mistakenly, as I awoke a few times to find her deep in slumber, that she lay in my arms, unmoving, dead. Startled, I broke her sleep at times to make sure she was breathing, relieved by her hearty cries. These are early days yet, I thought to myself. We will soon grow used to each other. I will soon know her various states by instinct. She will teach me what I need to do, and I will do it.

On day six, I felt empowered by her, fierce in my role as protective mother. The world, I thought, had gained a sense of possibility and hope. She allowed me to see things anew, from a different angle. I pledged to return to my older, bolder self with this new little someone to love and to love me. I would never drink again. I would do everything I could for her. And no one better rouse my fierce tigress mother within. They would regret it.

At the end of that first week, with Billy avoiding our room except to bring me food and small beer, and with Little John still thankfully away, she and I fell into a routine — *our* routine, *our* little rituals.

But what was natural inside was not natural without. As I well knew from experience, dark shadows lurked beyond our room. I knew this sense of security couldn't and wouldn't last, do what I might. I could dream and build sandcastles high into the air, but an impending, brutal reality was knocking at the door.

I came to understand that God hadn't answered my prayers when I least expected it. The timing was

234

wrong. It couldn't have been worse. He had made a terrible mistake giving her to me. She was too precious and innocent for this fallen, treacherous world and I was too jaded and lost. Any hope I once had in this life had been committed to, and buried in the grave, corrupt and mouldering. Sustained battery and belittling will do that to a person.

No one ever wants to believe it, but God does sometimes make mistakes. Even God. I am living proof of such errors, as was Maeve.

It would have been better for her had she never been born, I along with her.

I remember praying during those first weeks, that our room, which I once cursed as a damnable dungeon, would fast close in on us, securing us away for all eternity from the vicious, treacherous world outside.

***

A few days later when Billy came to the door with a look of concern, I knew something was wrong. He had been impatient and agitated over the past few days, arriving and leaving with rags for the baby, and food and drink for me.

I couldn't look him straight in the eye given what he'd forced me to do with Maggie, the old Irishwoman. We hardly spoke except to exchange information about what the baby and I needed. It is true that he had shown some care towards her and attention to me. Still uncertain as to his intentions, I remained anxious. I now knew what he was capable of and how I had to be strategic if Maeve were to be safeguarded. While I tried to appeal to him, my attempts to convince him to reconsider our becoming a family and leaving Edinburgh fell on deaf ears.

'Let's get away from this place before it's too late,'

I said in earnest. 'Let's start over. Please, Billy, I'm begging you. If you've never listened to me before, listen now. We need to put this nightmare behind us.'

Speaking from the heart, I added, 'Your nightmares especially. I know you have to be haunted by what you've done,' I said. 'I've heard you crying out in your sleep.'

But I was but a ghost to Billy, who said nothing in response, asking only if I needed anything from the shops.

Was there anything she needed? he asked, after I'd said no.

This last inquiry surprised me as he'd finally acknowledged her. This perhaps signalled a concern. Perhaps next time, he might even look at her — or touch her — or wish to hold her. I could only hope.

As I lay, breastfeeding, I prayed we had reached a turning point.

But my inner voice spoke a very different language — I had clung to the skirts of hope so many times before, they were threadbare.

***

All I heard each day was Billy going in and out. And each day, he poked his head in the room, as if we were contaminated, sick with some disease, to ask if there was anything I needed beyond the food and drink regularly brought in by little John. I decided to take the time and bond with the baby, to work on gaining strength before I made a major decision about our future.

Being locked in together, as if we were avoiding infection, took its toll on me after a few weeks. I started to lose track of what day it was and even what time of day. The ritual was repetitive — eat, feed, sleep, change rags (hers and mine), and swaddling clothes.

Realising I was feeling ill locked inside and growing desperate, I resolved to take it up with him the next morning. We'd been indoors for far too long.

Lying in bed that night, several hours after breastfeeding her, I awoke suddenly to voices next door in Billy's room. I was sure I could hear a woman laughing and speaking on the other side of the wall. I listened intently, more concerned than upset, to her gruff voice. I didn't worry as long as I heard her voice and Billy responding to her. What I dreaded was silence. Who it was, I didn't know, but I sensed a tension in the apartment. When, after about ten minutes, I heard a thud on the other side and a woman crying out in pain, I grew more worried and curious. A few minutes later, making sure Maeve was asleep, I decided to creep quietly out into the hall to investigate. Unbeknownst to Billy, John had agreed to leave the door open that night so I could use the bucket to pee outside the bedroom. He was going to his sister's, he'd said, and would return the next day.

Tiptoeing quietly, I made my way to the doorway of Billy's room. The interior was visible thanks to a candle on the stool near the wall. Although I was terrified and afraid of being seen, I edged in closer and warily peered in. The woman lay sprawled, immobile, at an angle across the bed. While some clothes lay on the floor beside her, she was still wearing her short gown. Her head was thrown back in an odd manner, I thought, hanging limply off the bed, her hair in disarray. At first, I felt uncomfortable as if I had invaded her privacy, a feeling magnified by the fact that Billy lay sprawled on top of her, his naked backside writhing up and down, as if she were still alive and responding. Shocked, I backed away immediately and out of sight just as I heard the last familiar grunt I had grown accustomed to over the years.

It was only as I hurriedly tiptoed back to my room with that horrible last image and sound imprinted on my mind that I realised who the familiar looking woman was — Mary Haldane's daughter, Peggy. She and I had shared, along with her mother, many a pint and a laugh. As I crawled back into bed and nestled myself in with the baby, I lay, at first, in shock. I began to cry as I thought back to poor Mary and her last evening alive. That Billy could victimise both women — first a mother, followed some months later by her own daughter — was sickening. It couldn't be more disturbing, impossible to digest.

I knew a drunk woman when I saw one. I knew a dead woman when I saw one, the distinctive blood and mucus running down Peggy's face onto the bedclothes, the same that I had seen with Maggie. To violate her after a violent death as she lay there vulnerable was the most despicable thing I had ever seen.

It unsettled me in ways unexpected, recalling my own earlier terrifying experiences with Rab when I was young and utterly powerless to fight back, so powerless I might as well have been dead. I remembered praying for any form of escape from him, even my own sudden death.

In a truly sobering instant, Billy and Rab no longer appeared in my mind as opposites. Instead, I saw them seated together, obscured by shadows at their own pub table, dead silence pervading the place. As they shared a dark joke together, the overpowering scent of liquor and decay commingled. In the image that arose in my mind's eye, I envisioned them turning their heads towards me, sinister smiles on both of their faces as each caught my eye and issued a low, macabre laugh as they placed their index fingers firmly against their lips.

As I lay there shaking, cuddling the baby, not

knowing what to do, I cursed Rab and Billy and every man who could violate a vulnerable woman. That Billy could find the abuse of a dead woman an experience of pleasure made me more terrified of him. This Other Billy clearly possessed wicked aspects I'd never before seen. He was a sick and sordid man, depraved and deprived of all sanity.

Sobriety in love is always accompanied by revelations and resolutions. My case was no different. There was no escaping what had to happen: while I didn't know how, Maeve and I had to get away. But first, Billy had to face his comeuppance. Now a mother with a newfound mission, I, Nelly McDougal, vowed, if it was the last thing I ever did, to have a hand in it.

**

Knowing what I know now, I wonder what words Billy whispered into the ears of other women, especially his chosen, inebriated victims. I used to imagine him in our bed in the back room in Tanner's Lane, his lips brushing softly against their flushed cheeks before methodically arranging his hands to ensure their suffocation while the Mute lay across them, securing their arms, to deter any frantic movement or breath.

Was it, *you're a braw wee lass?*

What beautiful eyes you have?

Lucky we ran into each other?

Or, perhaps, *sweet dreams?*

There are some things I should never contemplate, some things I really shouldn't know, that no one should know besides God.

But everything about Billy has long been my obsession. I have endlessly replayed our time together and painstakingly unpacked his finely strung sentences. Sequences have become muddled to the point where I can no longer tell which of my memories are based on reality, and which on fantasy.

I would give anything to stop thinking, especially about the women — their last moments and his parting words, his face their final mind's-eye image, his heavy breath foul with whisky and cheap, stale tobacco, his voice urgent and rasping.

What does he do with the ones he kills alone? my inner voice has insistently and repeatedly asked me.

I haven't dreamt properly in a long time. Years.

This is the stuff of which my nightmares are made as I assume the place of those women as Billy tells me, in his deep, seductive voice, that he adores me and wouldn't hurt me for the world.

'Here,' he says, 'I think you need a little bit of this — something special to calm you down,' as he places his firm, purposeful hands over my face and throat while Hare and Margaret watch in fascinated anticipation, smiling and visible from the doorway.

Such violent nightmares are nothing compared to the nightmare of my life, the nightmare I am reliving in these pages in a desperate attempt to overcome plaguing memories.

Recovery.

It's a loaded word and a damnably long road, one strewn with the wreckage of my life.

***

It was at this desperate juncture that I took desperate measures. All I recall now is falling on my knees before him the next day, pleading for him to bring Alice to the house as Maeve was in danger and looked jaundiced.

'I don't know what's wrong with her, Billy, but if she isn't seen to soon, she might not make it, and there would be a lot of explaining to do.'

Despite my frenzy, Billy just looked back at me

stony-faced and unconcerned, saying nothing. So, I was surprised when, a couple of hours later, he returned with food and drink and Alice, and then left us alone to talk. Perhaps it was because he wouldn't want word to get back to Connie that I was being mistreated so he had to be on his best behaviour. I didn't really know or care, as long as my plan was working. I'd thought through what to do before Alice's arrival. Having given her a bit of money that I had secured away, I sent her, a woman who could neither read nor write, out to buy notepaper, a quill pen, and some ink.

In this way, I managed to get a short letter out to my cousin Ann, asking her to come as soon as she was able. I prayed the note would arrive and she would follow the instructions I'd given her, which were specific: I asked her to stay at a nearby tramp hotel, not Margaret and Hare's. I didn't want Billy seeing her or anyone else knowing she had come to see me. I also told her to send me a note through Alice at her address in the Canongate once she arrived, a note consisting of three simple words — I am here.

Ann's was one of the only addresses I knew and my best option under the circumstances. I told Alice that the letter told Ann I needed help with the baby who seemed sick, something I knew Ann could help with.

Alice also helped me convince Billy to let us walk up to Holyrood with the baby. We needed to walk every day, she told him, so that Maeve could get some air and regain her health. Following this regimen, I also managed to bury some more dolls up near Arthur's Seat. I would drop Maeve at Alice's some days, visits I knew Alice enjoyed, and made my pilgrimage up the Radical Road. I needed to keep doing my special work — now for Maggie and Peggy — just as I had done for the others. Meanwhile, I prayed there would be no others.

Those walks also helped me stay well. Maeve also grew to like the exercise, her dark observant eyes taking in all of the faces, sights, and sounds of Edinburgh.

The truth of the matter was, despite feeling worried about what Billy had planned for us, our walks also kept my spirits up as I worked out next steps and prayed and waited for Ann's arrival.

18.

Billy

Some have said Nelly and I make a curious pairing. But I know better — that we are twins of a sort. The damaged, Mr. M—-, are survivors and have a way of finding each other. I could have found Nelly in a crowded pub while blind-folded, just as she could have found me. She is not only sharp but sharp-witted, a rarity in these parts; she is headstrong like my mother but thinks herself weak, especially in love. I have worked hard to keep things that way. I learned early on that the luring and the loving must come first, or the women will leave.

So much of our lives, including the decisions and choices we make, is bound up with what we believe to be true, about ourselves and the world. I am thankful that Nelly thinks little of herself. It makes my life easier.

Which returns me to my life philosophy and study of character. As anyone knows who's stopped to think about it, character doesn't exist on its own. Things happen to it over time — many things, most of them bad. It's called circumstances, most of which test our mettle and are beyond our control. Over the course of my years as a soldier, a navvy, a cobbler, and a seasonal labourer, I have heard countless life stories that have been — through their retelling — refined over time, down to their most enticing details. Edinburgh is a town filled with such stories, both speakable and unspeakable, told by so many characters arriving from God knows where, individuals containing a vast world of desire and dreams, marked by character-altering experiences. On any given evening, you can be entertained — in the pubs, in the streets, in the markets — by people recounting such tales until the wee hours of the morning, stories I have painstakingly drawn out from each of my shots. Last suppers and drinking sprees always go best with a funny, touching, or enthralling tale, especially when they derive from life experience. Like nothing else, stories offer release.

While I am fast filling the pages of this bloody notebook, Mr. M—, there are thousands of other life stories that remain untold. Can you imagine how the last tales of the shots would sell? If I had another life to live — if only — just think of the money to be made.

We begin as children who think life holds fantastic possibilities. It's a sad and sorry shame that our story changes as the world grinds us down. How many are laid low, brought to their knees by the harsh realisation that they are no longer who they once thought they were or could be? Just look at what I've done that I once swore never to do. I have become, over time, a very different character.

What stories did I hold out for myself all those many years ago, before I left Ireland? What stories did Nelly hold dear before Rab set his filthy, defiling hands on her? Can we conceive of a world where more people had the opportunity to tell — and to realise — their dreams and stories, and others cared to listen and help them achieve their dreams?

I can tell you one thing for certain — had I received a hand up and more support to pursue my education, you'd be reading a very different story right now.

***

And someone who should have written all of her stories down was Mrs. Hostler. I'm almost sorry that she came to do the wash that day because otherwise she would still be alive and sharing those stories. Her tales were usually melancholic and made you rethink your life. They were her stories, told from the heart and born of a hard life with many losses. What she spoke of that last day as she prepared the lye and ash in the metal tub to wash our soiled laundry were some of her most painful stories, ones I'd not heard before. One, in particular, stood out.

As Mrs. Hostler spoke, she squeezed, scrubbed, and batted the wash. Then followed the rinsing, wringing, and hanging, a process that reminded me of my mother doing the laundry back home when she would sing old folk songs. Connie and I used to play at her feet and listen as she worked.

Mrs. Hostler was a similar storyteller, only this time was different because her tale was personal. It even ranged — like the stories by yours truly — into the philosophical, although I know she wouldn't know what that meant. She recounted a painful story that day about the loss of her two wee boys — Alec and Richard. How it happened, she never did find out, but her husband was supposed to be watching them that morning after she'd gone off to work. By the time he realised they were missing and was frantically searching for them down the road, they'd been discovered by neighbours in the canal floating face down and lifeless in their wee tartan jackets. Desperate attempts were made to revive them, but to no avail. They were buried beside each other the next day in the matching wooden boxes they once used as beds.

'I knew they'd not be needing their blankets anymore. No one else could use them now. That would be bad luck. So, they served as their winding sheets. I was always fearful of the water. I'd told Jack I didn't like living so close, and here was the result of it. People should pay more attention to other people's forebodings. But Jack never did pay me much heed when it mattered most.'

A few moments later after wiping away tears, she added, 'But I know Jack paid a heavy price too. He isn't the same man now. Something in him died that day along with those two laddies. He says nary a word now about what happened. I think the guilt ate him up afterwards. I know I've been drowning in grief ever since.'

As was the way with her stories, she tried to close on a positive, final note. 'At least we still have John, our eldest.'

She then recounted how she'd suffered several miscarriages before and after John, fervently praying to God to safely deliver her twins. Her prayers were answered then, and thereafter, as God also brought them through several bouts of illness. Until their deaths, she had called them her miracle babies, believing they could survive anything because they had lived through what other children had not. There was even something miraculous in their deaths that day, she said, for when they were pulled limp and bloated from the water, they were still holding hands. While she took some comfort knowing they went into the hereafter together, Mrs. Hostler hadn't been the same since. She had struggled most days and wished she had died along with them.

'I can't comprehend God's ways,' she said. 'Why someone like my father, who was a brutal man, was allowed to live into old age, while my mother was robbed of life in her thirties. It never made much sense to me. I know it's not right to question the ways of the Lord. We must simply trust to His plan. I knew it wasn't right to wish myself dead either, but that's the sad truth about how I felt after being robbed of my children,' she said, looking over at me as I sat listening quietly. 'I lived for them. I was put here to look after them.'

She wiped away more tears as she spoke.

'I'd never say that in front of John and Jack. I know I have the two of them to live for as well. Although we never speak of it, I think Jack feels the same way — that he'd be better off dead.'

And then a philosophising Mrs. Hostler completed her thoughts, 'I sometimes wonder why God didn't take me instead. I've wrestled with that question ever since and suffered untold sorrows thinking through what happened. A big part of me died that day anyway, and I've been dying slowly ever since. I think we, each of us, die little by little each day in this lifetime. We are all taking baby steps towards the grave. We can be said, each of us, to die more than one death. Some of us are lucky to have anything left to bury. There may be a body there, Billy, but, for those of us who have suffered greatly and have lived a long life, there is little else. And what's a body without a spirit after all? It's not much of anything.'

Moving on to the final rinsing and wringing, Mrs. Hostler concluded her story:

'Some days the only thing that keeps me going is knowing that one day I will see them again. My husband doesn't believe in God or the next world, but I do. I have to hold on to that promise as there's precious little left in this life to hold on to.'

'And some folk might call me superstitious, but my boys have sent me many a sign — I kept finding ha'pennies in the oddest places for months after they'd died, and I can't count how many children I have met named Alec and Richard. I know they haven't forgotten me. Children never forget their mothers. I have seen them in dreams sometimes and held them both again. Those powerful dreams have brought tears of astonishment and joy to my eyes. In the most vivid image, I see them, as clearly as I'm seeing you, standing in their wee plaid jackets on the other side of that river, their arms held out towards me, calling for their Mama. One day — after John is all grown up, God willing — I will cross over and embrace them on the other side.'

Listening intently, I was willing, as was God, to answer Mrs. Hostler's prayers. After thanking her for sharing her painful story, I told her I needed to step out and would soon return to pay her. I had to go and get Hare. I knew exactly what had to be done. The signs were clear, and we'd need some strong drink for a good send-off. Young John was gone until the next day, and I knew Nelly wouldn't return until later that evening with the baby, well after supper.

I knew I'd be wanting a change of clothes afterwards, so I was glad Mrs. Hostler had just done the wash.

With God's blessing, it was time to send her home to her children.

19.

Nelly

My walks soon came to an end because Billy put a stop to them. I was staying out longer and later. He was worried I might leave, never to return. I had certainly thought about it, but the truth was I still felt vulnerable and was waiting for Ann. Until that happy, anticipated moment, I was trying to gain strength and regain my sense. I needed to clear my head, continue to put one foot in front of the other, and make a detailed and decisive plan. There were now two of us involved — me and Maeve. I knew the plan had to be foolproof. It had to be Billy-proof.

But I made a fatal error. I was tired and careless in what I said to him one afternoon, which always got me in trouble. It showed me how much I was still under his control, how much I quickly reacted when he acted, something I always tried to resist; something I was now, more than ever, made to regret.

What came up was sex, the fact that I wouldn't lie with him because I was too busy feeding and bonding with the baby. I first wondered at the comment. Over the whole of the past year Billy hadn't been the lusty Billy of bygone days. He had often rejected my advances. I said nothing about that as I knew he was sensitive. It was a miracle I was pregnant. But when he provoked me about sex again, verbally prodding me until I reacted, I told him to go and have sex with another dead woman, *just like you'd done with Peggy*.

At first, I could tell he was shocked that I knew anything about what happened. Then, I could see he was disturbed by what I'd said. He went on the defensive, insisting she was alive during the encounter and *where*, he demanded, *was I when I should have been fast asleep? Did I like what I saw?*

I told Billy I had watched from the doorway and I assured him Peggy was dead. Thanks to him and the horrible episode with Maggie, I insisted, I now knew a dead woman when I saw one.

His response was both shocking and laughable. 'She was really drunk,' he said. 'It was hard to tell from where you were standing.' Then he added as an afterthought, 'That just goes to show, Nelly, how you are, true to form, jealous and full of hate. You've always had some very sick ideas in that head of yours.'

I could see, after his numerous denials, that he actually believed what he said, and so I let him believe it. As for my sick ideas, I had no clue what he was talking about. And, I knew, neither did he. This was proof he'd entirely lost touch with me and little did he realise how this was helping me disengage from him.

'What I can tell you,' he said further, aiming to silence and hurt me, 'is that she was a far better partner than you've ever been. I thought of you every minute and what you haven't given me in some time. Peggy was a damn good substitute, dead or alive.'

As challenging as it was, I bit my tongue and cowered back, retreating to my room with Maeve. I felt sick as Billy denied his grotesque violation of a dead woman while ensuring that he humiliated me.

I knew what I saw, and what I had long known was once again confirmed: Billy was a morally depraved man.

***

Finally, in answer to my prayers, and when I least expected it, Ann arrived, but it didn't happen as I had expected. Just as I left to walk home one night, Alice handed me the note with the three words I had instructed Ann to write — *I am here.* I was thrilled yet terrified as I held that small scrap of paper, my heart racing the entire walk home. While I felt I was on the cusp of escape, I knew Billy could be ruthless if thwarted and duped. He would make me pay if he figured things out.

Sadly, I realised straightaway that my plan wasn't as foolproof as I'd hoped as I'd failed to provide Ann with clear instructions about what to do next. Over the whole of the next day, I made my way through the Grassmarket with Maeve strapped to me, trying to be as inconspicuous as possible as I looked for a nearby tramp hotel. I knew how these could spring up at times when people with an extra room needed a bit of money. There were dozens scattered across the area.

As my bad luck would have it, Billy came in that night with Ann in tow. Apparently, in desperation, she had gone to Hare's inquiring about where I was living, and Hare had contacted Billy to send her in my direction. It was a confounded mess, all of my own doing, and now I feared the worst.

I decided, after my initial surprise and some thought, to remain calm and pretend she had come into Edinburgh to visit with me and help with the baby.

She seemed more peaceful than I remembered her, older, but the way she smiled when she first saw me returned me to our younger days.

'Ann,' I said, overjoyed to see her and thankful to have her nearby, 'I can't believe it's you. It's been so long but it feels like yesterday.' I don't know that I actually said these last words, but they went through my mind as I hugged her, the tears rolling down my face as we sat down together. I brought the baby in just as Billy went to get food and drink. Once he was out of hearing, I told Ann how worried I was in Billy's presence and that he had yet to acknowledge Maeve. As she fawned over the baby, she told me how difficult it was for some men to become fathers. Perhaps I just needed to give him some time.

I could see she wasn't understanding the severity of my situation and the extent of Billy's sickness and depravity. How could she? My situation felt impossible to explain. As time was of the essence, I decided to speak more openly.

'He's truly dangerous, Ann,' I said. 'You must believe me. He is violent and threatening. It's not like you think. You don't know what he is capable of. For a long time, I didn't either. Don't be fooled,' I said. 'He can be very charming but trust me when I tell you, he has done many horrible, unforgivable things.'

Ann looked unsettled as she digested the severity of my words. Her voice took on a more serious tone, which suggested she was beginning to understand.

'No need to worry. We'll make a plan to get you and the baby out of here. You'll have to figure out how you'll feed yourselves, but we can answer that question when the time comes.'

I struggled to hold back tears as I contemplated the prospect of my escape with Maeve into freedom. I hadn't recognised my intense need for friendship until Ann's arrival and this conversation. 'I've missed you so much,' I told her, struggling to hold back tears.

After she told me about her children, who were now young men, I asked the question I most wanted to ask. 'How is our grandfather? Is he still alive? It took all of my strength me to leave him, especially so suddenly, but I had no choice.'

Ann looked past me at the wall after I'd said this, and swallowed hard a few times, the tears welling up in her eyes, as she said, 'Nelly, I'm sorry to be the one to tell you, but he died about five years ago and it wasn't a good death. It was slow and drawn out, like most deaths from the cancer. What I can tell you is that every time I visited him, and especially the last time, he spoke about you and how much he loved and missed you and wanted to see you again.'

And as she told me he called me *his special one, his sweet wee Nelly*, Billy returned with the food and whisky. Although I suspected he'd died, it was painful to hear that he'd suffered at the end. If anyone deserved a peaceful departure it was my grandfather. An overwhelming sense of life's unfairness rose up in me, along with so many other painful emotions and memories. What I wouldn't have given to have helped him in his final months and days. But it was too late now for regrets and there was no time for grief. Maeve and I were in danger. I had to focus on the here and now, and my plan with Ann.

After I fed and changed the baby and put her down to sleep, all three of us ate and drank in uncomfortable silence. True to form, Billy got a conversation going about men from around Maddiston who had worked on the Union Canal. He shared some of the best stories he'd heard over the years from them, and some of the best jokes. A few glasses in, just as I was wondering what was putting him in such a happy, storytelling mood, I realised something was afoot. Billy had his own dark plan and was outsmarting me. I should have warned Ann not to drink too much. But it was too late. Despite what I told her, she'd let her guard down. Perhaps she was trying to gain his trust. I don't know, but I didn't trust Billy for a minute. So, when it came time for Ann to return to her bed that night and Billy said she could stay with us, I urged her to sober up a bit before making her way back. As we said goodnight, we made arrangements for her to return the next day.

I knew one thing for certain now: walking through

the West Port at night was far less dangerous than staying with Billy. There were many others who wished they would have known better.

***

After Ann and I had spent time during the day with the baby, the next night seemed a repeat of the previous, with the exception that Ann seemed to be getting drunk faster. Billy had kept a watchful eye on us that day and I had advised Ann to go along with Billy's need for a couple of drinks before his usual departure for the pub. But he never left. Given Ann's noticeably slurred speech, I suspected Billy was secretly feeding her laudanum.

At that point, a couple of hours in, I told Billy that Ann didn't want anything more to drink. This proved to be a bad move as the conversation suddenly shifted its tone. Billy grew provocative and rude, referencing the time I showed up at Ann's house needing help and she directed me to Jeannie's.

'Billy', I interrupted, visibly upset, 'that was a story told to you in private. Leave it alone. Ann was a married woman then with her own responsibilities and two wee weans. She had no way to help me. I understand that better now.'

But Ann had been upset by the comment and told me, through slurred speech, how much she regretted what had happened that day. Although I had increasing difficulty understanding her, she told me that she now lived apart from her husband and that it had been a long time coming.

As I soothed her, I shot Billy an angry look. I told Ann never to think or speak of it again. 'I'd managed perfectly fine,' I told her, 'because you sent me to Jeannie. You actually saved me that day,' I assured her. 'It was a blessing finding Jeannie. I can see God's

254

hand was in it.'

I then shifted the track of our conversation to reminiscing about our childhoods but it was clear that Ann was totally drunk. Within the next half-hour, she was fast asleep on the floor from where I could neither rouse nor move her.

'Billy,' I said desperately, 'I know what your plan is. Please, I'm begging you, don't hurt her. She doesn't deserve any violence.'

'Well then,' he answered, laughing, 'you should have thought of that sooner — before you invited her here. Do you think I didn't figure things out? You're a stupid fool, Nelly. Now, you'll both have to pay.'

'Or maybe all three of you,' he added, knowing that would unsettle me further.

As he began dragging Ann, who was groaning, into the bedroom, I kept begging him, my voice growing hoarse, 'Please let her alone, Billy. Let her leave here alive. I'll do anything.'

But Billy remained stony-faced and silent. Upon his return from the bedroom, his demeanour had changed and he said to me, with a smile, 'Thanks for luring this one in, Nelly. It's about time you earned your keep. It took you long enough. We might be able to do it alone together after all.'

He then gestured for me to follow him into the bedroom. 'The hard work hasn't been done yet though, he said, and it's your job to do it. And if you don't, Nelly, I'll do it alone and then I'll take care of Maeve afterwards. If I were you,' he added, 'I would want this one dead.'

'This one?' I repeated, horrified. 'This one is one of the only ones who ever truly loved me, along with my grandfather and Jeannie. I trusted you with my story, Billy. This one is very special. Please, leave her be, Billy. I'll do anything.'

I realised these were dangerous words to say

to him, but he responded as if he were operating a business, saying we needed the money, that he would direct me, and that it wouldn't take long. Otherwise, he reminded me, menacingly, Maeve will have to go too. 'And I know you don't want to take that route, Nelly.'

Minutes later, I was shaking uncontrollably as I was made to lie down beside Ann on the bed. I remember being barely able to breathe, feeling faint, as I repeatedly begged Billy, between sobs, not to do *this terrible thing*.

But he ignored me, and then left the room briefly, returning with a newly opened bottle of whisky. He held it out and told me to take a few swigs. 'That's usually all that's needed,' he said, 'when I can't face the work. That, and not thinking about who's behind the face. I'm the one who has to look at them, Nelly. Mine is the hardest bit of business. Over time, I've trained myself up for it. I imagine the good doctor faces a similar challenge with dissection. The greatest difficulty lies in erasing the face.'

'And when it gets really bad, I have to keep reminding myself that God has helped me do the choosing, and I'm doing the shots a favour.'

If ever Billy's words shocked and unsettled me, this was the time. What man was this who spoke of God in relation to the act of murder? How, if God were involved, could Billy justify treating people like animals to the slaughter? The devil's in this, I thought to myself.

And then, not able to hold myself back anymore, I challenged him and blurted out —

'What type of God are you serving, Billy? What happened to "Thou shalt not kill"? You've truly lost your mind,' I added, at which point he reached across the bed and slapped me hard across the face, as if he were trying to recall me to myself.

He then said something inaudible about *his calling*. And then he became angry. 'I'm not answerable to you,' he snapped. 'And we haven't got all night. Take those few swigs and let's get on with it, Nelly.'

He proceeded to position himself at the top of the bed again, and barked a command at me, 'Roll over on top of her, Nelly. And if you can't manage that, just hold her legs down and I'll do the rest,' he said.

Sensing Billy's impatience and anger were fast ramping up, I trembled at his threats against Maeve and followed his orders. I rolled over on top of Ann and, as she groaned and struggled for release, I placed my arms around her, hugging her close. I wept softly into her gown. Laying there, I remembered being in the bed with my dead mother and our last goodbyes.

At that point, I broke down.

'I can't, Billy,' I sobbed. 'Have mercy and ask God's forgiveness. You are torturing me.'

'Just hold her bloody legs,' he fired back, ignoring my pleas. 'It'll be over soon.'

As he began the operation, Billy's next words stunned me.

'You're my assistant now, Nelly,' he said, with pride, 'an assistant to the great, good Dr. Burke.'

Stunned by these words and trembling, I whispered the Hail Mary as I lay there. I remember the horror and the accompanying sensations that followed. I could sense, physically and spiritually, when it was all over. I felt Ann's body convulsing beneath mine as we lay there, my heart pressed up against hers, before she lay still. Refusing to look up at Billy, I wept aloud, as I recalled my fond memories of girlhood and my great love for my beautiful cousin.

A few minutes later, as I lay shaking and sobbing beside Ann's dead body, Billy said, 'They can't be delivered with clothes on. I'll take care of that later. You won't need to touch her.'

He spoke as if he were doing me a favour and sparing me the worst part. But I knew that the worst part was yet to come — when I realised Ann could never be recovered, that her loss was final.

Later that night, as I lay in bed numb, rocking Maeve to sleep, I wondered if Billy was trying to push me over the edge. I also wondered if he was trying to get caught. The choice of Ann would certainly call attention to us. Others must have known she had come to visit me. Surely Billy, *the great, good Dr. Burke*, had thought of this liability.

In the hours that followed, I lay sleepless, tormented by how much I loathed and despised Billy, how much I wanted him dead. I also realised how much I feared him. He not only posed an incredible danger to me, but to Maeve, his own daughter.

I asked myself, *How had I ever loved such a man, such a monster?*

And just before I drifted off to sleep, I wondered what he might be doing to Ann's naked body.

20.

Billy

On so many occasions, I could have throttled Margaret Hare — Maggie, the old witch, the harridan — for so many good reasons, but especially for her risky, opportunistic choices of the wrong victims. After the torments I went through over killing the old Glasgow grandmother and her grandson — a mere innocent child — Margaret made her worst move in luring Daft Jamie Wilson to the tramp house. As soon as I saw him, my heart sank, a voice in my head cursing Margaret once again. We should have done the decent thing and let him go. I tried to reason with her, but common decency is a feeling unknown to Margaret, words that should never come out of her filthy, stinking mouth.

Jamie was just a young lad, a harmless, snuff-loving simpleton who lived for a good joke and through the great good charity of his sister, her husband, and the people of Edinburgh who gave him small change and snuff. I knew him well, as did Nelly. To kill him was the height of cruelty and indecency. Perhaps most disturbing of all, to kill him was a tremendous risk. A familiar figure on the High Street, he was an easy, unsuspecting target for Margaret that early October morning as he stood outdoors waiting for his mother. Margaret promised him a warm fire, a late breakfast, some whisky and his beloved snuff, assuring him that his mother would soon join them. Jamie, trusting and shoeless as usual, walked alongside Margaret, his slouch and gait recognisable to all regular Edinburgh folk, as they made their way down the West Bow into the Grassmarket.

While Hare distracted him with food, snuff, and some fireside chatter after his arrival, Margaret sought me out at Rymer's to tell me whisky was wanted as Hare had a shot detained in the house. Jamie grew increasingly uneasy in the hours that followed, refusing to drink, anxiously pacing around the room, and asking after his mother. When might she arrive? Did she know where Margaret lived? Anxiety soon turned to aggression when he found he couldn't leave. At one point, worried something must have happened to his mother and that she might be in need of his assistance, he pinned Hare up against the wall and tried to escape. To keep him from making any further commotion, we had no choice but to make a shot of him quickly and prepare the body. It took every bit of strength we had to secure and suffocate him, Daft Jamie being the only shot who required additional violence — in this case, a blow to the head — to put down. I worried thereafter about his head injury being detected and being charged with murder.

I have never been able to forget the details of that long and harrowing day. I must resist reliving them. What I can say is that, without consuming the noteworthy amount of drink usually imbibed by our other victims, Jamie proved especially difficult to manage. Daft as some thought him to be, I believe he had a sixth sense and knew, at one point — far too late to save himself — exactly what was afoot. He fought with every fibre of his being to escape us, not so he could survive, I believe, but to see his beloved mother again and alleviate her worry. It destroyed me to discover after our arrest that she had wandered the Edinburgh streets in quest of him for months afterwards.

And I will let you in on a sad truth, Mr. M—, one

unknown to a single other living soul, including Hare. The very last word on that child's lips was 'Mother' — not 'stop' or 'have mercy', but 'Mother'.

It disturbs me to relate this now, and to tell you that I had no further visitations from the spirit of my own mother after that day. She had told me to attend to the signs, assuring me that God's signs were recognisable to the chosen. There were no such signs in Daft Jamie's case. I violated my calling, then and there, and have damned Margaret Hare to hell ever since.

The Good Lord surely made his signs clear thereafter as we were arrested just a few short weeks later.

I have often thought back to how my repeated requests to Margaret to let us release Jamie fell, as I knew they would, on deaf ears. She feared our exposure after he'd been in the tramp hotel for such a length of time. She insisted that he had to be killed. But we had a ready excuse to let him go — his mother had not yet arrived and must have gotten lost. We may have faced questions from Jamie's mother afterwards, but Margaret, who never faced the horrible labour, was greedy for the money.

Who, I might ask, could target the disabled with no remorse, Mr. M—?

Margaret Hare.

And I have another, related, question. Who, in response to concerned comments from his closest assistants that Jamie's body was publicly recognisable, could simply place the laddie on his belly, turn his face away from onlooking students, and perform the surgical anatomy of his spine? Who could have brutally cut off Jamie's deformed feet in order to conceal his identity in advance of that barbaric exhibition?

Who then do you think should follow me to the gallows given the wealth of evidence that the bodies delivered to him were fresh, some in the prime of health, making their purchaser an accessory to multiple murders?

Dr. Robert Knox.

You and I both know, Mr. M—, that up and down this country there are many more guilty parties besides.

As it stands, I will go by myself to the gallows, a fate I well deserved for Jamie's death alone.

I will swing by myself, Mr. M—, unaccompanied by Hare or Margaret or the good doctor and his keen assistants. With Daft Jamie's special snuff box tucked away in my trouser pocket, I will swing alone.

21.

Nelly

A few days after Ann's death, I awoke early, in the wee hours. It took me time to get my bearings but as I did and remembered what had happened, I faced another nightmare, this one the worst revelation of my life — my baby was gone!

Where I had fallen asleep cradling Maeve's small swaddled body against mine, I now awoke groggy and in a state of shock, alone in an empty bed, the world a stark, dark dream.

I reacted immediately, as any mother would, feeling so horribly dizzy that when I tried to get out of bed, I fell onto the floor. My balance regained, I began — desperately — tearing around the apartment looking for her. I choked as I repeatedly called her name and scrambled through the rooms out into the passage, and then back again. My whole world fell away as I traced and retraced my steps before collapsing in tears. When I managed finally to stand, I returned to our bed, hunting desperately through the straw for any vestige of her swaddling clothes. And yet nothing — not a single trace of her — was to be found. And neither Billy nor John were anywhere to be seen. I vaguely recalled John being sent away, so perhaps, I thought, Billy took Maeve outside for some air? But a sick gnawing feeling in my stomach and a worried voice in my head told me otherwise.

Still suffering the effects of the drink, my head throbbed terribly while my heart raced wildly in my chest. I tried to focus my mind and memory on the last few days, but found myself barely able to recall the night before. What I did remember came in disjointed fragments: there had been several days of endless drinking as I grieved over Ann and railed against myself and my sick monster of a partner, Billy stopping in only to replenish the drink. I had consistently refused food.

I vaguely remembered a nasty argument where I threatened him with the police. He laughed as he told me I'd only be implicating myself. I recalled Billy pushing me into the wall at one point, manhandling me just as he used to before Maeve's arrival. It had been some months since he'd done anything like that and I was in shock that he could do so now, after I'd had a baby — *his* baby — and was still recovering, and breastfeeding. How could he hit me after tending to our needs over those many weeks? At least he hadn't hit her. But then, my mind returned to the horrifying present — *where was she now?*

I knew in the throes of my grief over Ann that I shouldn't have drank any liquor, but there was nothing else for it. I was devastated and distraught over her loss and the fact that I'd been forced to have a hand in it. She wouldn't have come into Edinburgh had it not been for my letter. I knew that was how Billy prepared his victims — with drink. How could I have run such a risk?

In the face of her devastating loss, I had turned to the bottle, as was my way, *our* way. Especially for Maeve's sake, I knew I shouldn't have touched a drop. And I had drank a lot, far more than any nursing mother should.

But some things still didn't add up, like how I had managed to sleep for so long. Had he slipped me some laudanum too? I certainly felt extremely unsteady, the dizziness unnatural. Perhaps I was so badly drugged I wouldn't have felt any disturbance that morning.

Something had happened. Babies don't just vanish.

As I strove to piece together the facts of Maeve's disappearance, two words relentlessly thrust themselves to the forefront of my mind despite my attempts to push them away — *the doctor*.

***

Some hours later, when Billy returned, he was surprised to find me awake. He didn't seem himself. He was unusually quiet, and when I begged him to tell me about Maeve — where she was and what had happened — he looked at me surprised and said, 'You don't remember?'

'No,' I answered, rattled by the question, confused by his bewildered response.

Desperate, and with my voice breaking, I begged him, 'Stop playing games with me Billy. That child is my life. You need to tell me what happened.'

But Billy looked past me, blankly. 'You really can't recall?'

At which point, he told me this story:

'You were upset about Ann and started raging at me,' he said. 'You threatened to contact a constable. And then you disappeared into the room with the baby. You gave no sign you were going to do anything, especially not to her. And I would have sworn you could never do something like that. Never. But when I looked in on you some hours later, there she lay, unmoving, like a stillborn.'

His words stunned me, and I fell to my knees at his feet, weeping and repeatedly screaming 'no'. For a time, I kept saying that word aloud, over and over. What Billy told me did not make sense. I knew it was a lie.

'That could never happen, Billy. Never. You know me and what I am capable of.'

Feeling as if I had to convince him of my innocence, anger and confusion jointly took hold of me. Still kneeling on the floor before him, I grasped Billy's hands, trying to connect with something human in him. I pleaded with him to reveal Maeve's whereabouts, calling him a liar and demanding he tell me the truth.

But Billy was adamant and stuck to his story. 'How can you not remember anything, Nelly? We even agreed that I would get up early and go bury her. We couldn't take a dead baby into police.'

I was still trying to process everything Billy was saying, when he added, 'You've been so withdrawn lately, Nelly, so unpredictable. I no longer knew what you were capable of.'

And then he calmly suggested, as if throwing me a lifeline, 'Perhaps you suffocated her without intending to. It can happen. Babies die every day by accident here in Edinburgh, Nelly. You were dead drunk. You could have fallen asleep and rolled over on top of her. Accidents happen.'

As he spoke, I had an image of Maeve lying dead in my arms, her head and body limp. Confused and disturbed by that vision, I tried to jog my memory again. But it was all to no avail. I couldn't remember what had happened, how she ended up that way. I just had a vague remembrance that something horrible had happened.

Billy interrupted my panicked thoughts, saying, 'We agreed I would get up early and go bury her. I did as I'd promised. I got up when it was still dark and laid her to rest up near Arthur's Seat — at that secluded spot where we used to stop and sit and look out over Edinburgh.'

Upset and unsettled, I kept shaking my head. Finally, I said, 'You know me, Billy. I never would have agreed to that. If anything would have happened to her and she had died, I would need to prepare her body and say my own private goodbyes. You know I would have insisted on that.'

'But there was no time for such preparations and you were wildly drunk,' he said, 'and we'd agreed not to bring a dead baby into police as it would raise suspicion.'

I knew Billy's words were a lie and my mind turned once again to the question of what had actually happened. Had he suffocated her, just as he had done with the others? I dreaded to think. Was I not able to save my own daughter? My mind was in such a state of confusion.

'Do you mean I slept with Maeve lying dead beside me, Billy, over a whole night?'

And then I added, 'And now you're telling me she lies buried up near Arthur's Seat? I don't believe that either. Not when there was money to be made from her, Billy. I know you too well. She's with that doctor! Don't keep lying to me.'

As I scrambled to get dressed to go outside, I demanded, 'Who is this doctor and where can I find him?'

'I need Maeve returned to me, Billy. Today. Even if all I have is her dead body. Give me her dead body. I'm begging you. I need her back in my arms, even if she's no longer alive.'

I choked on sobs as I uttered these last statements, just the mention of my baby's dead body sickening me.

As I grew more agitated and desperate and thought through Billy's story, I pleaded with him again.

'She needs me, Billy. I'm begging you to take me to her.'

But he just spoke to me condescendingly, 'Try not to fall apart again, Nelly. What has happened is all for the best. She's in God's hands now. Have a shot of whisky and some laudanum and try to calm down.'

267

Scoffing and angry at his words, I pushed him away. 'Who are you to talk of God? He should strike you down dead the next time you do so. I pray He does.'

And, despite my fear of him, I had more to say.

'And you know I'm not crazy, Billy. If anyone is mad, it's you. Over these last many months, while I was carrying a child you claimed wasn't yours, you tried to drive me to madness. You seemed to delight in it. I'm going out to find this doctor, even if it's the last thing I do.'

And although I could see that my words had registered with him and he looked concerned, Billy was true to form. He remained calm and fierce in his response, 'Margaret was right. We should have done you in a long time ago. I'm sorry we didn't do it when we had the chance.'

As I threw on my shawl and prepared to exit, Billy laid me low with these words:

'If you dare go to the doctor, Nelly, he said, menacingly, I promise, you will end up on the same slab.'

And in that final threatening statement, I read Billy's admission of guilt and retreated into my room.

***

Many days of sleeping endless hours followed, during which I clutched Maeve's other set of swaddling clothes, and drank bottomless glasses of beer, gin, and whisky laced with laudanum. I vomited profusely from time to time. I wept until my body ached and my heart was numb.

And then, after several helpless, hopeless weeks, we moved again.

For reasons of guilt or the purposes of concealment, or both, the sack of assorted shoes and boots that

268

should have been hawked on Candlemaker Row, accompanied us.

As I couldn't possibly remain where Ann and Maeve breathed their last, I was the one who insisted on that move, although we remained in the West Port. It was a much smaller space, a single room with a fire and two large straw-beds but, most importantly for me, it contained no disturbing memories. I became a ghost of myself over those weeks, self-murder never being far from my mind. Every waking minute was a torture, Maeve's name being forever on my lips. I was lifeless without her, tormented by memories I continually replayed of our time together. My body ached with the absence of her, my breastmilk still being released and soaking my clothes despite using rags to absorb it. I was incomplete, forever changed, as was the world around me, now emptied of love.

As the days passed, my hatred and anger towards Billy grew, he who had taken everything from me. In the face of Maeve's death, he was entirely unfazed and I prayed, with a venom I'd never before known, that Maeve would be vindicated and haunt him to his grave.

How do you repay a person who has robbed you of your very self and divested you of your most precious thing? You do what I did. I, Nelly McDougal. You repay them in full measure and in good time. I painstakingly prepared to show William Burke that he had misjudged me as weak and forgiving. I had nothing else to lose, so I bided my time. Although I know Billy would baulk at the comparison because I was a woman — and a *fallen* woman, as he was always so very quick to remind me — I had the patience of Job.

22.

Nelly

Looking back, it is fitting that everything came undone on Hallowe'en. Some have said there were supernatural forces at work, that it was fated to occur following the night when the boundary between the worlds of the living and the dead is crossed. Could it be that the ghosts of Billy's victims returned to thwart him at that time when the ghosts of the dead return to walk the earth, appearing among the living? Could it be that Maeve was at the helm? Certainly, had the discovery of their crimes happened in an earlier age, it would have been said, given my hand in the matter, that I was a witch.

Let them say what they will. I will revel in it.

The men began drinking early in the day, immediately after the arrival of Margery Docherty, an elderly Irish beggar-woman, also known by her married name of Campbell. Earlier that day, Billy had played one of his usual tricks and lured what was to be his last victim, this vulnerable old woman, in from a nearby shop where she was begging. He did so — as he had done with others before — under the pretence of their being long-lost relatives, his mother's maiden name, he said, being Docherty. There was only one difficulty — another couple, James and Ann Gray — had slept the previous few nights in the room's other straw bed, their infant daughter accompanying them. Ann, a woman I had met in Falkirk, had sought me out for assistance in the form of a short stay. Complaining privately that the Grays hadn't paid for their keep,

Billy sent them to Hare's to make room for his new-found relation. In contrast to Ann and James, the unsuspecting Margery would pay her way.

Margaret and I were cleaning the room in preparation for a Hallowe'en party, one I suspected would actually be Margery's wake, although I had other plans. The dancing and singing started soon after and the party went on for hours, with the Grays briefly returning mid-evening to retrieve some of their forgotten belongings. Billy treated them rudely, failing to invite them in for the party, violating traditional Irish custom. While Margery and Margaret Hare continued the celebration, I took the opportunity to walk with the Grays back to Hare's where I obtained several two-penny candles and informed the couple that I was glad they and their baby daughter had departed as I'd seen some suspicious things recently at the house. Refusing to go into detail but certain I'd raised some concern, I returned alone to the room in time to hear old Margery, thinking an altercation between Billy and the Mute was about to erupt in violence, shout *Murder*. But the violent end was Margery's as Billy and the Mute suddenly gave up their fight and turned on her, shouting loudly all the while in order to drown out the sounds of the old woman's dying.

And so, the unravelling began when Billy — fool that he was — brought the Grays over to breakfast the next morning and Ann inquired about the curious absence of old Margery. When no one responded, I attempted a cover-up, telling Ann that Margery had been put out after showing herself too fresh with Billy. When Ann approached the bed seeking some stockings she'd left behind, Billy snapped, telling her to get away while he began, suspiciously, to sprinkle the remainder of a bottle of whisky around the bed in order, as he said, *to freshen the air*.

Some hours later, when Billy and Hare were away

at the doctor's making arrangements to transport Margery's body, Ann and her husband secretly returned to the room. When I encouraged her to search the bed for the stockings, Ann first spied blood on the pillow slip, a very concerning discovery. The blood was actually my own as a drunken, angry Billy had hit me hard in the face the night before. I reminded Ann that she and her husband had witnessed the assault. Ann had later commiserated with me about it on our walk over to the tramp hotel, letting me know, privately, that she was sickened and disturbed by what she'd seen.

'I hope you're alright, Nelly. I didn't expect that of Billy, who is usually so charming. While I've seen you two argue, I didn't know he could erupt into violence like that. I don't know why you stay with him, Nelly. But that's none of my business.'

As I set the pillow slip aside to be washed, Ann, still on the hunt for her stockings, reached deep into the straw and drew out, much to her complete shock and surprise, Margery's right arm. Her voluble shriek was followed by further alarm and commotion as her husband pushed more straw away and raised, by the hair this time, an entirely naked Margery, now divested of her dark printed gown and red-striped bedgown. Examining the blood around her neck and mouth, he asked Ann if the woman who lay concealed there was in fact the old woman Burke had brought home the morning before.

Ann's wild nods confirmed it, after which, visibly shaken and breathless, she implied my involvement and demanded to know what we had done.

'My God, I cannot help it,' I said, trembling and in tears, to which Ann responded, 'You surely can help it or you would not have stayed in the house.'

This moral pronouncement stunned me into silence. How could I possibly begin to recount my side of the story — my harrowing tale of torment with Billy and his catalogue of abuses, my own beautiful child a victim of her own father?

I managed to say, feebly, 'But I have tried to help it, despite his violence. I was the one who allowed you entry and urged you to search the bed.'

No sooner had I said these words to Ann, who looked at me in sympathy, than Margaret suddenly appeared in the doorway. My situation was now precarious. Having heard the commotion, Margaret demanded to know what was going on. She approached the bed and shot me an accusatory glance, suggesting I had led them there. I knew now there was no stopping what I had painstakingly set in motion. As Margaret pushed Margery's body down deep into the straw, I tried to bribe the Grays into silence, promising them money well into the future. My offer had the desired effect as Ann exclaimed, 'God forbid that I would be worth money at the expense of dead people.'

Alarmed by the situation and the prospect of police, Margaret said she needed something at Rymer's before suddenly making an exit. I knew she was flying to tell Billy and Hare about the discovery of the body. The Grays then left for the police station but not before I told them, privately and in exchange for their promise not to reveal the source, 'If the body is gone from here when the police arrive, be sure to check at the doctor's. The police should know what is meant.'

I made the last statement in desperation, as I had many others during our conversation, entirely uncertain that the police would know where the doctor was or what was meant. But I knew once they heard the Grays' story, they would be willing and able to investigate and find out.

23.

Billy

I have replayed the last death, that of Margery Docherty, over and over again, to try and understand what happened that day. I had heard the Grays' testimony in the courtroom, listening intently, but there are parts of their story that have never added up for me. Did Hare tip off the police to check at the doctor's? And if not Hare, then who? It isn't something the Grays would have figured out on their own, although they did seem very suspicious over the time they stayed with us. Why had they come back to the house from Hare's a couple of times, unexpectedly, over the course of that last night and the next day? I can make no sense of it. I can't imagine Nelly had a hand in it. She wouldn't dare. She would never have implicated me or put herself in harm's way. She had everything to lose. It is confounding, Mr. M—, and you've been no help as I've tried to work out this mystery. Perhaps Nelly might have shed some light on the subject that day when, as the sentry told me, she and Constantine came here to Calton Jail to visit me. But I was too busy making my other confession, and they were turned away.

***

As you suggested during our conversation of yesterday evening, Mr. M—, it must be terrifying to be me, a man about to face his maker, a man who has done and seen such indecent and horrible things in his lifetime, a man who, in your eyes, is guilty of vicious and despicable acts. With the exception of your suggestion about how God intends to deal with me, I agreed with you during that conversation, but I have one final confession to make before I ascend to the gallows tomorrow morning at Libberton's Wynd.

This, as I see it, is the place to make it.

There are many things seared into my memory, some good and some bad. In this, I am like all common, decent folk. What I once regarded as horrible — the faces of the suffocated dead — fast became comforting as I recognised that, with their deaths, their suffering was at an end. Suffering, you see, is located on this side of the grave, my dear Mr. M—, the gracious good Lord guiding my hand to take them down easy and send their eager souls heavenward.

I will close my account with a very short story about the worst thing I have ever set my eyes on. This horrible image is forever etched in my memory and I will be thinking about it as I say my last prayer tomorrow preparing for my execution.

Last summer, my Nelly gave birth to a stillborn child. I was away at the time and she was alone as she delivered it, fully intact, with all of its fingers and toes, with the cord wrapped tightly around its precious wee neck. She was indeed a perfect specimen in every way, but I thought then, as I think now, about how fitting her image was of the working poor in Scotland with precious little air to breathe from the cradle to the grave. Nelly was, as you can well imagine, devastated, and I have never forgotten her grief at the loss of Maeve, who was named after Nelly's long-lost mother. Perhaps it was a sign for yours truly, a desperately suffocating man whose neck will soon be fitted with a different cord.

To advance the cause of science, I sold the baby to the doctor. I never revealed this to Nelly, although I know she guessed the truth and could never forgive me. I hope the good Lord will as I can see clearly now that this flesh trade is the most sinful and pernicious aspect of this whole affair. Someone must put a stop to this body business.

She was a beautiful baby, Mr. M—. None could match her. Born into a different class, she would have had the world before her, at her feet. But that was not to be. She was born into poverty.

I know Nelly blames me for her death, for not being there to assist with the birth. But I blame her, a woman guilty of abortion, an act the good Lord, rightly and without exception, condemns.

I hope to meet Maeve on the other side, and perhaps one day, the world on this side of the grave will be the kinder, gentler place that I strove to make it by *wiping away all tears from their eyes*. It is my ardent prayer that, like St. John the Evangelist, the shots I have delivered have each *witnessed a new heaven and a new earth: and the former earth shall not be remembered, nor come into mind.*

24.

Nelly

Today, in the wake of unbearable loss and sadness, I will take my last lonely walk up this Radical Road, carrying Ann's and Margery's single wee box-beds in my apron pocket. These are the last of the coffins I will lay to rest. I have suffered painfully alone and for long enough. It is over — at least, for Billy who was hanged, his skull carved open, his brain removed and examined, his body dissected, and his skeleton prepared and arranged for display. It is said that Doctor Monro dipped his quill pen into blood from Billy's head to chronicle his execution. After thousands filed past his corpse on the very slab where his victims were each dissected in Knox's surgical theatre, Billy's skin was cleaned and treated and used to make a pocketbook — like that of the horses in Tanner's Lane. Edinburgh has since heaved her collective sigh of relief.

Today, I carry my journal, the one containing this story and my final confession. It too will be laid to rest in the coming days deep in a neighbouring crevice I spied during my last walk here. I will undertake that ritual after I place Billy's uncoffined doll on top of those of his sixteen victims. Brutalised by me over many months, it once lay in pieces, anatomised, like the bodies of his victims, just as he was by the mad butcher, Monro. But I have granted him some mercy by binding all of his separate body parts tightly together in cotton gauze, his wee winding-sheet. The final touch sees his shrouded body secured with my luckenbooth brooch. Whether or not God will resurrect him, I leave to God to decide. I confess that this undertaking gave me boundless pleasure — to not piece him back together, to swaddle and smother him the way he smothered me and Maeve and all of the desperate, defenceless others.

It is right and fitting that my story be buried separately. Only my mother's coffined doll and Maeve's doll and wee box bed will remain in my safekeeping.

Undertaking my final funeral march towards Arthur's Seat, I will consider the unfulfilled promise of this sprawling monster of a town, of the tens of thousands who built and maintained it, who paid for it with their very lives. Their stories remain untold, deemed by many not to be worth telling, not to be worth listening to — the Radicals, the navvies, the countless brutalised and degraded women. Their tongues all lie silent now beneath this rocky sod, unlike those desecrated on the dissecting table. Billy, the cobbler-storyteller had a gift for pulling people's stories out of them — their darkest, most shameful, most comic, and most joyful. He recounted many of those tales to me and the attentive and devout pub-goers over the years.

There was a time where he respected and cherished those lives and those life stories. But they are lost now to history, dying with him on the gallows on 28 January at Libberton's Wynd, he who missed his storytelling calling in this lifetime, he who, like me, was short-changed at every turn. He should have been remorseful about short-changing others, but I never saw a hint of it.

There were, and are, so many like us who were robbed of any opportunity and hope. Like my mother. Like my daughter. Like me.

I will sing my coronach as I ascend the Radical

Road, its Gaelic words a mystery to me, keeping pace with my rhythmic step, as has become my ritual as I gaze out across a misty Edinburgh on this early May morning. I will sing for those killed to assist the doctor, alongside the thousands of forgotten, inglorious dead of this country, *the very bastards of creation*, as Billy once told me they were called and degraded by a despicable Englishman. My tears fall for the great waste in this great wasteland, for the tremendous multitudes of human beings treated and discarded like waste, just like Billy treated Maeve and me — with a level of shameful, unspeakable carelessness.

Doesn't the Bible say, *Do unto others as you would be done by?*

Billy would snigger at this idea, I know. He would snigger and then spit. Ever quick and clever with his turns of phrase, he would have retorted, Do unto others as has been done unto you.

He had a lot of nerve, my Billy, right up until his parting breath. He must have had nerve to do everything that he did to me, and to his many other vulnerable victims as he conducted his so-called *body business* heartlessly, just like clockwork.

We were well-matched in one sense, at least: I too have a lot of nerve. I doubt he ever knew that I was behind his arrest. I have smiled privately to myself about that before realising I am now utterly alone, without my Maeve, as I regularly cry myself to sleep. I made my way with Connie one afternoon recently to visit Billy at Calton Hill Jail where I had planned to let him in on my little secret, but they wouldn't let me see him. More's the pity.

No one wishes more than I that Hare would have swung with him, along with that harridan Margaret, and Dr. Knox, but I know they chose the worst criminal with Billy, the manipulator, the mastermind. Hare, the brute, just did as he was told. William Burke

279

was, by far, the greater terror. He could lure you into your own death chamber, smiling all the while, blaming you afterwards for succumbing to your own undoing. Self-murder he would have called it. Such a deadly trick. His charisma and ruthlessness were a lethal combination.

I've seen his ferocious inner bulldog up close many a time. I've done costly battle with him. Mine is a bruised, well-bitten body, thanks to Billy, a man who was warm and charming on the outside, always up for a laugh; cruel, heartless, and bloodthirsty on the inside. The same passion and charm that attracted me then, repels me now. *Always beware, ladies,* I want to say to the women, *of the mask.* That would have been my foremost warning to Maeve had she survived. It is best that she is now cradled by God.

Beware of the mask because of what lies behind it. Don't be seduced. Don't fool yourself. Get away as fast as your feet will carry you.

All I crave now, like a lover, is peace. I receive little rest. The worst torments overtake me in my box-bed. My nights tend towards the sleepless and when I do find sleep, my nightmares are unspeakable, haunted by painful memories of Maeve, my perfect, most beautiful, most sacred daughter.

I know one thing for certain: *Execution was the easy way out.*

***

I would be lying to say I hadn't fantasised about killing him.

I had done so dozens of times. Just as I brutalised a toy soldier in the likeness of Rab those many years ago, imagining his demise in various painful, tortured ways, I visited various acts of violence on Billy's doll, each of which involved his knowing that I was watching his final moments, able to intervene and possibly stop the horrible event, but choosing never to do so. These are the twisted fantasies he nurtured in me after years of neglect and abuse.

Even after forcing me to participate in his crimes against Maggie, the old Irishwoman, and Ann, I kept my hands to myself. I feared for my baby, so I never left. I couldn't leave. Nor did I poison him — that Other Billy — despite possessing the knowledge to do so. Margaret may have escaped the law after poisoning Lucky, but poisoning Billy would have marked the end for me. The hateful Mute and the venomous Margaret would have gleefully informed the police of their suspicions. I would have ended up on the gallows.

Despite all he had done to me and Maeve and the many innocent others, I didn't want his blood on my hands.

But taking Maeve to the doctor was beyond a crime. It was an act of pure evil, one that sought to ensure that she and I could never be reunited in the next life.

Thankfully, my God doesn't work that way. No one is chosen. No one is beyond redemption. The world of men may be rotten to the core, but the world beyond this one is of another order. It is a place of peace. I have to believe that, now more than ever.

What he took from me by selling her to the doctor was my chance to retreat peacefully, far away from this mad asylum of a world, laying her to rest where I could visit her daily.

He robbed me of consolation, of an ongoing dialogue with my daughter, which is beyond forgivable for *it was actually I who took her life after Billy forced my hand*.

It sickens me to write those words down and revisit those events, and yet I must lay my soul bare in this journal, this full and true document of confession.

*I, Nelly McDougal, can now confess to murder —
child murder.* Like Billy, I have never been prosecuted
for my greatest crimes. My life is a testament that
sometimes our greatest crimes go unpunished.
Although Billy was the madman who forced my hand,
I am the person who robbed Maeve of life.

The night Billy discovered that Ann had come to
rescue us, he beat and bullied me. Ann had returned
to the room where she was staying, entirely unaware
of Billy's brutal plans.

'You will help me tomorrow when she returns,' he
threatened. 'You will help me get her drunk. Trust me,
she'll be far better off that way. You will be helping to
ease her. You love her, don't you?'

Not hearing any confirmation, he redoubled his
threats. 'If you don't do as I tell you, Nelly, the baby
dies.'

After years with Billy, such threats were familiar,
although this threat was by far the worst. His violence
followed a pattern: he raged when he had no control,
ramping up the terror several notches at a time until he
felt he had me completely in his grip. In this instance,
instead of firing back, I responded first with silence,
then with sobs. I thought of Ann, my beautiful soft-
spoken cousin who had shown me, along with my
grandfather and Jeannie, the only true love I'd ever
known. I would sooner have slit my own throat than
lay a finger on her. She may have turned me away
when I saw her the last time, but I knew she had her
reasons, her own concerns, as every woman does.
Despite judging me at the time, she hadn't abandoned
me. It was she who had directed me to Jeannie. In
doing so, Ann had saved me.

As I considered Billy's nefarious plans, I imagined
Ann already dead. I broke down, pleading with
Billy to spare her. 'She has children,' I begged, 'and
grandchildren to come. Her children may be older, but

she is loved dearly and needed by them, as mothers are.' He gave a sharp, cruel laugh in response to these words and then struck me, one fist landing directly on my right breast. Warm breast milk seeped out onto the bed clothes as I winced in pain.

The next thing I knew, as I lay sobbing with Maeve asleep beside me, Billy rolled over on top of me and placed his hands firmly over my mouth and nose. I was unable to breathe while in his vice grip. With the world fast disappearing from my eyes, and his body a leaden weight, I was suffocating.

This may be the best thing, I thought as I recited my last prayer, *a blessing in disguise.* When Billy released his hands, allowing me to catch my breath, he laughed as if he had just been playing a joke.

As I struggled to get some air, I turned to ensure Maeve was still safe beside me. Billy proceeded to speak in that calm, steady, godlike voice he reserved for such moments. 'It's not your turn yet, Nelly, but it will be tomorrow if you don't do as I say. And if something happens to you, who will see to the baby? I certainly won't, although I have some ideas for her.'

He laughed again before leaving the room and said, 'Get some sleep now. Tomorrow is an important day. Remember, you tried to outsmart me and invited her here. You brought this on yourself.'

I lay there in abject fear, trembling, after Billy left. While I was thankful he no longer slept near us, I found no rest that night. Instead, I lay there, desperately chasing my thoughts, plotting how to save Ann from a dark fate at the doctor's. Her love of me would soon cost her life, and I was to blame. How mad must I have been to try to dupe Billy? I was the one who had sent her my desperate message with a plan. But that plan had failed. Although I was aware of Billy's rages and madness, I ignored them and contacted her.

I prayed that night that Ann would return home

and leave me to my fate. Had I been able to sneak out and warn her, I would have done so. But it was too late.

When morning came, Ann came with it. Ever a sensitive soul, she knew something was wrong. I have never been a good liar or capable of disguising my feelings. She could see I was exhausted and terrified. She was clueless about what lay ahead. Whenever Billy left my side over the course of that day, I told her urgently and repeatedly to leave, but this made her even more protective of me and the baby, ever more determined to stay. She sensed something terrible had happened and thought she could outsmart Billy by complying with him. Late that afternoon, she accepted her first drink from him. Others followed.

The rest of that horror story has already been told.

A few hours later, I lay, in agony, in the adjoining room with Maeve snuggled up against me, as Billy dealt with Ann's dead body, a part of me dying too as I heard him raving aloud about how much he hated me. He knew I could hear him through the thin partition between the two rooms. He knew, and he gloried in it. I focused on nursing Maeve, soothing and stroking her soft fuzz of hair, shutting out as best I could — as I had tried throughout our entire relationship — the sick disturbance that was Billy. I wept uncontrollably. Despite my exhaustion, I failed to fall asleep. I could find no release from my Billy nightmare.

When he entered the room the next morning, he smiled as he recounted the events of the night before and the crime I had been forced to help him commit. Looking at me with contempt as he spoke of killing Ann, he said in the low, menacing voice I had come to know so well, 'I pretended she was you the entire time.'

***

Sick and exhausted, I slept through the whole of the next day, waking only to feed and change the baby. I tried to return to our routine over the next few days but found myself fast drowning in sorrow and tears. Knowing Billy as I did, an internal dread increased by the day. Between feedings, I prayed over Maeve, asking God to watch over and keep her safe as I struggled to determine next steps. Billy continued dead silent the entire time, only coming in twice a day with food, drink, and supplies, and to remove the refuse.

I knew him well and sensed he was plotting something.

And then it all happened.

Billy startled me awake early one morning. He had a very strange look on his face as he leaned in close where Maeve and I lay together on the bed. He seemed different, almost possessed. Maeve, who was growing more aware by the day, reacted with tears as he suddenly placed his face right up next to hers in a way he'd never done before. As I soothed her, Billy pretended to be an endearing father. Look at how beautiful she is, 'Nelly,' he said. 'You finally managed your wifely duty.'

It was his next statement, uttered in a menacing tone, that sent a foreboding chill through my heart.

'But I still can't help but wonder, Nelly, is she even mine?'

As he stroked Maeve's head in a slow and sinister way, he added, 'You didn't fully cooperate when it came to Ann. The business can't be managed properly like that, Nelly, so some training is in order. You have a decision to make, and I promise, this one is easy.'

Billy leaned in close again, kissed Maeve for the very first time, and said, 'Either you kill this baby while I am out today, Nelly, or I will, after I return.'

Billy's words hit me like a series of closed fists. As

I struggled to make sense of what he'd demanded, a horrified voice inside me asked, *What type of person – what type of father – is this?*

But Billy wasn't done.

'I'll take care of her if she's still alive when I return, or I will deal with you first and her afterwards. Either way, we will rid ourselves of this burden. Like most people barely surviving in this city, we could never afford children, Nelly. You knew that. We were blessed without them.'

And then he added, as if it were an afterthought, 'And don't try to outsmart me this time, Nelly. Rest assured that you can't get out of here. The door is firmly secured. Don't even bother trying.'

I remember hearing the door close behind him, his footsteps retreating, and my stunned confusion as I tried to process what I'd been directed to do.

It devastates me to recall the next few hours.

I began by sitting upright in the bed and breastfeeding Maeve and then gently and rhythmically rocking her back and forth in my arms, smoothing her hair and kissing her forehead and face. I soothed her as she slept, rubbing her back and feet, arms and legs, blessing this beautiful body that I had carried inside me for those long, harrowing months as I became aware of Billy's atrocities. I told her through my tears how much I loved her, how very special she was to me. She was, I whispered, the realisation of every dream of a child that I'd ever had. I told her she was pure and good and that I loved her unconditionally and forever.

Billy's menacing words and ultimatum hung in the background, recalling me to my senses. I couldn't bear the thought of what he might do to her. I vowed to Maeve that, no matter what happened, she was not going to the doctor. Over my dead body, I repeated.

With the clock ticking, I focused again on Billy's

horrible threats and the matter at hand.

I couldn't bring myself to touch or mar her perfect body. She was sacred to me. I determined she remain as pristine in death as she was at birth. I made the necessary preparations. I wrapped her up snugly in several swaddling clothes. Then, I cradled her close again, holding her tight to control her movements. With one final prayer to God, I clasped one hand firmly over her swaddled mouth, knowing it wouldn't be long before she could no longer breathe. For a moment, she managed to release some cries, and then writhed in struggle. I held her more securely, soothing her at the same time. I sobbed and shook uncontrollably while rocking her during this excruciating operation. As her cries turned to choking gasps over the next few minutes, I prayed once more and pictured myself handing her over to God.

Nothing will ever erase her last few sounds, or my memory of the moment she stopped moving in my arms.

Several minutes later, I gingerly unwrapped her body, the reality of what I had done overwhelming me. Her beautiful serene face looked as if she were just sleeping, a precious wee doll. Despite feeling nauseous and endlessly trembling, I was comforted by her peacefulness. I kissed her through my veil of tears, vowing to find her a final, secure resting place.

I remember nothing after that until Billy's return.

When he entered the room, Billy neither looked over at us nor spoke. He simply deposited two bottles of whisky and laudanum inside the door before quickly withdrawing and closing the door again. That he knew I would succumb to his threats told me everything about our relationship. Billy's silence spoke volumes in other abusive ways, suggesting that no demand had been made by him, that I had willingly killed Maeve with no threat from him, no ultimatum, that I had acted independently and alone. In his quiet return to our room, Billy signalled that he'd had no hand in this atrocity. The guilt and sin were completely mine.

I cursed him endlessly over the course of that night. The bastard had once again outsmarted me. I poured the entire small vial of laudanum into the bottle of whisky and began drinking heavily, believing I had finally and completely lost my mind. I drank both to numb and to sober myself, and wondered, had the demand actually been made? This and a slew of other questions tormented me. It must have been hours later — after I'd raged and cried and punched my fists deep into the straw bed and hammered the walls, desperately moaning and crying, cursing Billy's name endlessly before falling dead asleep in the aftermath of a whisky and laudanum haze I hoped would kill me — that he snuck in, quickly and quietly, and removed her precious, delicate body as she nestled into me, and transported her to the doctor's. *His own daughter.*

He had no right to touch her. He hadn't even acknowledged her as his until his terrible ultimatum. She was too good for him. Maeve's purity brought Billy's vile nature — the evil of her own father — into full relief.

No one could have written a more disturbing tale. And no one could have told it so well, unflinchingly, as Billy could have done, to a rapt, inebriated pub audience.

It was as if he'd had no hand in it.

But I know better. And unlike the good folk of Edinburgh and those who uphold the laws of Scotland, I also know that sometimes our greatest crimes go undetected and unprosecuted.

The saving grace — thanks be to God — is that they don't go unpunished.

For Billy, Maeve was expendable, just like me.

I had been forced to kill her, so I did so with the kindness that only a loving mother could have shown.

Most will condemn me. Few will understand. And only God may forgive me for this act undertaken unwillingly.

And although but a baby, my Maeve proved to be my daughter. She outsmarted him by stepping out, fearlessly and triumphantly, through the daylight gate, towards the life to come.

I have continued to speak to her from this side, always through remorseful tears, knowing my crimes to be unforgivable. 'Your mother showed you her tender mercy, my wee angel. God will lend you His grace.'

I have mouthed those sentences every day since her death, through the endless waves of my suffocating sorrow, remorseful and penitent about what I have done, tormented to be alive.

Once again and as always, Billy forced my hand, mine, Nelly McDougal's, a shattered, broken shell of a Scotswoman against whom criminal charges were found not proven.

I whisper into the darkness each night as I lay myself down to sleep and pray the Lord my soul to keep.

'But we both showed him, my wee sweetheart,' I whisper to my beloved Maeve, the angel who now watches over me. 'Together, we both showed him.'

This has become my latest ritual, part of my nightly prayer as I settle in, peering into nothingness as I imagine her, in all of her sweet, precious innocence, in a far, far better place. I imagine Maeve cradling into me, finally at peace, her eyes looking intently into mine, her warm, wee hands at rest on my breast. Thanks to me, her loving mother, she now lies well beyond the veil of this cruel, cold graveyard of a world, the world of her father.

I have laid her doll to rest in its wee box bed. I cannot bear to think of her beautiful body, cut up and violated. In my mind's eye, she remains mine, forever intact, and that is how I shall meet her again.

From this side, I have comforted Maeve with the promise that one day we will rise up, gloriously, thankful, and blessed at our blissful reunion, mother and daughter.

'Until then,' I whisper, mouthing words of heavenly promise in the still darkness, 'rest your weary head, my wee hen, and go to sleep.'

'One day soon, we will walk our Radical Road together, on the other side, God willing.'

Acknowledgements

Various books were consulted as I conducted background research for this novel, the three most important of which were Thomas Ireland, Jr.'s *West Port Murders* (1829), William Roughead's *Burke and Hare* (1921), and Owen Dudley Edwards's *Burke & Hare* (1980).

I would especially like to thank everyone at Ringwood Publishing for their infectious enthusiasm and unwavering support in bringing this book to life and placing my first "baby" between book covers — Sandy Jamieson, Chief Executive Officer; Isobel Freeman, Chief Administrative Officer; Mridula Sharma, Assistant Managing Director (Editorial); and Skye Galloway, Graphic Designer extraordinaire, who was extremely innovative and attentive to my suggestions in creating the cover design. I was drawn to Ringwood Publishing because of their integrity, objectives, and Scottish-based mandate, and they never failed to deliver on any front.

I am especially indebted to the amazing editorial and marketing teams at Ringwood, as overseen by the brilliant and well-organised Managing Director, Simon McLean, who kept us all on track as this book went into and through production. I gained so much from the intrepid editorial team of Aria Tsvetanova (head) and Dora Grabar, who were incredibly astute readers who were never afraid to ask the tough questions or make the uncomfortable comments, vastly improving the novel as a result. The marketing team, comprised of Olivia Jackson (head), Rosie Watts, Bronte Kwek, and Shalika Kotha always brought their A-game to the table and were ultra-creative at every turn and on various platforms. If these keen young interns are any indication of the future of the publishing world, it looks very bright.

I would also like to thank various friends and family members for reading and/or commenting on sections of this novel and/or encouraging me to keep writing: Marg Bisetto, Sandy Davison, William Davison, Susan Lindsay, Susan McLean, Marie Mulvey-Roberts, Chelsea-Brooke Pascual, Jaime Pascual, Jasmine Pascual, Andy Smith and Glendora Watkins. Special thanks go to Ray Robertson, Canadian novelist and former Writer in Residence at the University of Windsor, who encouraged me to finish this novel, and my University colleagues, André Narbonne, Tom Dilworth, and Mark Johnston, whose support and optimism buoyed me up when necessary. Mark's suggestions about the book cover were especially helpful and greatly appreciated.

I am forever indebted to Corey Evan Thompson for his unflagging support and wise advice. He was my first reader through until the novel's completion, and it was for him alone and his reading pleasure, at several points, that I kept writing. I am also grateful to my dear friend, Elizabeth McAteer, who loved Nelly and Billy's story from the first, and who helped sustain me during a recent painful and challenging time of horrible personal challenge. I would like to extend my eternal gratitude to my mother, Alexandra McLean, who served as my sounding-board during the early stages when I worked out the Nelly plot trajectory, and who, along with my father, imbued me throughout my life with a sense of the tremendous powers of love and possibility, even – and especially – in the face of adversity.

It is my ardent prayer that all victims of domestic and sexual abuse may find the fortitude, necessary supports, and solace to carry on with their lives, one small baby step at a time.

In support of that aim, a portion of the royalties from the sales of this book will be donated to Glasgow Women's Aid.

Other Titles from Ringwood

All titles are available from the Ringwood website in both print and ebook format, as well as from usual outlets.
www.ringwoodpublishing.com
mail@ringwoodpublishing.co

Inference

Stephanie McDonald

Natalie Byron had a steady job, supportive friends and a loving family. Or at least, she thought she did. The morning after a date, Natalie wakes up inside a strange house, in a strange bed, sleeping next to a man named Jamie who claims he is her boyfriend.

Fearing she's been kidnapped, Natalie flees, but not one person on the island will help her. When everyone around her insists that her life is nothing but a delusion, Natalie begins to doubt her own sanity.
ISBN: 978-1-901514-84-1 £9.99

Embers

Stephanie McDonald

When the shy and mild-mannered Graham meets the confident Angie he is instantly besotted. The two soon embark on an all-compassing love affair, later marrying and settling down. But Angie has a past unknown to Graham – one which threatens to shatter the loving family they have created together. When their marriage eventually crumbles, and Angie succumbs to the trauma of her former life, Graham is left to try and rebuild a life without her.
ISBN: 978-1-901514-99-5 £9.99

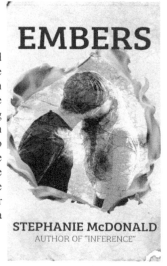

Raise Dragon

L.A. Kristiansen

In the year of 1306, Scotland is in turmoil.

Robert the Bruce and the fighting Bishop Wishart's plans for rebellion put the Scottish kingdom at risk, whilst the hostile kingdom of England seems more invincible than ever.

But Bishop Wishart has got a final card left to play: four brave Scottish knights set off in search of a mysterious ancient treasure that will bring Scotland to the centre of an international plot, changing both the kingdoms of Europe and the course of history once and for all.

ISBN: 978-1-901514-76-6
£9.99

What You Call Free

Flora Johnston

Scotland, 1687. An unforgiving place for women who won't conform.

Pregnant and betrayed, eighteen-year-old Jonet believes nothing could be worse than her weekly public humiliation in sackcloth. But soon she discovers that a far darker fate awaits her. Desperate to escape, she takes refuge among an outlawed group of religious dissidents. Here, Widow Helen offers friendship and understanding, but Helen's own beliefs have already seen her imprisoned once. Can she escape the authorities a second time?

ISBN: 978-1-901514-96-4
£9.99

Murder at the Mela

Leela Soma

DI Alok Patel takes the helm of an investigation into the brutal murder of an Asian woman in this eagerly-awaited thriller. As Glasgow's first Asian DI, Patel faces prejudice from his colleagues and suspicion from the Asian community as he struggles with the pressure of his rank, relationships, and racism.

This murder-mystery explores not just the hate that lurks in the darkest corners of Glasgow, but the hate which exists in the very streets we walk.

ISBN: 978-1-901514-90-2

£9.99

The Carnelian Tree

Anne Pettigrew

A dead body, a disappearance, and an epic lost in time. Unrelated incidents on the surface. Judith Fraser's Oxford sabbatical quickly takes a sharp turn when she gets tangled in the mysterious murder of a colleague. With threads leading nowhere, conflicting impressions about people around her, and concern for increasing risk to her loved ones, whom can she trust?

The Carnelian Tree follows the journey of Judith Fraser as she unravels mysteries of locked doors, missing computers, cat's collars, and Reuter's reports, with the help of DCI Keith Steadman, her potential love interest. Judith probes into people, power, politics, and sex, only to discover that some things remain unchanged.

ISBN: 978-1-901514-81-0

£9.99

Stirring the Dust

Mary McCabe

A corpse left unburied for fear of infection; a paranormal great-great aunt; bigamous and incestuous marriages; a runaway wife and her gypsy rover. Dramatic episodes in the past are linked with the present. A sense of something missing in events now has its echo in the rich cast of characters standing behind down the generations. Mary McCabe should know the cast in this drama. They are the author's own family.

ISBN:978-1-901514-57-5
£7.99

Two Closes and a Referendum

Mary McCabe

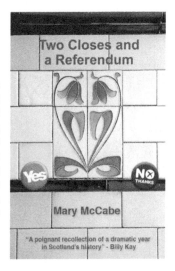

Two Closes and a Referendum is an engaging tale of ordinary people in an extraordinary time. This novel brilliantly captures the growing excitement and fervour of the 2014 Independence Referendum that changed Scotland for ever, as ordinary citizens explored their identity and wrestled with the hopes and fears that surrounded the choice they were asked to make.

ISBN: 978-1-901514-48-3
£9.99

Made in the USA
Las Vegas, NV
02 October 2023